DISCARD

The
Unforgotten

The
Unforgotten

A Novel

LAURA POWELL

GALLERY BOOKS

New York   London   Toronto   Sydney   New Delhi

Gallery Books
An Imprint of Simon & Schuster, Inc.
1230 Avenue of the Americas
New York, NY 10020

This book is a work of fiction. Any references to historical events, real people, or real places are used fictiously. Other names, characters, places, and events are products of the author's imagination, and any resemblance to actual events or places or persons, living or dead, is entirely coincidental.

First Gallery Books hardcover edition February 2018

GALLERY BOOKS and colophon are registered trademarks of Simon & Schuster, Inc.

For information about special discounts for bulk purchases, please contact Simon & Schuster Special Sales at 1-866-506-1949 or business@simonandschuster.com.

The Simon & Schuster Speakers Bureau can bring authors to your live event. For more information or to book an event, contact the Simon & Schuster Speakers Bureau at 1-866-248-3049 or visit our website at www.simonspeakers.com.

Interior design by Bryden Spevak

Manufactured in the United States of America

10 9 8 7 6 5 4 3 2 1

Library of Congress Cataloging-in-Publication Data

Names: Powell, Laura (Writer and editor), author.
Title: The unforgotten / Laura Powell.
Description: First Gallery Books hardcover edition. | New York : Gallery Books, 2018.
Identifiers: LCCN 2017031033 (print) | LCCN 2017040027 (ebook) | ISBN 9781501181238 (ebook) | ISBN 9781501181221 (hardcover : acid-free paper)
Subjects: LCSH: Man-woman relationships—Fiction. | Life change events—Fiction. | Psychological fiction. | BISAC: FICTION / Psychological. | FICTION / Thrillers. | GSAFD: Suspense fiction.
Classification: LCC PR6116.O947 (ebook) | LCC PR6116.O947 U54 2018 (print) | DDC 823/.92—dc23
LC record available at https://lccn.loc.gov/2017031033

ISBN 978-1-5011-8122-1
ISBN 978-1-5011-8123-8 (ebook)

The
Unforgotten

Part One

1

Early June 1956

The girl runs along the promenade and around the lighthouse keeper's derelict cottage, her ponytail whipping the air and new tears flying down her face. She stops at the topmost step that leads down to the crescent of shingle, cups her hands around her mouth, fixes her eyes on the pair of figures below—the size of thumbs from here—and she bellows.

They don't turn around. The shorter of the two figures raises his arms and flips over on his hands. His body cartwheels a perfect circle. The second figure, a head taller and wearing a black-and-white-striped dress belted at the waist, turns away as if trying not to notice the cartwheel or its impressiveness. The girl on the promenade tries again. She calls louder this time, but her words are carried off by the wind. The girl below raises her own arms. For a moment she is a cloud of whirling stripes and cotton and ivory stick legs, then she is back on her feet, dusting sand from her hands.

The girl on the promenade inches down the steps, changes her mind, and leaps back up again as though the steps are scorching hot. She opens her lips, and she shouts a third time.

"Betty, come up here quick. They've found another girl. Dead!"

Seconds pass. Betty is pleased she executed the cartwheel well; her hips had stayed straight as they rolled in a neat circle. She glances sideways at George, who is cramming broken gingerbread from his trouser pocket into his thick lips. Something about him makes her stomach curdle. She turns away from him and notices the girl on the promenade.

"I think Jennifer's calling me—"

"There was me thinking you were too frightened to go upside down," George cuts in, still munching. "But now just look at you, cartwheeling about like a clown."

"I wasn't scared. You only dared me because you wanted a look at my knickers."

"Your knickers, indeed," he says, and his eyes swim over her body. "One day you won't speak to me like that."

"Like what?"

"Not when I have a Bentley S1 and drive us to the South of France, then back through London for tea with the queen herself. You'll wear a dinging silk scarf. And my child'll be growing in your stomach."

He jabs his eyes into her middle. Betty turns away and kicks up a toeful of sand. A seagull shrieks. Jennifer waves her arms madly.

"I'd better go back up. Jennifer wants something."

"Fine. You go," says George. "As long as you come with me to the dance. Pa'll drive."

"But—"

"No buts. You're coming with me."

Betty sighs; if she protests, he will spend the next three weeks trying to persuade her. She gives a small nod and skips off across the sand.

"Your ma sent me," cries Jennifer as Betty reaches her. Her voice is raspy, as if the words have been pulled out of her throat and over a grater. "A busload of up-country men have arrived at the hotel."

"Calm down."

Always so urgent; Betty would like to stitch pebbles into her hem to slow her down.

"But that man what stabbed Maureen," pants Jennifer. "He's struck again on the New Road. They've come to write about him for the papers. Didn't you hear me calling?"

Betty shakes her head. She tries to look calm, but she feels sick.

"Who?"

"They don't know yet. She's not local."

"Why didn't you come down onto the sand to tell me?"

"No." Jennifer's voice drops to a whisper. "Maureen's blood is probably still wet on it, God bless her soul."

"Don't be silly," snaps Betty, but she walks faster.

"My da said he stabbed her in the neck with a bait hook. And my ma said—"

"Right," she interrupts, not wanting to know more. "Get yourself home safely. I'll help Mother."

x

PARKED MOTORCARS LINE THE street and a man wearing a spotted bow tie lolls outside the hotel sipping a glass of something amber. His left arm blocks out half of the hotel sign. Eden, it reads now.

"Fully booked, love," he mutters without looking up.

"I live here," says Betty curtly, and she squeezes past him.

Inside, the big room is misty with tobacco warmth. Men stand shoulder to shoulder, still wearing their overcoats, and Mother wriggles between them doling out cups of tea and cinnamon slices of loaf cake and toothy smiles.

"Want your grushans topped up with a drop of stout?" she calls to a man in an armchair with an empty teacup balanced on his knee. He ignores her.

"The killer has to be a local," another of the reporters is saying to no one in particular.

"Apparently her blood was still warm when they found her," chips in a younger one with a cigarette wedged in the gap between his front teeth. "And the inspector just told me that the first poor lass was stabbed in the stomach forty times . . . or was it fourteen?"

"Mind your lip, Tony," says the eldest with an Irish accent. "There's ladies about."

"I'm just saying it like it is."

"Well, don't," snaps the bow-tie man, stepping into the room. They all quieten. His face is stern, but he slips Mother a wink. Betty pretends not to notice.

"All warm enough in your rooms?" chirps Mother, giving the bow-tie man one of her special smiles. "Enough blankets on your beds?"

"My darling, the only way we could possibly be more comfortable is if you hopped into our beds with us."

Mother pretends to look coy and sashays into the kitchen as the men fall about laughing, all except the silent man on the armchair, the teacup still balanced on his knee.

"What's wrong with you?" snaps the bow-tie man, glaring at him. "Silver spoon still stuck up that backside of yours?"

They all laugh harder and stare at the armchair man. As Betty squeezes between them, making for the kitchen, she glances at him, too. His eyes are low and he doesn't speak. He seems to want to keep himself in a separate bubble. He skims through a stack of papers, each covered with black words inked in tight orderly shapes. She can't quite make out his eyes, just the steep curve of his forehead and the black curls jostling for space on his crown. He has narrow shoulders, she notices. A long face, too. He looks strangely streamlined.

She stares at him, fascinated at how the teacup still balances while his right hand holds a pen and the other supports the wad of papers. He cocks up his left eye and locks onto her.

"Yes?" he grunts, but not altogether unkindly.

His voice is deeper than she expected, startling her to silence. His eyes are glassy blue puddles of cold water, and pink capillaries thread across his face. Beautiful, somehow.

She fumbles for something to say. She is usually so composed around hotel guests.

"Ever so sorry," she manages.

She wants to know why he doesn't talk to the others, why he wears a jet-black trench coat like a Soviet spy and what seems to be a wedding ring but on the wrong finger. His face looks younger the more she stares. It is unlined and hasn't the creases of the other men, but it is pock-marked, too, and threaded with those veins, as if he has worn it harder than he should have.

"I'm Betty. Betty Broadbent. Pleasure to see you. Or perhaps meet you. Though we haven't quite met yet."

She stops, embarrassed, and waits for him to say something. He looks down at his papers, pausing before he glances up again.

"Gallagher." He clears his throat. "I have to . . . These things don't read themselves, you know."

She wonders whether to laugh, but he is still frowning. He picks up his pen and writes something in those blockish letters. His curls bob as his hand moves.

"Right you are, then," she says, and feels silly; like Mother, or a parody of her.

The room is very hot suddenly. She squeezes between the other reporters to the cool galley kitchen at the back of Hotel Eden, where Mother is standing in a pile of carrot skins and thwacking a cleaver through a heap of potatoes so that there are enough to go round for the men's suppers.

"What's the matter with you? You look all pink and funny," says Mother with a frown. Suddenly she brightens. "But you've been out with George again today, I hear?"

×

AT SIX O'CLOCK IN the morning Betty pads into the kitchen, still groggy with sleep. The air is yeasty, and Mother is up to her elbows in greasy dishwater. She sings along to Fats Domino on the wireless, not quite keeping up with the words.

"I couldn't stop thinking last night about that poor, poor dead girl," says Betty.

"Nonsense, too busy for idle gossip," snaps Mother, then she grins and her voice changes. "But you slept like a little angel. I watched you and watched you but you didn't wake once. And look, what a day! Sun shining, birds singing just for us." She lets out a little whoop.

Betty kisses Mother's forehead, but her insides prickle. The only days Mother talks this fast and wakes this early are the days before a crash, before her mood springs high and crumbles, leaving her in bed for days, weeks sometimes, until she can pull herself upright.

Betty clears an empty gin bottle and a lipsticked tumbler from the floor. She is wondering whether to ask Mother about them, when a cough cuts in. She whips around. Gallagher is standing in the kitchen doorway staring at her.

"Mr. Gallagher," gushes Mother, cutting between them. "Early riser, aren't you? Sit yourself down in the big room and I'll bring in breakfast. Kippers all right for you?"

She crosses the kitchen to stroke his arm, the way she does with all of her favorite male guests before they fall in love with her for a week. Betty looks away. Suddenly there is a loud pop, as boiling water spits out of the kipper pan.

"Whoops-a-daisy," squeals Mother, flapping a tea towel and giggling.

Betty looks back to see Gallagher's reaction, but he has slipped into the big room. He sits at a breakfast table, his long back facing her and his head pointed at the window covered with yellowing net curtains.

"Do something, take him tea," whispers Mother, pushing a cold teapot into her hand, and Betty can see how desperate she is to get it right.

They aren't used to making a dozen breakfasts at once; there might be two couples or sometimes a family, but Betty has never seen Hotel Eden so crammed full that men are sandwiched in, two to a room. Only Gallagher has his own bedroom. He paid triple rate for it, so Mother said.

"Betty, today, please. We're brewing a pot of tea, not a bloody thunderstorm."

Mother pinches the bridge of her nose as Betty fills the pot and hurries into the big room.

"Lovely morning, isn't it?" she says in a high-pitched voice that doesn't sound like her own. "Some tea?"

Gallagher doesn't seem to hear. Betty watches his face as she pours. She doesn't notice that there isn't a teacup on his saucer, or that hot black tea fills it and dribbles onto the place mat.

"Whoops. Crikey. Sorry."

"Christ," cries Gallagher, pushing back his chair. He jumps to his feet before the tea runs into his lap.

"I'm so sorry."

"Let me do that. You're making a real pig's ear."

"I can do it."

"Suit yourself." And he sits down again with his chair pushed far out from the table and his jaw grinding.

Betty mops the tea with her handkerchief and pulls across a teacup from another setting.

"I really am sorry about that," she says again, rummaging in the dresser drawer for a place mat.

Her finger has a red dent from the heavy teapot, and her hand pulsates with pain.

"Tell me what you know about Nigel Forbes the butcher," says Gallagher sharply.

She sets down the teapot, stunned by the question.

"Mr. Forbes? I hardly know him," she says, trying to sound unruffled.

"Never mind that," he snaps. "Just tell me what you do know."

She frowns, irritated. Did your mother never teach you manners? she thinks. Then she realizes with horror that she has spoken aloud.

Her tongue seems to swell and fill up her mouth. Gallagher raises an eyebrow. She would like to run back upstairs, to remake the bed, wash her face again, pull on a different skirt, and start the morning over. It is as if some strange spirit possesses her and causes her to behave quite out of character around this man. If Mr. Eden found out, Mother would lose her manageress post and their home at Hotel Eden.

She pours tea carefully into a fresh cup and is about to apologize again when the bow-tie man strides in. He rubs his chin, curved like that character from *The Dandy*, and takes the chair opposite. Gallagher's face darkens. Betty looks from one to the other.

"Marvelous, a lovely cuppa to start my morning," says Reggie loudly. He turns to Gallagher. "My, my. Isn't she a corker? Just the ticket to perk up a dull day."

"Never change, do you Reggie?" snarls Gallagher. Reggie turns back to Betty.

"Say, what's your name, sweetheart?"

"Betty," she mutters.

"Leave her alone," hisses Gallagher.

"First dibs, eh?" Reggie stretches his fingers behind his head. His knuckles crack. "Didn't know you had it in you, boy."

"You make me sick. She's a child."

Betty turns to face the dresser so they won't see the tears pool in her eyes. She blinks them back. She shouldn't care if Gallagher thinks her a child; he is just a rude man who asks too many questions.

"Your problem, Gallagher, is that you're so damned forgetful," sneers Reggie.

"Is that so?"

"Because you seem to think you're a cut above the rest of us, but what you're forgetting is, no matter who your daddy is or how many prime ministers he gads about with, we're all chasing the same story. And we're doing it from the same gutter."

The room is silent but for Reggie's wheezy breathing. Gallagher stares into his cup like the gypsy woman who reads Mother's tea leaves every birthday; the gypsy woman who stopped coming to St. Steele last year after she saw something so black in the leaves, she almost choked on her gumdrop.

Betty pours Reggie's tea. She wishes she had a clever phrase that would defuse the awkwardness, the way Mother would. Tea tinkles into Reggie's cup, but she has forgotten to strain it. Black leaves float to the surface.

"Sorry," she says, flustered. "I'll fetch you a fresh cup."

She lifts the teacup, but Reggie pushes her wrist back down. "Don't you worry, my precious. I'll drink it as it is."

His sausage fingers linger on her wrist. She wants to pull away, but she can't make a fuss. She freezes, but then Gallagher swats away Reggie's hand.

"Anyway, tea leaves aren't poison, are they?" continues Reggie, as though no one has touched or swatted anyone else. "Or have you poisoned mine, Gallagher boy?"

He slurps and pulls back his lips. Clumps of tea leaf have lodged in the gaps between his teeth. Betty looks away. Gallagher stands abruptly and pushes back his chair, just as Mother totters into the room with two plates of steaming kippers and doorsteps of bread.

"Breakfast's served," she squeals.

"You beauty," winks Reggie.

"None for me," says Gallagher.

Mother's smile wavers.

"But you'll enjoy these lovely kippers. They'll set you up for the day."

Gallagher storms out of the room. Betty tenses as the front door opens and slams shut.

"Well, now. There's a gentleman," sneers Reggie.

Mother does her trilling laugh, but it sounds thinner than usual. Betty wants to hug her until she is bright again, but Reggie is patting her bottom and gesturing for the extra kippers to be scraped onto his plate.

"There's a good girl," he says to Mother, tucking a napkin into his collar and shining his fork on the hem of her apron.

Betty hurries into the kitchen. She picks up two apples and runs out the back door, through the yard, and onto the lane. At the end, where it picks up the promenade and curves down to the cove, she can make out the back of Gallagher, his hands pushed deep in his pockets.

"Mr. Gallagher," she calls.

He strides on without looking back, his coat hem swinging.

She trots to catch up. "Mr. Gallagher!"

He stops and turns, his face still hard. She reaches him and extends a hand with an apple in it.

"Breakfast," she says softly. "And thank you . . . for earlier. That man, Reggie . . ."

He glares at the apple as if there is a hidden message in it, then accepts it. She bites into her own apple and tries to chew quietly. They walk in step the rest of the way to the shore, and Betty allows herself little darting glances at his jaw. The shingle is damp against her feet. She realizes that she is still wearing her indoor slippers and hopes he won't notice.

"You asked earlier after Mr. Forbes the butcher," she says, emboldened. "Mother sometimes buys shin and ham from him, but his cuts are dear so we buy it from Spoole most of the time. But if you're asking because you think he's the killer . . . It wasn't him."

Gallagher's face still looks uninterested, but his head half turns toward her.

"Yes?"

"That's all."

"That's not all. There's something else you want to say about him, or perhaps don't want to say," he says, and a lump clogs up her throat. "I could tell back at the breakfast room."

"There's not . . . Just . . . The policemen don't think it's him, do they?"

"Between us, they do."

"It can't be."

"You said you hardly knew him."

"I don't," she continues more carefully. "But why would he hurt anyone? He might look frightening—and I know that the children joke he turns into a monster at midnight—but that's only his way. He's . . . He likes to keep himself to himself."

She tries to invent a stronger reason. Their eyes meet again. Gallagher's glare is piercing.

"He's stopped going to church, so I've heard," he says. "Something must have changed for him to have lost his faith."

"He hasn't gone out much at all since Mrs. Forbes died; it isn't just church."

"And I'm told he returned from the war a changed man. A loner," presses Gallagher. "Didn't he attack his wife once?"

"I don't know who'd say such nasty things," she says, frowning. "But he spends his time working and doesn't bother anyone. He has his own farm and an abattoir and—"

"Wait, an abattoir?"

"Only a small one."

"You've seen it?"

"Yes, but—"

"He invited you there?"

"Of course not. Why would he invite me to look at dead bits of cow?"

She blushes. He can probably see straight through her lies.

All she knows is that no one must suspect Mr. Forbes.

"It can't be him, I just know," she repeats firmly. "And I only really came here to say that I didn't mean to upset you earlier. The things I said about your manners."

Gallagher doesn't look at her; he is still staring at the sea. She shouldn't have followed him. He probably thinks her dull or difficult, and now she must stand here in this excruciating silence or else slink away, embarrassed either way. A flock of angry seagulls circles overhead. She wishes they would dip down and carry her off.

"Upset me?" he says after a long silence. "Pah ha."

It is such a strange barking noise that Betty stops twisting the apple core in her palm. She wants to laugh, too, but she keeps her eyes on the horizon.

"But still," she says. "I'm sorry. I'm sure your mother and father instilled very good manners in you. . . . I suppose you just forgot them for a moment this morning."

His lips twitch. She thinks he might smile, then he is serious again.

"Mother'd have liked you," he says, and Betty curls up her toes inside her slippers. "Yes, she'd have called you spirited."

"I'm not usually," she mumbles.

"But it's a fine quality to have."

Her hands are clammy. She wishes she had something fascinating to reply with, or that she was beautiful like Mother and Mary and her Sunday school teacher Miss Hollinghurst so she wouldn't be expected to say anything fascinating at all. She clears her throat.

"One summer we had no fish here at all," she begins, trying to sound like Mother who has told this story many times before. It's a good talking point if you're stuck for chat with the guests, she once said. "Whole armies of seagulls came and ate them all. Lots of the fishermen had to move to the cities for work . . ."

Betty trails off. She can't remember how the story ends or even if it is true.

"Yes, seagulls are the biggest predator here in St. Steele, never mind the Cornish Cleaver."

Gallagher spins around to face her. "What did you just say?"

"That hundreds of seagulls came, so we had no fish left."

"No, no. The last bit?"

"Um, I don't know," she says, nervous again.

"The Cornish Cleaver. You said the Cornish Cleaver," he says, leaning so close, she can smell his aftershave and hair oil and the damp wool of his suit.

"Yes, I meant the man who killed Maureen and the second girl, Elsa."

Gallagher squeezes the tops of her arms in a sort of hug. Her stomach leaps into her mouth.

"Thank you, Betty. That's your name, isn't it?"

She nods, certain that her cheeks are the color of Mother's boiled beetroots.

"The Cornish Cleaver. Utterly perfect."

He pulls out a tiny notepad from his inside pocket and writes something, then stops and looks cautious.

"Wait, you didn't hear that expression somewhere else, did you?"

She shakes her head, and his face relaxes again. Her skin still tingles from the hug—it was dry and tight, as though they had slotted together for a moment. But when Betty collects herself, Gallagher is striding away; he is striding away so fast, she is certain he can't wait to be rid of her.

2

Fifty years later

"Mary stop it, you're scaring me."

Mary sits upright in bed and gasps. Her arms are pimpled with cold perspiration and her nightdress has twisted around, straitjacketing her. Her throat stings, too.

"What time is it?" she croaks.

"Four," says Jerry, handing her a glass of tepid water. "The same one again?"

She nods.

"Who were you shouting at to let you go?"

"I can't remember," she lies.

She gulps down the water and replaces the glass on the carafe that sits on the bedside table exactly where she left it. There is something comforting about its solidity, about the row of perfume bottles arranged beside it at perpendicular angles, about her brush without a single hair caught in its teeth, and the handheld bone-inlay mirror that smells of polish. It is the one she pretends she inherited from her mother to show Jerry something tangible from her past.

"They must be linked to something."

"They'll pass." But she sounds defeated.

"But something's not right," he continues, fumbling for his reading glasses. "It's been every night for almost three weeks now. There's definitely nothing bothering you?"

She shakes her head. He struggles out of bed and limps away, rubbing his stiff left knee.

"What are you doing?"

"You can't live like this," he says gently. "There are people who can help."

"It was probably just the brie. You know what they say about cheese and nightmares."

She watches him pull his silver pen and diary from the pocket of his suit hung over the wardrobe door ready for morning. He scribbles something in the diary, frowning as he does.

"What are you writing?" she says. "Don't do anything, I don't want a fuss."

"Just reminding myself to call Dr. Griffiths in the morning."

"No doctors. Please! You know how I feel about them."

"But he might recommend something."

"No doctors," she bellows, surprised at the strength of her own voice. He stops writing and looks at her. "I only want to help."

"I'm sorry," she says, washed with guilt. "I know you do. I'm so sorry."

His face, lit by the streetlamp glow that creeps into the bedroom through a gap between the curtains, is thin and drawn. He has aged without her noticing. That happens sometimes; she looks at the curled leaves and the naked trees and realizes that two whole seasons have passed without her registering them, as though she has slept through a great chunk of life.

Jerry clambers back into bed. He wraps an arm around her middle and kisses the back of her shoulder with dry lips.

"It'll be all right. I'm here for you."

He slips back to sleep while she lies rigid, counting the rings of plaster around the brass light fitting on the ceiling until her eyes scramble.

x

Autumn sun streams into the bedroom. Mary stretches and touches Jerry's cold, flat pillow. Morning terrifies her these days: how to fill another day? She snaps on a bra with gentle underwire, a blouse buttoned to the throat, and a slick of rose blusher, then sweeps a comb through her long hair that age demanded she shorten long ago. As she pins it in her usual chignon, she registers that the house is so silent, it hisses.

To fill the emptiness, she hums tunelessly and looks at the framed photographs on the dressing table, careful to appreciate the faces smiling at her as she does every morning, but then the brown envelope lying flat beside them catches her eye. She grabs it and stuffs it into her bottom drawer beneath a ball of nude stockings. Careless of her to have left it out where Jerry might have seen it. She closes the drawer and walks downstairs.

In the kitchen is a mug with a tea bag inside, a cereal bowl with a spoon poised beside it. The kettle is already filled; thoughtful Jerry. All she needs to do is flip the switch and add milk; kind Jerry. She pours herself a sour black coffee instead and chews a dry crispbread, leaning against the patio door and watching a family of sparrows hop around the breadcrumbs on the bird table. Something about them makes her queasy.

She will do something special for the family today. For her family today. Yes, she will prepare a supper and invite them around this evening. She will do it well for once without forgetting a vital ingredient or burning something, and without Cath having to rescue it all. She will marinate lamb, serve Jerry's favorite Rioja and a chocolate tart for Holly. She will even write a shopping list.

If it all goes well, maybe she will tell them over pudding. "It's nothing to worry about," she might say reassuringly, the way a mother and a grandmother and a wife ought. "The nice lady consultant said I have a good chance of making a full recovery." She did say that, didn't she? Though Mary had planned not to tell them at all.

She had thought she might reverse Jerry's little automatic car out of the back of the garage and drive herself to the appointments—surely one never forgets how to drive—then park it back behind his Jaguar before he comes home from work. She would take a handbag full of magazines with her as company and treat herself to some of those boiled toffee sweets to suck on for the nausea.

Stepping onto a ward again will be the worst part, she reassures herself, pouring a second coffee; after that it will only be as painful as going to the supermarket or the dentist or doing any other chore. That moment the phantom smell returns—bleach and stringent detergent and that gelatinous gravy she was once force-fed—making her drop her coffee mug. She leans over the kitchen sink and retches.

X

HOURS LATER, MARY FLIES back home along Richmond High Street, a heavy grocery bag cutting into each hand and a wide smile on her face. She had found everything she needed in the supermarket and didn't even go into one of her strange mind freezes, where she wanders vacantly around the aisles and forgets what she is looking for.

She gulps big mouthfuls of the meaty, pasty air that pumps out of the bakery and swings her shopping bags, exhilarated to have been so decisive for once. She will stick to her original plan and do without their help; without them having to divvy up lifts to her appointments, without Jerry incurring a premium on their private health insurance, and without Cath waking in the night to worry and trawl the internet for herbal cures or complementary oncologists. Yes, she will manage it herself, and when she has recovered, she will tell them. They will be surprised—impressed, even—at how well she coped.

Mary looks around at the other fast people on the street. She must look purposeful, just like them, and she is elated that it is all going so well. Why did she ever find such a simple task as going to the supermarket so daunting? Then her eyes fall absentmindedly on the newsstand across the road, just outside Star Newsagents.

Mary stops dead. She opens her lips. She screams.

It is a strange scream but a scream nonetheless, yet no one else seems to notice. Swarms of shoppers shoulder past without registering Mary. She doesn't register them, either. All that exists in this second, in this street, is that newsstand and the poster displayed there. At first, Mary thinks she must be hallucinating, but she reads it again, and she screams again, and again it comes out as a peculiar, raspy cough.

A double-decker bus draws up, and Star Newsagents is blocked from view. Mary doesn't move. People trickle off the bus. It slides away again. The poster reappears and, that same moment, the bottom of one of Mary's polythene bags gives way as if it too is strained by the shock of it all. Lamb cutlets, crème fraîche, a box of aspirin, a bunch of asparagus, and a tart tumble out. Jerry's Rioja crashes to the pavement.

"Are you all right?" says a girl with blue mascara, gathering up the asparagus.

"Sweet Jesus," breathes Mary.

She doesn't see the groceries on the pavement and hasn't registered that one of her bags is weightless.

"I'm doing my nurse training, so you're in safe hands. Do you need to sit down?"

Mary crosses the road without hearing the question and without looking for traffic, her eyes still on the newsstand. She doesn't notice the crescendo of horns, the sharp brakes, or the bald man who leans out of his car window and shakes a fist at her. She reaches the newsstand and touches the metal frame that holds the poster in place, just to be sure it really is there. It says:

CORNISH CLEAVER SPEAKS

3

The Irish reporter slams his fist on the afternoon newspaper spread out on the dining table.

"How the hell did Gallagher come up with that?" he yells.

"The Cornish Cleaver," reads Tony, spitting out each syllable, and Betty almost drops the decanter. She stops dusting and listens. "It's good," he continues. "But I'm not buying that he came up with it himself. Reckon his daddy paid someone to write it for him?"

"Calm down. It's hardly a story," snaps Reggie.

"Easy for you to say. Your editor's not threatening to pension you off if you don't come up with the exclusives," slurs Irish, his glasses steaming up. He wipes the lens with a corner of the tablecloth. "And it had to be him, didn't it? Sodding Gallagher."

Betty grips the neck of the decanter. She couldn't feel more exposed if she were standing there in her nightdress. She wants to scream: Those were my words; that was our private conversation, but another bit of her isn't sure why she should be angry at all.

"Enough shop talk boys, we're done for tonight," says Reggie, hoisting himself to his feet. He tucks his stomach into his waistband and shuffles toward Betty, carrying their four empty glasses. "Top these up will you, Betty love? And have I told you that you're looking as pretty as a picture again today?"

She ignores the last bit and pours the whiskies.

"I couldn't help overhearing," she says in a low voice when the others are talking. "That you said something about the Cornish Cleaver . . . and Mr. Gallagher."

Reggie leans a thick arm around her waist. She stiffens. He smells eggy.

"We were just saying that he came up with that rather good nickname for the murderer and now everyone's using it from here to Timbuktu. Nothing for you to worry your pretty head about. Probably just given to him by some cheap source or other."

Betty runs very cold. Reggie drains his glass and belches.

"Now, where's that delectable mother of yours?"

x

FOUR DAYS LATER, BETTY is home alone. Her hands tremble slightly as she polishes the silver spoons in the dresser drawer, her ears trained on the moan of the floorboards and the burble of the restless water pipe. She hates being home alone now. The carriage clock sings and she jumps; the two spoons in her hands ting together.

It is the third time it has chimed since Mother left for the greengrocer's, her lips slashed with scarlet lipstick and her breasts bulging over her tight coral dress. Betty isn't sure how long she should wait before alerting the inspector or Joan next door that Mother still isn't home; she tries not to panic, but the greengrocers is only three miles away, so she should be home by now. Eventually the front door clicks open, and Betty exhales with relief, but then two feet that don't sound like Mother stamp on the hall mat. Betty freezes, gripping the spoons.

"Staring at your reflection in the silver, are you?" booms a voice and she jumps again.

"Mr. Gallagher," she exclaims, relieved and embarrassed at once.

"Did I give you a fright? That was cruel of me."

He leans against the doorframe between the hall and the big room with a small smile.

It is peculiar; his face sat in her mind for days—she was furious at him for stealing her words and she has waited to confront him—but now that they are finally alone she wants to squeeze herself inside the dresser to hide. It is painful, somehow, to stand so close to him.

"I'd love a tea," he says, friendlier than she has heard him before.

She nods, relieved for an excuse to disappear into the kitchen. She runs her wrists under the cool tap as the kettle boils. When she returns to the big room he is pert on the settee, his left calf draped over his right knee. She rests his teacup on a coaster and returns to polishing.

"You might try soda crystals on those. A trick from Father's housemaid," he says.

She nods, but it is strange for Gallagher to tell her how to clean, as if Hotel Eden itself has tipped upside down. He sips his tea. She tries to concentrate on the spoons, but the room is stifling. She juts out a lip and blows cool air onto her forehead. She would like to open the stiff windows, but she will do it when he isn't there to watch.

"Look, I didn't thank you for your help," he says after a silence.

"You've nothing to thank me for."

"The Cornish Cleaver thing. You're annoyed . . . You've barely said a word."

"I'm really not."

"Let me take you for a spin this evening."

"There's no need."

"I need to take my car for a run anyway. We could stop by the flicks."

Betty grips the rag and imagines Mary's face if she saw Betty strolling into the pictures with a man at her side; her eyeballs would pop right out of her skull.

"I can't. Mother wouldn't like me going out when we're this busy."

"Nonsense, she has that other girl who helps," he says, and Betty is pleased that he doesn't remember Jennifer's name.

"Mother's out this evening, so I have to—"

"There, all the better," he says quickly, then looks taken aback at his own words.

"Thank you, but I shouldn't."

The front door bangs open and Gallagher's face falls, or perhaps she imagines it. He picks up his cup and swallows the tea fast, making his Adam's apple bob, then jumps to his feet. She still wants to ask him why he stole her expression without telling her, and part of her would like to apologize for seeming so cold and uninteresting around him, but there isn't time.

"All right, the pictures. Six o'clock," she says suddenly, surprising herself.

He raises one eyebrow, gives a small nod, then sweeps into the hall and up the stairs, just as Mother breezes into the big room with a string bag of vegetables.

"I hope he wasn't giving you any trouble. Reggie says he's a high-and-mighty pain in the backside, that one."

"He's fine," mutters Betty, not meeting Mother's eye. Then she remembers her panic. "Where've you been? You were gone so long, I almost called Inspector Napier."

X

AT HALF PAST FIVE, Betty still can't decide what to wear to the pictures. She is standing in front of the bedroom mirror, wrapping Mother's best raccoon stole around her shoulders, when Mary bursts in.

"Only me," she squeals, draping herself across the bed. Betty rips off the stole, embarrassed. "Guess what? Gray's asked me to supper. I think I'm going to die with happiness."

"To supper? That's so exciting," says Betty, trying to sound enthusiastic.

"We're courting! At least we will be when he asks me. Can you believe it? He's the second best boy in all the villages. Except George, obviously, but I won't fight you for him."

Betty rolls her eyes and glances at the clock. Its second hand seems to beat louder than usual.

"I just don't know how to behave around him," continues Mary. "I wish I could be more like you, Bet. More, you know, aloof and get boys to want me without even trying."

Betty nods, only half listening. She still hasn't dressed properly, and she didn't arrange where to meet Gallagher. What if he has changed his mind? Then she registers what Mary said.

"Wait, aloof?"

"Yes, to make George mad about you. You know, you're all frosty around him and pretend not to care. It's George Paxon, for goodness' sake. Any girl would want him."

A coldness sets in Betty's stomach.

"That's not what I do. I don't even like George."

"You needn't play coy with me, Betty Broadbent. I haven't time. And anyway, I only came here because my hair's a fright, and I thought your mother might set it for me, but that sourpuss girl let me in and said she's not home."

"Jennifer? She's all right. But yes, Mother's out, so—"

"So I'm stuck looking like this, that's what," finishes Mary. Betty looks at Mary's hair, curled strangely like a plumed bird.

"It's fine."

"I suppose I do look quite pretty, don't I?" says Mary, twirling before the mirror. "And I'm going out with GRAY." She lets out an excited little shriek.

Betty tries to look excited, too, but she feels very old suddenly, as though she is Mary's elderly aunt instead of her oldest school friend.

"You should probably ignore Gray for a while," continues Mary in a serious tone. "He talks an awful lot about you. He obviously likes me more, but you still shouldn't speak to him, just to be sure. You know how you encourage them sometimes. You need to be fair, Betty."

Betty sighs. She likes Gray. They have long conversations without him staring at parts of her body, the way George does. She can be herself around him. Gray confided in her recently that his parents are thinking of moving to Devon to be closer to his grandparents, but she won't tell Mary that; she would be crushed. She wonders whether to tell Mary about going to the pictures with Gallagher. No, it would be gossiped around in minutes and get back to Mother.

"Now, what dress shall I wear? Bottle green or pink?" continues Mary.

"Green, I think. And make sure he walks you all the way home. It's not safe."

"Do you really think green? Because I prefer the pink. Do you think Gray likes pink?"

By the time she has followed Mary down into the hall and waved until she is a smudge at the end of the street, the hall clock is chiming six times. Betty runs upstairs to change, just as Gallagher's bedroom door opens. He steps out, blocking the landing.

"Who was that visitor of yours? The Eskimos could probably hear her in Siberia."

"My friend Mary," she says, and stifles a laugh.

He shuts his bedroom door and turns the key, his black spy coat slung over one shoulder.

"Come on, now, the pictures won't wait for us."

"But I'm not dressed."

"Nonsense. You look splendid as you are."

Her heart pounds. Splendid, that's what he said.

At the front door, he helps Betty into her coat. Jennifer is humming in the kitchen. Gallagher puts a finger to his lip and they walk out, closing the door softly behind. The street is empty; Betty's hands are sticky with nerves. She walks two steps behind him, and he stops beside a black car with no roof and a shiny silver bumper.

"My baby. Miss Austin Healey," he says, and smacks the hood. "Beauty, isn't she?"

"I didn't realize motorcars had surnames," she says. Or Christian names, she thinks.

Gallagher laughs as if she has made a joke, and Betty blushes.

"We've never had a motorcar," she explains.

He opens the door for her. She climbs in, drawing her coat tighter around her.

"Father spotted her," says Gallagher, slotting in beside her. "He happened to be at Silverstone shortly after she was launched and met some chap who had tired of her already. Out there with the Grand Prix, the lucky devil."

Betty doesn't know who Grand Prix is, only that he must be a very important Frenchman. She nods intelligently, and Gallagher starts the engine. He speeds along the road, and she clutches the edge of her seat. Her stomach churns, and she bunches her legs near the passenger door, far from his.

"I should have brought my camera," she says to make conversation.

But he doesn't hear her over the throaty engine and the rumble of the road, and they drive the rest of the way in silence.

x

THEY ARRIVE FOR THE film fifteen minutes early. Gallagher hands her a peppermint, still warm from his pocket. She fiddles with the paper. He chooses seats in the front row.

"It's empty," she says, surprised.

"He's terrified them all away; it's always the businesses that suffer first," says Gallagher in a matter-of-fact tone, and it takes Betty a moment to realize who he means.

"Have you any leads?" she says, her eyes on the red velvet curtain.

"Leads?" He half smiles, as though she shouldn't know the word.

"So have you?"

"None apart from Forbes. Napier's focusing on him, though I'm not convinced."

"Who do you think it is?" she says quickly, hoping he won't ask her any more about Mr. Forbes.

"Never you mind, little lady."

"I could probably help."

"Aren't you a tease? I'm sure you'd make quite the KGB interrogator."

"I'm serious," she says crossly.

"Why are you so interested?"

She shrugs.

"Because all the ladies in this village seem awfully scared but not particularly inquisitive," he continues. "Whereas you're quite the opposite."

"It's just . . . Mother's not safe until he's caught."

"Your mother? What about you?"

"Oh, I'm fine, but Mother's a blonde."

Gallagher raises one eyebrow. It is that funny eyebrow with the life of its own.

"Just like poor Maureen and Elsa," she explains. "He's picking blondes, isn't he?"

"Who told you that?"

"No one, but I saw their pictures in the newspaper. And if there's nothing else linking them . . . They didn't live in St. Steele, they weren't related, they didn't even go to school together. So he must have chosen them because they're both pretty and look a bit alike. Unless it's a coincidence. But is anything in the world ever a true coincidence?"

"Sharp as a tack, aren't you," he says, watching her. "I think I've my next story."

"No, don't listen to me," she says, blushing. "Maybe it is just a coincidence."

"Gentlemen prefer blondes, and so does the Cornish Cleaver," he says, nodding in the direction of the screen. "How's that for a timely headline?"

Betty frowns. It's tasteless, she wants to say. And, Why do you always write about our private conversations in your articles? But he is too busy rummaging in his trouser pocket to notice her expression. He pulls out a fistful of peppermints and banknotes.

"I've been meaning to give you a little something." He pushes the notes into her hand.

"What are these?"

"For the tip-off, the Cornish Cleaver suggestion. I look after all my sources."

"But I'm not a source."

She drops the money on the floor in surprise. A cheap source, Reggie's words return to her. She jumps to her feet.

"Sit down, for goodness' sake. What's the matter with you?" he hisses.

"I—I need to get back."

"What are you talking about? The film's about to start."

The door swings open. A group of girls, a little older than Betty, files in. They speak in high voices. Betty's throat tightens. The peppermint seems to have lodged itself between her tonsils, but when she moves her tongue, it is still on top of it.

"Betty, it's perfectly normal. Reporters often tip their sources," whispers Gallagher in a hard way. "Just accept it. Then we can watch the film, and after I drive you back, we need never speak again if that's what you want."

She opens her lips to explain what she means: that she didn't want to be his source, that he should never have stolen her words in the first place. She wants to know why he is warm one moment and frosty the next; why the other reporters dislike him so much; and why he pays attention to her at all, when all she does is spill tea over him and say daft things. Her eyes well up and Gallagher looks blurry. He probably looks at her and sees a silly girl. She should never have come. She rushes out of the picture house.

Outside she runs faster, pounding the pavement with her feet. One mile closer to home, the movie theater far behind her, she slows to a walk and wipes her eyes with her fists. The street is empty; the air is mild and choking with gnats. She tucks down her head as she passes Mr. Forbes's closed-up shop. Someone has thrown eggs at it. Stringy yellow yolk dribbles down the glass shop front. Half of her would like to wash it off for him, but then she thinks of Mother and she isn't sorry for him at all.

Betty had pretended not to mind when she saw Mother kissing him in the kitchen of Hotel Eden two months ago, and when Mother didn't come home from his shop until eleven o'clock for six nights in a row. When she did, she smelled of meat and grease and smiled too much, making Betty smile, too. But one night she didn't come home at all.

Just after two o'clock Betty had locked up the hotel, run along the black streets, and knocked on Mr. Forbes's shop door. He hadn't answered, so she had walked around the back to the abattoir and noticed a bit of Mother's green skirt fabric caught on a jagged broken window. She had climbed through after her and found Mother lying under the meat hooks on the red stained concrete, a bottle of sherry in one hand, a handful of white petals in the other. She was barefoot and sobbing and chanting his name. Betty had put her too-big shoes on Mother's ballerina feet, laced them, and walked Mother home, her arm around Mother's shoulders. Her own feet were slashed with gravel by the time they reached Hotel Eden.

Mother had gone back to his butcher's shop the next night, and the next. On his back doorstep, she had left dozens of letters and Victoria sponge cakes cut into heart shapes, but Mr. Forbes only ever sighed at her and said in a tired voice, "Please stop this, Dolores. I'm sorry, but it really is over."

Betty had wanted to tell Gallagher every bit of it and explain that Mr. Forbes was so cowardly and un-killer-like that, even when he changed his mind and stopped loving Mother, he wasn't violent or nasty with it. Instead he ignored her letters and door knocks and pretended she was a ghost like his dead wife. But then Betty had reminded herself that if Gallagher wrote about it, and the inspector found out about the love affair, Mother would be questioned about him, and her nerves might not stand it, so she had pledged to tell no one.

Betty glances at the butcher's shop. The upstairs curtains are drawn, but there is a snake of light in the gap between them. She thinks she sees a silhouette at the window, but it is probably just her imagination. Still, she walks on a little faster. She passes Woolworth's and turns onto the main carriageway with nothing but fields on one side and sea on the other, all wrapped up in black night. The first flutters of fear fill her chest, and she starts to trot.

Minutes pass, and a car engine fills the silence. She glances back and sees two enormous headlamps. It is bulkier than Gallagher's car and it slows as it nears her. Something about it makes her break into a sprint. Her chest heaves and the thick air clogs her lungs, but she runs harder, imagining that each breath of wind is a blade swiping at her.

The car crawls along the curb beside her and she tries to sprint faster but she can't. She looks at the car but can't make out the driver; the windows are too dark. She isn't certain how much longer she can run for. At some point she will have to stop and give herself up to him. But then the car whooshes off and she is alone again.

Tears slide down her cheeks. She slows to a jog, and to calm herself, she pictures Hotel Eden with the stone water jar heating the bed and Mother singing along to the wireless. She is still trotting when a second car rumbles up to her and the passenger door swings open.

"Betty?" says Gallagher in his short, cool way.

She stops. She is so relieved; she could throw herself down and hug his ankles.

"There was a car . . . ," she begins.

"Are you getting in or not?" he cuts in.

He is hunched over the wheel, his face white and taut in the moonlight. She is about to thank him when she notices a slash of red across his knuckles. She freezes, one leg inside the car, the other out of it.

"My nose bled," he says roughly.

"Your nose?"

"It does that when I'm . . . Look, that's what kept me, so will you get in?"

He rubs his fist with his handkerchief. Betty looks at the dark road, then at him. She isn't sure what to believe, but she thinks again of the big car and clambers inside.

"I'm sorry," she mutters.

"I'm sorry about all of that," he says, and she isn't certain whether he heard her.

"I shouldn't have run off like that."

"Yes, well. I've never had a free source."

She wonders whether it is a joke, but neither of them laughs. He drives on. They reach a roundabout and he circles it twice.

"Shall we go back and watch the end of the film?" he shouts over the engine. "It looked quite good, but don't tell anyone I said that or it'll ruin my image."

She nods and tries not to think about the blood on his knuckles or the other car. He shoots back to the picture house, so fast, the night and the trees and the streetlamps merge into one.

✕

BETTY IS WOKEN JUST after dawn by a rustle of voices outside. She climbs out of bed and peeks between the curtains. The moon and the sun still sit side by side, but on the street below is a crowd of her neighbors, all wearing their dressing gowns and slippers. Joan stands in the middle, her head piled with rollers and her hands flailing as she talks to her husband Richard.

"Mother," whispers Betty, nudging her.

"Don't," grunts Mother, her eyes still closed. "Leave him, he's mine."

"Wake up, something's happening outside."

Mother groans and rolls over. Betty pulls on her bed jacket. She makes for the bedroom door and trips over two empty wine bottles that weren't there when she went to bed. There is no one on the stairs or in the hall, but the men rattle around in their bedrooms. Betty slips through the front door and heads for Joan. Black mascara trails down Joan's cheeks, and her eyes are pink and puffy.

"What happened?" says Betty.

"Everyone's leaving," cries Joan. "It'll be a ghost town; he's driving them all out."

She points at Mr. Gwavas from number twelve; he is stacking suitcases in the trunk of his car while Mrs. Gwavas tucks blankets around their twin girls, asleep on the back seat.

"My Richard wants us to leave, too, just until the police find him," continues Joan, her teeth chattering. "But I told him: no one but the Lord himself will drive me away from my home. Not even the Cornish Cleaver."

Richard crosses the pavement wearing flannel pajamas and carrying a steaming teacup. Betty draws her bed jacket tighter around her, blushing.

"You're in shock," he says, handing Joan the cup. He turns to Betty. "Tell your mother I'll fit an extra lock on her door this afternoon. No charge."

"Has something else happened?" says Betty.

"These shouldn't even be up," cuts in Joan bitterly, nodding at a poster on the lamppost. "It's disrespectful to the families."

With her long red fingernail, she picks at the loose corner and peels it off. *Newl Grove Residents' Association Annual Day Trip*, it reads. *11 July.* Below are lots of words stenciled at skewed angles. *Torquay. Pier. Pavilion. Pleasure steamers.*

"Haven't you heard?" says Richard softly to Betty.

"Last night," whispers Joan.

"Not another?" says Betty, her mouth dry.

Joan nods.

"Who was she?"

"The niece of one of the factory workers," says Richard. "One of Napier's men found her in the early hours. Pretty little blonde thing, so he said."

Joan picks the last gluey bits of the poster off the lamppost.

"Napier was just here," continues Richard. "He said the constabulary is finally drafting in fifty more troops to patrol, but it's three murders too late if you ask me."

"Stop it," hisses Joan. "We should stick together, not criticize our own."

"Where did they find her?" says Betty, looking down at her cold bare toes.

The yellow headlights and the wide car flash back to her. She should tell them, but something stops her. What if it was just her brain tricking itself with fear? What if the car didn't slow down at all? Even if it did, maybe the driver was just lost. She would look silly; they would think her a scared little girl, and worse, they would ask why she was in Spoole and with whom.

"Somewhere on the embankment up by—" sniffles Joan, mopping her nose.

"The New Road," finishes Richard.

"Not by the Spoole Picture House?" mutters Betty, and a cold hand slides down her spine and squeezes.

"That's it. The very place."

4

Fifty years later

"What happened, dear?" says an elderly lady.

Mary twists away from her and stares harder at the headline stand: "Cornish Cleaver Speaks."

"She dropped her shopping," puffs the nurse girl, reappearing with Mary's aspirin and asparagus and two salvaged lamb cutlets balanced on top of her wheel-along suitcase. She carries Mary's full grocery bag in her other hand. "Don't worry. I'm a trainee nurse. I think she's just in shock. Unless it's a stroke." She turns to Mary and speaks louder, "Sugarplum, can you tell me your name?"

Mary realizes that her coat is hanging off one shoulder and that she is crouching. A huddle of shins has gathered around her.

"Can I call someone for you?" the nurse girl is saying.

Mary shakes her head, confused. She pulls her coat straight, stands, and walks on.

"Your shopping," the girl calls after her. "Your tart's a goner but the veg is okay."

x

INSIDE STAR NEWSAGENTS, MARY picks up the top newspaper. "Sicko Cleaver Speaks," says the red-and-white front page. She forces herself to read on:

> Sick murderer, the Cornish Cleaver, spoke out for the first time ever yesterday, exactly 50 years after he stabbed to death his pregnant ex-girlfriend. Family of the victim branded the newspaper's decision to print the interview "downright disgusting."

"Do you want to buy that?" calls the newsagent in a chalky Indian accent.

Mary blocks him out and tries to read the next sentence, but the words swim around the page.

> . . . was imprisoned for 20 years for stabbing pregnant Maureen Cardy in the stomach 14 times. She was found by a fisherman on a blood-spattered beach in St. Steele, a village on the south coast of Cornwall. The attack was so savage that the victim's body was dismembered. Her body parts and internal organs were found across the sand.

"I'm sorry," whispers Mary.

"There's something the problem?" says the newsagent, but gentler. Mary shakes her head, losing her place again.

> Defending her decision to publish the interview, Editor in Chief Elaine Riseborough wrote in her editorial comment: "Is the freedom to respond not a right to which every human is entitled, no matter how heinous their crime—or alleged crime?" She added: "After all, this man has been painted as the bastion

of evil in thousands of articles, books and reports published over the last 50 years, yet he was convicted on a single piece of circumstantial evidence and has quietly but persistently appealed ever since."

The shopkeeper calls out in a foreign tongue to someone in the back room and a tissue is pressed into Mary's hand. The doorbell jangles and the nurse reappears, pulling along the squeaky-wheeled suitcase.

"There you are," she says with a thread of frustration. "I've brought your groceries. I'd help if I could, but I'm going to miss my train and I don't think you've had a stroke, anyway."

Mary's knees ache. She realizes that she is kneeling and that the girl is still talking at her, but she doesn't hear what's said. The noises have all merged; her ears could be underwater. She turns back to the newspaper, pushing herself to read more.

"It's absolutely disgusting," said Taylor Cardy, the victim's nephew. "Printing the interview gave that monster the attention he wanted. It's all very well to talk about his human rights but what about Maureen's rights? What about her unborn child's right to live?"

Released in 1976, he was given a new identity and round-the-clock security at an estimated cost to the taxpayer of £350,000 per year. His identity was uncovered in 1990, shortly after he married a woman 15 years his junior. The pair have since been given a second set of new identities and are believed to live in Spain.

"I did the right thing," whispers Mary, but her voice doesn't sound like her own.

It isn't that she forgot or that she lived easily with her decision. Rather, the memory of it all has been compressed for so long, it takes her a while to unpack it.

> Maureen had arranged to meet him on the night she died, apparently to tell him that she was pregnant after their brief affair. He admitted meeting her but denied the affair and killing her.

"The right thing," she repeats more firmly. "I did, didn't I?"

> He was acquitted of the murders of five other young women, all killed in similar circumstances in the surrounding villages in the summer of 1956. Their killer has never been brought to justice, and the victims' families have repeatedly called for a retrial.

Mary retches again. Vomit spatters the chipped vinyl tiles. "Mital!" calls the shopkeeper, then more foreign words.

Another tissue is placed in Mary's hand, a warm palm rests on her back, then she is being helped up and steered through a door toward darkness.

x

MARY SITS ON A stool in a windowless back room stacked with boxes of chocolates. The newsagent's wife hands her a mug of hot milky tea that smells of cloves and cinnamon but tastes acidic. Her mouth is coated with bile, and her vision is gluey. It sticks onto anything in front of her, making her seem starey and odd. Her eyes lock onto the round red spot between the newsagent's wife's eyebrows. She forces them away.

"Thank you," she says, ashamed, nodding at the tea. "I'm not usually like this."

She should mop herself up and go home, but somehow she can't.

"No English; my wife speak little English," bellows the newsagent, poking his head around the door and waving a mop.

The shop door opens, and he disappears again before Mary can say "thank you for your help" and "sorry for spoiling your shop floor." His wife dips her head. She has a long ponytail and wisps of black girlish hair. Only the crisscross of wrinkles betrays that they are similar in age. What must she think of her: a bedraggled, vomiting old woman?

"You have done not bad thing," says the wife, surprising Mary.

"But I have."

"No, my husband clean floor. He is good man. Not angry."

Mary manages a watery smile. The woman slides down from her stool; she is surprisingly short—tiny, even—and she reaches for a brown notepad covered with rows of shapes.

As she moves, Mary sees that her groceries have been transferred into new blue polythene bags. Something about the woman's kindness makes her eyes sting. She is wondering how to show her gratitude—perhaps she should explain the significance of the article—but then she notices several bundles of newspapers, bound up with white tape. A sheet of paper on top of the tallest stack says "old stock" in blue felt tip pen.

On the cover is his mug shot taken fifty years ago. It is the same photograph the newspapers rehashed throughout his trial and when he was released, and even when he was given a second new identity. Even now he is caught in time; still a man of thirtysomething in his old age.

"Exclusive Interview with the Cornish Cleaver," says the headline. On the line beneath it: "I am innocent—my only deathbed regret is that I didn't fight harder to prove it." Mary reaches down and picks up the newspaper. She is about to read it, but his eyes bore into her as though he is looking her in the eye again, the way he did that day he knelt on the pavement and pleaded for her help. She rolls him up and stuffs him to the bottom of her handbag so he can't look at her like that, and she jumps to her feet.

"Yesterday newspaper. Old newspaper. No good this day," says the newsagent's wife, pointing at Mary's handbag.

"I have to go," says Mary, picking up her grocery bags.

"My husband say these word to me when I cry," continues the woman tentatively, looking at her notebook. "What is the use of crying when the birds ate the whole farm?"

She reaches forward to touch Mary's hand, but Mary pulls back.

"I'm—I'm sorry to be rude," stammers Mary. "Thank you for— you're very kind but I need—"

"No crying when birds ate farm whole," repeats the woman firmly.

Mary half nods and smiles vaguely at her, then she turns and hurries out of Star Newsagents.

She steams along Richmond High Street, but in the other direction this time, and is breathless by the time she arrives. She has stood outside this building at least one hundred times before and thought of going in but always changed her mind. Today, without pausing, she heaves open the double doors and steps inside.

The doors clank shut behind her. Her heels clack against the parquet, echoing, bouncing off the stained glass and reverberating against the copper organ pipes. It takes a second for her eyes to adjust to the murkiness. She notices a figure at the far side of the room. He—though it is impossible to be sure—is cloaked in shadow. He holds a candle in his right hand, and his left peels back a curtained doorway.

"Wait," she calls, as he steps toward it. "Don't go. There's something I have to— Could you take my confession?"

5

The day of the dance arrives too soon. Late afternoon, Mother shuffles into the kitchen with purple rings under her eyes. She smells of gin. Betty stiffens.

"Are you feeling better?"

Mother doesn't reply. She unfolds a copy of the *Cornishman* with a plea on the front page from Lord Mayor Oates to the killer himself. "Dear Cornish Cleaver," it reads. Mother laughs at it in a scraping way.

"Silly, isn't it," agrees Betty. "Do they really think he'll read it and just turn himself in?"

"I haven't forgotten the dance tonight," cuts in Mother, tossing the paper into the rubbish bin.

Betty is surprised that Mother remembers the dance at all. She hasn't left her bed for five solid days, ever since Betty snuck to the pictures. She won't tell Mother that another girl died; she is fragile already, and another worry might make her crumble again.

"George'll be here soon to collect you," continues Mother, beaming.

"I'm not going," says Betty. "I need to make the breakfast bread and buy in fresh meat. The men can't live on carrots and parsnips forever."

She has put off leaving Hotel Eden the whole time Mother has been in bed. She locks the door with a bolt when the men leave after their breakfasts, and she only opens it again to let them back in at supper-time or to bring in the box of vegetables that Richard has taken to collecting for her. She reminds herself that she isn't scared of going out, just busy.

"You're not missing the dance," says Mother firmly. "You can't lose George when we're this close . . ."

Betty rips the leaves off a cabbage and frowns. Blow to George, she wants to say, but she must care for Mother, and that means not upsetting her.

"Go for me, dance for me," continues Mother. "God knows I wish it was still my turn."

She waltzes around the kitchen wearily, her oily hair flicking out, and bangs into a saucepan handle. Wet carrots tumble to the floor. Betty picks them up wordlessly as Mother pours herself a thimble of sherry. She tips back her head and swallows. Betty would like to pull the glass from her hand and straitjacket Mother with a hug.

"Have another nap if you like. I'll make supper," says Betty softly.

"You know I won Miss West Country before the war?" says Mother as she pours another sherry. "It's not your fault you drew the short straw with your father's looks, but you must compensate. You need to dance well and make the best of yourself, Elizabeth. Marriage proposals don't come easily, especially ones from a catch like young George."

"I'm not going . . . I don't think it's right to dance when those girls have only just died."

Mother pinches her cheek.

"You must go," she says in a fierce voice that Betty has never heard before.

Betty pulls away, but Mother clamps her cheek tighter. The side of her face numbs.

"You're hurting me."

"You will go and you will have a smashing time. He's a Paxon," says Mother firmly.

She bangs her other hand on the countertop, so hard that Betty is certain her bones will crack.

"Don't look at me like that; you know it's true," continues Mother, rubbing her palm. "You must seize your moment and snare him before some clever little slut snatches him from under your nose. Do you hear me?"

Mother releases her and tips back a third sherry. Betty rubs her cheek back to life.

"That's better," sighs Mother when the glass is empty and she sounds like herself again.

She sets down her glass and strokes Betty's other cheek now but in a tender way, as though Betty is an egg and if she is handled too roughly she will crack.

"You'll listen to your old mother, won't you? She knows best."

Betty nods, her eyes damp.

"I knew it. You're looking forward to having a little jive, aren't you?"

"Yes, Mother."

"Excellent. You've made my day."

x

AN HOUR LATER, a car horn toots. Betty pulls closed the front door and steps out into the drizzle, just as Mother appears in the big room window, her red lipstick painted on and hard blocks of rouge on her cheeks. She waves madly and Betty waves back, then realizes that Mother isn't looking at her at all. Her wave is directed at the wide, black car parked on the other side of the street. She seems to be looking at Mr. Paxon, who sits on the front seat, holding the steering wheel and keeping his eyes in his lap.

Betty crosses the road to the car and wedges herself into the back seat beside Mary. Inside it smells of petroleum and sugar and a familiar perfume.

"Excited about the dance?" says Mary shrilly, and Betty nods.

"You're looking lovely," says Gray, leaning around Mary to catch Betty's eye.

"I'm not really," she mutters.

She ignores Mary's glare. Mr. Paxon starts the car, and Betty turns and waves out of the back window until Mother disappears. George swivels from the front passenger seat, making the skin on his neck twist around like a helter-skelter, and he hands them each a pale cookie with fluted edges.

"Try one," he cries.

"What is it?" says Mary, examining hers.

"Pa invented it. He's a genius," squeals George.

Mr. Paxon half turns in his driving seat and cocks an eyebrow at Betty. She wishes he would concentrate on the road instead. She doesn't swoon after him like Mary and Miss Hollinghurst and the other girls who all jostle for a space in his church pew every Sunday, ignoring tight-lipped Mrs. Paxon. Betty sees that they might like his striking jaw or his thin, reserved smile that probably makes them feel special, but his hair is flecked with silver, as though it has already started to die. Not at all like Gallagher's hair, which is shiny black and curly. She blushes at the thought.

x

THE CONCERT HALL IS already full when they arrive. On the opposite side of the dance floor are two doors, flung open onto a grass verge that slopes down to a long, empty beach. Sea air gushes in, flirting with the girls' hemlines. George and Gray buy orange juice from the bar while Betty and Mary hover near the dance floor.

"I've news," squeaks Mary when they are alone. "Aunt Irene found me a position. From next week I'm to be a telephone operator in Spoole. Fancy that? Me, a working woman!"

"You're not going to secretarial college anymore?"

"No need. Mr. Cripps's other girls will train me up. He said I'm a natural."

"I'm so pleased for you," she says in a high voice, and hugs Mary.

She wishes she was pleased inside, too, but it is all happening so fast. Only three weeks ago they were at their school desks, whispering and planning this—their future. Now it has snuck up on her.

"I'm pleased for me, too. Isn't it the best news?"

"And how was your night out with Gray?" says Betty.

Mary wrinkles her nose and gives a little shake of her head, just as George and Gray reappear. The microphone crackles, and a man wearing a butter-colored suit announces the start of the dance contest.

Betty tries to focus on the girl dancer's trippy footwork and the boy dancer's carrot-orange hair, but George stands too close to her. Beads of sweat cluster on his brow. His hand reaches out and finds hers. It is wet and pudgy, like a toddler's. She pulls away and clasps her hands behind her back. Mary whispers something to Gray, but his eyes are on Betty, too. Mary scowls. "I need some fresh air," Betty whispers to George, and hurries to the beach doors before he can reply; something is squeezing closed the opening of her throat.

Outside the air is thinner and the sky is bruised with angry storm clouds. She inches her way down the verge, relieved to escape, and her breathing eases. She scans the beach: to her right is a shoulder of cliff that juts out into the sea, and to the left is a long worm of bleached sand, with a huddle of stick men on it. Two of the men break away from the pack and walk along the empty beach toward her, while the others clamber over the dunes to a dozen cars parked haphazardly on the roadside. Applause wafts out of the hall and needles of warm rain pick down. She looks harder at the breakaway pair, their heads bowed in conversation. One wears a policeman's custodian helmet and the other wears a fedora and long black coat that flows out behind him. Betty's throat tightens again. She knows that coat. Mr. Gallagher.

She hasn't seen him since the pictures. Were his bedsheets not rumpled up every morning and his wardrobe not filled with a neat line of shirts, she would think he had left St. Steele altogether. She has almost managed to block out their last confusing moment alone together, but now she sees him, it replays in her mind: How he drove her home in silence after the film and they tiptoed back into the dark hallway of Hotel Eden. How the door to the big room was shut fast, but they could hear a drone of voices and clinked glasses from within. How he hung up his fedora and wordlessly leaned forward as if to kiss her, then jerked away and strode past her up the stairs, careful not to brush skins. She still isn't certain what she did wrong or why he has avoided her since.

"Betty!"

She glances back and sees George making his way down the damp verge, his arms outstretched to keep his balance.

"Come back up, Bet. I want a dance."

"Soon, I just need some air."

"But I want to dance now. And a storm's brewing."

The wind sighs and seawater sprays their faces. George wipes his eyes. The pair of figures on the sand creep closer. Betty points at them.

"Haven't you heard?" says George. "Napier just had a meeting with the newsmen. They wouldn't all fit in the station, and he didn't think the cove was right, what with Maureen, so they came out here. That's what Pa told me, anyway." He pauses. "So who d'you think the Cleaver is?"

"I don't want to think about it."

"Well, you've nothing to worry about. Not when I'm here."

He steps closer to her so the hairs on their arms brush. She leans away.

"I don't bite," he says, and jabs her middle with his elbow.

"Go back up to the dance or they'll be wondering where you are. I'll come in a bit."

"Stop playing with me, Betty. I know you want me really."

If he jerked forward another inch, his lips would touch hers, or perhaps her chin. She can smell his fish breath and see the jewels of rain clinging to his horrible eyelashes.

"Look, I know you're nervous, but I've done this before. Just let me show you."

"You'll show me nothing, George Paxon."

But he grabs her wrists and pulls her toward him.

"Stop it."

"You're such a cocktease," he snaps.

"No, let me go."

"Yes," he insists.

His lips pucker in a comic book sort of way. He moves forward slowly—so slowly, she is certain she would have time to run to the other end of the beach before his lips reached hers, were he not holding her wrists so tightly. His eyes are squeezed shut. He inches closer.

Suddenly a cough cuts in. George's head jerks back. His eyes open and he looks around, releasing her wrists.

"I'm afraid this area is out of bounds," says a voice.

Betty looks up and sees Gallagher in front of them. His trench coat is belted and a notebook is poised in his hand.

"Dreadfully sorry, Inspector," says George in a formal voice. "Part of the investigation, is it?"

Betty waits for Gallagher to correct him.

"That's right," says Gallagher with a stern look. "Make your way inside."

George holds out his hand to help Betty up the grass slope that is slippery with new rain.

"Actually I'll need a minute with the young lady," says Gallagher.

She tries not to smile and searches Gallagher's face, but he still doesn't look at her.

"Of course, Inspector. And you'll see her safely back up to the dance hall afterward?"

Gallagher nods. Betty watches George struggle up the verge. He loses his footing and steadies himself with his hands, looking back sheepishly. She almost feels sorry for him.

"Why do I get the impression I saved you from a sticky situation back there?" says Gallagher when George is indoors. His eyes are all crinkled up and twinkly.

"Nothing I couldn't manage."

"There, that's the spirit."

She stares at him, confused by his friendliness.

"You're cold," he says tenderly.

"I'm fine."

Gallagher unbelts and removes his coat and arranges it around her shoulders. She lets him, holding her breath in case she smells fishy like George. Why are you being so kind to me, she wants to ask.

The raindrops fatten. They watch the real policeman pace across the beach toward the jutting cliff.

"They've questioned Forbes and released him for now," says Gallagher. "I thought you might—"

"No," she cuts in. "I've told you, I'm not your source."

She is pleased at having stood up to him, but he gives a grim smile.

"I was just going to tell you what Napier told me after the others had gone . . . That whoever killed Maureen probably knew her. She was expecting. He suspects that she and Forbes were a couple; that the child was his."

Betty looks at him stunned, but she swallows the hundred questions that are ready to leap out of her mouth. She should get back to the hotel. Mother will be crushed when she finds out.

"No one knows," adds Gallagher, as though reading her thoughts again. "Napier told me in confidence."

"Why would he tell only you?"

Gallagher shrugs.

"I suppose I'm decent to him. Not like those dogs." He nods at the patch of beach where the other reporters had been.

"Did you pay him, too?" she asks.

He looks hard at her. "No, Betty. I didn't. And if I'd known it would upset you that much, I wouldn't have offered you a penny."

His arms wrap around her, and her face is pressed against his chest. It is firm. She sucks in her tummy, and her head fugs up with the smell of his bitter soap and cigarettes and Brylcreem. She would like to stay in his warm arms, not caring if anyone sees them, but then there is a bleat of trumpets in the dance hall, and Gallagher drops his arms to his sides. Betty glances back at the doors.

"I ought to go back up there," she says.

"Why?"

"He'll want me to dance with him."

"You don't have to do anything you don't want to."

"You don't know my mother," she says, and lets out a half-hearted laugh.

She would like to add that there is nothing she would like to do more than stay in the rain with him, but she is terrified of saying something wrong or foolish, so it is safer to leave him now before she spoils everything.

The rain comes harder. Betty clutches a bunch of her wet dress to keep her hem from the grass.

"You'll need a walking stick to make it back up the slope," he says, handing her a fallen tree branch.

She reaches for it and skids. Gallagher steadies her.

"I can walk by myself," she says, flustered, making him grin. She tries to step forward, but her foot slides again, and he catches her arm to keep her upright, taking the branch from her.

He presses the tip of it into the muddy grass to steady himself and arches forward.

"Jump up," he says.

"I'm sorry?"

"On my back. Jump up. I'll carry you to the top."

"No you won't."

"Do you see a better way of getting up there in those silly little shoes of yours?"

Betty doesn't think about it. She propels herself forward and lunges onto his back. Scared of tumbling straight back off again, she wraps her legs around his waist. His hands sit under her thighs. They are warm, even through the taffeta. She panics. It is wrong somehow. She unwraps her legs again and pushes her hands against his back, struggling to get down.

"Put me down!"

Gallagher loses his footing. He topples forward, and the two of them tumble down the grass verge, Gallagher on his front, Betty over his head. They land on the beach, inches apart and just a few feet from the foamy waves that beat the sand. Betty's mouth is gritty with wet sand. She blinks, winded. Her tongue tastes of metal. Pain shoots through her right arm. Gallagher hauls himself upright and brushes sand from his coat, his face stormy. Betty can still feel the broadness and heat of his back pressed to her thighs. Mortified, she tucks her chin to her chest and hobbles away.

The rain pounds, and liquid mud dribbles down her dress. The sky cracks with lightning. She wipes her eyes and glances back at Gallagher. His face is twisted in a strange grimace and his skin is white. She marches on toward the paved pathway that leads back up to the dance hall. She reaches the top and winds her way around the building, pausing near the front door. Her cheeks are scalding with embarrassment.

Gallagher catches up to her. He stops, too, and gazes at the window. Dancers whisk past and music wails out. Betty wishes she could read his thoughts. He is probably looking at one of the pretty girl dancers, and she is gripped with a strange balled-up angriness. Their eyes meet in the glass.

"You don't have to go back in there," he says, his voice brittle. "We could just drive."

There is another growl of thunder, louder this time. You're his cheap source, she reminds herself. He only wants you so he can squeeze another article out of you. As if someone like him would really notice a silly girl like you otherwise. Betty turns and runs back indoors.

Mary stands on the corner of the dance floor, her arms crossed and her face stony. When she sees Betty's dripping hair and dress, soiled with sand and mud, she sniggers, but then remembers her anger.

"You all just basically left me," she cries. "You ran off goodness knows where, George went off to the bar with some blonde, and I haven't seen him since. And Gray . . ." She groans.

Betty is about to reply, but Mary cuts over her.

"Do you know how tedious it is? Being taken to a dance, then aban-

doned by your three friends—or so-called friends. You don't, do you?
No one would dream of abandoning you."

A trumpet wails, and the man in the butter-yellow suit taps his microphone.

"I tripped down the verge," says Betty weakly.

Mary rolls her eyes. The butter man screeches something, and the band fires up.

"All he talked about was you," shrieks Mary over the music.

"Who did?"

"Gray," she cries. "When he took me to supper the other week. You're so greedy, Betty. You encourage them, and it's just not fair on me."

She stamps her foot and is about to continue, but George appears with two cups of orange juice. He hands one to Mary, not looking at Betty.

"Your little friend's gone, then?" snaps Mary, but George doesn't hear.

"Want a dance?" he says, and Mary nods eagerly.

She shoves her cup in Betty's hand and glides off with George. Betty is glad to be alone—her back aches, her knees are grazed, and her hair is still dripping. She drains the last of Mary's orange juice and wonders how to explain to Mother that Mr. Forbes loved Maureen. She will be broken, but better she hears it from Betty than from the newspapers or gossipmongers.

Betty is looking for somewhere to set down the cup when a scream cuts over the music. The piano stops. The trumpet belches and dies. A second later, the dancers all stop whirling, and the hall falls silent but for murmurs and gasps. Mary tucks herself in George's arms, and Gray appears at Betty's side. Every head turns toward the beach doors where the scream came from.

A girl stands in the doorway. Her long raven hair is drenched and her dress is muddier than Betty's. She screams again, then crumples into a heap on the dance floor. Betty squeezes the orange juice cup. It cracks. Whispers rustle across the dance floor. The pianist crosses the room and cradles the raven girl. He says something that Betty can't hear. The girl sits upright.

"On the sand," she bellows, her voice shaking. "I just saw her."

"Saw who?" says the piano man.

"Blood still coming from her neck, I just saw her," repeats the girl.

"What's happened?"

"I don't know, but she's out there. She was dancing earlier. I don't know her name, but she could have been any of us. She's dead."

Gray presses his lips to Betty's ear.

"I just saw George's father parked outside. Let's get you home," he whispers, but Betty is transfixed by the girl.

"Dead," she wails again. "I've never seen so much blood."

Someone screams. There is a wail and another whimper. Mary pulls away from George and lunges at Gray.

"You left me," she shrieks. "It could have been me. You all left me, all three of you, especially you, Gray. I could have died, too. You wouldn't have even noticed. Or cared!"

Mary beats Gray's chest, crying and sniveling, until George pulls her away and hugs her.

"Let's get to the car," says Gray gravely, wrapping an arm around Betty.

Betty nods this time. The crowd of dancers disperse, some to the beach doors where the raven girl is still sobbing loudly, others to the main exit. Betty and Gray are carried out with the crush.

"You all left me," Mary is still saying somewhere. "It could have been me, just at the start of my new job and my new life in Spoole."

They pass from the stickiness of the dance hall to the sheets of cold rain outside. Betty looks around for Gallagher, but he has disappeared. For a strange moment, a picture bubbles up in her head of his red-stained knuckles and his face, all taut and white. She pushes it away—his nose bled, she reminds herself, and she glances down at the beach.

"Don't look at her," says Gray, sidling up.

At first she doesn't know what he means, but then the crowd on the beach parts and Betty sees her: a Sleeping Beauty figure spread out on the sand. She is half covered with a crimson shawl but her gray feet poke out beneath it. A halo glows above her head, but when Betty squints harder, she sees that it is the girl's bright golden hair fanned out and beneath it, a horseshoe of sand soaked red.

6

Fifty years later

Mary sits in the box listening to his slow, steady breaths. It is dark and empty inside, just a splintered bench and velvet curtain and lungfuls of dust. There is something comforting, though, about being swallowed up and stowed here, with no doctor's letters or newspapers or husbands to worry about.

She listens harder to his breathing. It is slow and even, though he has been waiting for her to speak for more than ten minutes. How can anyone be so patient? She would like to ask him that, but it is not what she came here to say. She digs her fingernail into the bench and considers where to begin, where it began. Old varnish curls up behind her nail, pushing into her skin.

"When you're ready," he murmurs from the other side.

She stops picking at the varnish.

"Thank you," she says. A pause. "But now I'm here, I'm not sure where to start."

"It's all right. Take your time."

"I saw a newspaper and I needed to tell someone. . . . It happened so many years ago and I was convinced I'd done the right thing, but after seeing his face again . . ." She gulps. There is another pause. "I should probably tell you that I don't go to church. I've never done this before."

"Everyone is a child of the Lord, Mrs. Sugden."

Her name surprises her, as though she had forgotten she carried it with her into this dark box.

"You said you had something to bring to confession," he continues. The word knifes her. Confession.

"Have you ever had to make a choice?" she begins. "One of those horrible life-changing choices between two people? Like those dreams where you can either save your husband or your daughter . . . I don't suppose you have children. Or a husband." She half laughs nervously. "But you know what I mean?"

His tongue clicks against the side of his mouth as he opens his lips to reply, but she interrupts him, scared of what he might say.

"Or that Bible story. I'm sure you remember it. The one with the baby and the two women—two prostitutes, or were they two queens? You know, they both say it's theirs."

She realizes she is talking very quickly; she isn't sure whether she even sounds legible or whether the sentence has merged into a single bloated, nonsensical word.

"Didn't the king suggest they cut the baby in half? And one said yes, the other said no?" She pauses. "I can't quite remember the rest or what she said—"

"And she said, 'O my lord, give her the living child, and in no wise slay it.' But the other said, 'Let it be neither mine nor thine, but divide it.' Then the king answered and said, 'Give her the living child, and in no wise slay it. She is the mother thereof.' Kings, chapter three."

"Yes," she whispers.

"You said you had to make a choice?"

"How do you know? If it was the right one." She can hear him breathe out slowly.

"That verse continues: 'And all Israel heard of the judgment which the king had judged; and they feared the king: for they saw that the wisdom of God was in him, to do judgment . . .'" He speaks a little louder, as if moving closer to the grid between them. "Sometimes we must listen and let ourselves be guided."

"Guided?"

"Sometimes a decision can be too great to make alone."

There is another long pause. She sits on her hands and wonders how to word it. How would you know about decisions and choices? What does guided even mean? Guided, how? What could you possibly know, sitting here and spending your days inside this little, safe box? Whatever she says will sound angry; best she say nothing at all.

"This was a mistake," she says, jumping to her feet and almost banging her head on the ceiling. "Jerry will be wanting his supper."

"It's all right, Mrs. Sugden."

"I need to get home and marinate the lamb."

"Mrs. Sugden, why don't you—"

She steps out and gulps the clean, pale air. The church is exactly as she left it, her two blue bags still on the front pew. She grabs them and hurries for the door.

The sky is still steely but the traffic has thickened. One streetlamp has flickered on, coloring the pavement a strange watermelon pink. Someone is pulling down a squeaky metal shutter over the door of a vegetable shop. A boy scoots past it wearing a blue raincoat and clutching the handlebars of his silver scooter while a woman, his mother probably, holds his hood. Mary watches them carefully as she walks behind them, or glides perhaps, for she doesn't notice her tread or the firmness of the pavement beneath her shoes.

Then she is off the high street and onto a quieter road of Georgian houses that she has passed countless times before but somehow never noticed until now. The traffic is thinner here and the pavement is slick with crunchless leaves. In front of her, no more than forty steps away, is the mouth of the cul-de-sac—her cul-de-sac: a deceiving word for something so plain.

Fifty-four steps and she could be at her front door, the key in the newly greased lock. Sixty-two steps and she could be in her kitchen, trimming fat off the cutlets, rubbing them with rosemary and that sandpapery sea salt Cath bought her for Christmas. Perhaps she could switch on the radio; that would shut it all out. But would it? If she concentrated hard enough, could she really make herself believe that she never saw those newspapers and that she has been nowhere all day but inside that safe, square kitchen of hers with her drawer of polished teaspoons and sharpened steak knives and neatly stacked salad forks?

"Give me a hand with this, love," says a hard voice.

Mary is suddenly aware that she is sitting down but has no recollection of doing so. She can still see the cul-de-sac, but it is farther away and slanted sideways. Her polythene bags are on the pavement, and her bottom and thighs and back are pressed against a cold metal patio chair—someone else's patio chair. She is reaching down, her shoes are kicked off, and she is rubbing her bunion through her stockings.

"Yoo-hoo, are you asleep down there?"

Mary notices a pair of feet, which must belong to the voice. They are squashed inside pink stilettos, a half-moon of blister spilling over the top. Mary looks up farther. There is a pink leather skirt, so shiny, she might see her own reflection in it if she stared. Above that are two balled fists on the figure's hips. Up more and she sees the tips of the woman's stiff yellow perm; a pair of soft chins; then two eyes, frowning and etched with age lines and kohl.

"I said, ARE YOU ASLEEP DOWN THERE?"

"I'm sorry," says Mary, slipping on her shoes quickly and pulling herself upright. "This must be your chair."

"Yes, and it's my pub an' all. So if you're not going to buy a drink or help me carry this table inside, you can bloody well move on."

"Oh," says Mary. And, to her surprise, she is ready to cry.

She reaches inside her pocket for a tissue and feels something gathering in her chest, pushing its way down into her stomach, then back up toward her throat, making her choke and splutter, but tears still don't come. Tears never come. She can't remember when she last cried.

x

MARY'S FEET DON'T QUITE reach the floor. They dangle off the high barstool, her elbows propped on the sticky bar.

"You look like you could do with one of these," says the landlady.

She stands behind the bar, pouring a bottle of something golden brown into two glasses.

"I should go home," says Mary, not moving.

"You live across the road, don't you? I've seen you walk past but you never come in."

Mary is wondering how to reply. There is a loud smack as the landlady sets down the tumblers on the bar.

"Chin, chin," she says, and flings back her head, draining her glass.

She looks at Mary expectantly.

"I don't drink alcohol."

"So that's why you look so uptight," says the landlady, and grins. Mary doesn't smile back. For so many years, its burning, chemical smell alone was enough to make her skin itch and her throat sting. There is another long pause.

"People tell me things, you know," says the landlady. "Whatever it is won't shock me."

Mary frowns. How do you know I have something shocking to tell, she wants to say. She automatically glances down at her left breast. Then she picks up the glass and necks the liquid. It stings the back of her throat, making her cough. But the burning is vaguely familiar, and soothing, too, in its way.

"You could tell me you'd just murdered a man and I'd have probably heard worse."

"What if I told you I covered up a murder?"

Mary is too shocked at her own words to meet the woman's eye or look for her reaction.

"Like I said, it's difficult to shock me," says the landlady evenly.

Don't you want to know why, Mary wants to ask.

"I've never told anyone that," she says instead, but more angrily than she intended.

"You look like a nice, God-fearing lady," says the landlady, pouring a second round. "So you must have had your reasons."

"I was protecting someone," says Mary, staring into her glass. "An innocent man went to prison for twenty years because of me." She wishes she could push the words back down her throat; she didn't even sound remorseful, just emotionless and factual, as though she were reading a definition aloud from the *Oxford English Dictionary*. The landlady still says nothing. If she were admitting all this to Jerry, she knows exactly what he would reply: "Go to bed, my dearest. You're just having one of your not quite right days." He and Cath said that a lot, as though not quite right days were in the *Oxford English Dictionary*, too, just above the definition of not quite right people.

Mary swallows the second glass of whiskey and enjoys the way it scorches her throat. She doesn't cough this time, but her eyes fog over, making the landlady look featureless and fuzzy.

"Aren't you going to ask why?" says Mary, staring at her but not properly seeing her. "Or how I live with myself?"

The woman shrugs.

"We all do strange things for the men we love."

"Love? I haven't said anything about men or love!"

She refills the glasses again without looking at Mary. This time, she only stops pouring when they are full to the lip. Mary sips it.

"I don't know why I told you that," she says eventually. "I haven't even told my husband."

"We all pick and choose what we tell our other halves, love," snorts the landlady.

"I'm not like you," she says, then flushes. "Sorry, that's not what I meant."

The landlady shrugs. Mary finishes her drink, then sets the glass on the bar. Her insides are very hot, as though a fire has started in her gut and is slowly curling its way upward.

"It's just . . . I was so sure I'd done the right thing. Then today I saw that poor man's face for the first time in goodness knows how many years—decades. And it made me think: How could I have done that? How can choosing one man's life over another ever be okay?"

"Listen love, it's done. You either live with it or you do something about it."

"It's a bit late for that," Mary says in a high voice, and half laughs.

"It's never too late."

The landlady swirls her glass and stares inside it. "This chappy you covered up for; he must have been something really special to be worth all that?"

Mary winces. Even now, she can't bring herself to picture his face again.

"It was a long time ago."

"Still, if you're not sure whether you did the right thing, find out."

"You make it sound so simple."

The landlady shrugs again and turns around to wipe glasses with a gray dishcloth.

"Anyway, that would mean . . ." Mary trails off.

She knows his address by heart, though she has never visited him. It was more a comfort to carry it with her, knowing she could see him if she needed to. She never imagined she would. Mary glares at the landlady's back, angry suddenly.

"Forget what I told you," she says curtly. "I was just being silly and emotional."

She rummages in her handbag for her purse and slaps a note on the bar, just as the pub door swings open and a man shuffles in, his chin buried into his chest and his back curled over his walking stick. The landlady glances at him briefly, then leans over the bar to Mary, so close Mary is forced to breathe in her tobacco breath and her perfume that smells of candy. Mary tries to focus on her, but she is gray and fuzzy; the whole room is gray and fuzzy. Mary grips on to the edge of the bar and holds herself upright.

"Listen," whispers the landlady in her smoky voice. "If I've learned one thing from spending half my life listening to people from behind this bar, it's that lies are worse than cancer. Trust me. They eat you up and poison you, so you either let them rest for good or you cut them out."

She fills Mary's glass, then totters over to the old man at the far end of the pub who is gripping the bar and singing a lullaby in German.

"One for the road," she calls.

"Thank you," says Mary, but it doesn't sound enough.

She wishes she could untangle exactly what the landlady had meant, but the words were woolly and had knitted together. All she knows is that this woman meant well, and, for that, she is grateful.

x

Two hours later, Mary spears the lamb with her fork and tries to focus on the conversation.

"The point of the matter is," says Jerry, smacking the table, "Tony Blair's had his day."

"Go on. I'm dying to hear where you're going with this." Leo smirks, raising an eyebrow at his father-in-law.

Mary fumbles for something to say, but her head is still cloudy, a silhouette of someone printed in the center. She presses her eyes closed and fights to see the figure's face more clearly.

"Look, you're giving Mum a headache," cuts in Cath.

"You might want to bury your head in the sand, Catherine, but those poor army boys on their way to Iraq can't," cries Jerry in a rare burst of impatience.

Cath glares at her father, then looks across the table to her daughter.

"Holly, why don't you tell your gran which universities you're applying to?"

"But I still haven't decided."

"We've talked about this," says Cath warningly.

"I don't see what's wrong with St. Andrews. You'd swear I was suggesting Australia from the way you talk about it."

Mary nods encouragingly at them both, but she has lost the thread. She can't tell why Cath's voice has an angry edge. Something about Iraq and St. Andrew?

"But I thought you agreed Reading would be far more sensible."

"No, that's what you said. Actually, didn't you grow up in Reading, Gran?" says Holly, looking at Mary. "What do you think? I mean, what's it like as a city?"

"Lovely," says Mary with a vague nod.

She hates lying. She could just blurt it out. She has never even been to Reading, everything I told you all about my past is a lie. She often wants to say that, but there would be too many questions. She chews on her lamb. It is tender, the way only Cath can make it.

"What, so we should turn a blind eye? Withdraw from Iraq?" cries Leo.

Cath groans and stacks the dirty plates.

"Let's leave them to it," she says, heading for the kitchen.

Mary follows, Holly close behind. They divide up the tasks without speaking: Holly at the dishwasher, Cath pulling foil from a dish of blackberry crumble, and Mary making custard from powder. She mixes it on autopilot, but when she comes to, the milk has stuck to the pan. Cath takes the wooden spoon from her, and the custard is rescued. Holly sprays the countertops clean. They move fast, too fast for Mary these days.

They carry in the bowls and dole out the crumble while Mary hovers behind, redundant. She realizes that her right hand is touching the side of her left breast, her fingers pressing into it, the way she has taken to doing mindlessly, to check that the lump hasn't grown bigger than an olive pit. She drops her hand quickly and looks around, but no one seems to have noticed.

Two more conversations tumble over one another, but Mary can't fully latch on to either. She looks at them all around the table; she should be proud that they are hers and that she brought them together this evening, but something is lacking, as though she is their cumbersome guest, welcome but a stranger.

She spoons up another mouthful of crumble. It sears the roof of her mouth, and a blister bubbles up.

"You're quiet tonight, Mum," says Cath.

Her mouth is full. Scalding blackberries scorch her tongue; the blister is ready to pop. She doesn't know what to say.

"Yes, quiet," she manages, but they still look at her expectantly. She rests her spoon on the lip of her dish. "There's something I must tell you."

It is the right time, only she isn't sure how to word it and which news to begin with. *Perhaps I did a terrible thing. I let a man go to prison knowing he was innocent. It's no excuse, but I did it to protect someone I love.* Loved, she corrects herself. She looks at Jerry: poor, loving Jerry. She picks up her spoon.

"I just wanted to thank Cath for saving the day and for making us such a delicious meal," she says. "And for marinating the lamb so beautifully and for this lovely crumble. Are the blackcurrants from the garden?"

"Mum, they're blackberries," says Cath, frowning. "I bought them from Waitrose. You watched me make it."

Cath looks worried. They all look worried.

"Oh, I was getting muddled. I made blackcurrant jam last week, didn't I, Jerry?"

Jerry smiles uncertainly, and the others look into their bowls. Better she hadn't spoken at all.

"Are you sure you're all right, Gran?" says Holly.

"Bit headachy, that's all."

"If you want to lie down, Mum," says Cath. "Dad said you—"

"Will you all stop fussing," she shouts.

The room is silent. Leo clinks his spoon against his dish. Mary blushes. She never raises her voice. Jerry mouths, "Are you okay?" but she ignores him.

"Did you see the news today?" says Cath in her diplomatic way, and Mary's stomach leaps into her mouth. "Something about a school of dolphins being found in the Thames. Must be some sort of odd PR stunt."

Mary relaxes again, but only slightly.

x

ONE HOUR LATER, CATH, Leo, and Holly pile into their minivan. After they have waved them off, Jerry locks the front door, and the house rings with that silence. Mary starts humming again.

"Are you sure you're all right?" says Jerry. "Maybe we should have Dr. Griffiths check you over, after all."

"I'm fine. Just a funny five minutes earlier," she says, giving him a reassuring smile.

"But you . . . ," he begins gently, then pauses. "You've been drinking."

"You drink all the time," she snaps. "Am I not allowed?"

"Mary, you haven't touched a drop for the forty-four years I've known you, and today you stumble home drunk, smelling like a brewery. What in God's name is wrong?"

"I didn't stumble. . . . And if I did, it's because the hall mat is askew."

"Did something happen today? At the supermarket?"

"Look, the corner is curled up. We should go to B&Q on Saturday and buy a new one."

"Or the nightmares. Is it to do with those?"

"What about John Lewis? They're probably nicer there, but they won't be cheap."

"Mary!"

He stands too close, peering into her face. She closes her eyes. If only she could step out onto the street and run along the dark roads away from this stifling house. She would keep running straight, her arms outstretched, until she hit grass and then sand and, at some point, the cold barrier of the ocean. She would keep running until she was beneath it, until it wrapped her up and held her.

"I love you so much, Mary. You will tell me if something's wrong?"

Mary nods, her eyes still closed.

×

IN THE END IT is not the newsagent's wife or the priest or the landlady or Jerry or even the pair of eyes staring out from the newspaper mug shot that prompts Mary to act, but the shiny-lipped newsreader on the breakfast program the next morning. Mary is pulling clots of potato peel from the sink and half listening to the small television on the wall when the woman appears, cutting into the jolliness with her news bulletin. At first Mary hardly notices her.

"More than one hundred complaints were made to the Press Complaints Commission about the decision to publish the controversial interview with Nigel Forbes, known as the Cornish Cleaver," she says, and Mary's head jerks up.

Her dishcloth falls to the floor, and for the next few seconds, she forgets to breathe. The newsreader bleats on, then the screen switches to a balding man with a puffy red face and watery eyes, speaking angrily into the camera. The bar at the bottom of the television screen reads, "Taylor Cardy, victim's nephew." Mary is frozen. She still doesn't move when the news bulletin ends.

When she finally comes to, the kitchen is cold. The sun has disappeared and a shadow falls over her. A different woman is on the television, stirring mussels into a yellow stew. It's done, that's what the landlady had said. But the landlady was wrong. You live with it or you do something about it. If you don't, it'll eat you up with the cancer. Had someone else said that, or was that the landlady, too? Mary pulls on her good wool coat, picks up her handbag, and closes the front door. The landlady or whoever said it was right; she must find out whether she did the right thing that summer—she will ask him herself. She keeps her head low as she passes the Three Hops and only raises it again when she reaches the station. She buys a ticket at a machine with a smudged screen and hurries to the platform.

Mary checks the clock. There are eighteen minutes to fill until the train arrives. She cleans her fingers with a wet wipe, maps out her journey in her head, then perches on the edge of the bench to wait. She is very weak suddenly, as though her bones have disintegrated and her body will flop over if she doesn't try very hard to keep it upright. She sits a little straighter, clutches her bag tighter, and smiles, hoping that no one will notice she isn't quite right, but it all takes an inordinate amount of effort.

"You're waiting for a train," she whispers, trying not to move her lips in case people think her mad. "Just sitting on a train station bench. Even you can manage that, silly old girl. Just waiting for a train."

And it hits her then, at that moment, as her fingers dig into her handbag and as the station caller announces the arrival of a train on another platform, that she really is going to see him again, finally. The thought of it makes her run cold and hot at once.

7

No one speaks during the car ride home from the dance, not even Mary. Betty watches Mr. Paxon in the rearview mirror. His eyes are red and drooping, as though he has been crying, and he doesn't seem to care whether her sandy dress spoils his upholstery. His eyes flick up and meet hers. She looks away, plaiting her fingers into one another.

They drive the long way to Mary's aunt's house. Gray steps out of the car to let Mary out, and she shoulders past him. Mr. Paxon doesn't honk as he drives off and Mary doesn't turn to wave. As they pull out onto the New Road, Gray touches Betty's arm lightly. She can sense him looking at her from the corner of her eye. She draws away her arm, wriggles farther from him across the seat, and focuses instead on the seam running along the back of Mr. Paxon's fedora.

She bargains with herself: if she keeps her eyes on that line of stitching for the whole car ride, her brain won't turn to jelly and everything will be all right. She will be back at Hotel Eden in no time; Mother will still be upright, and they will toast bread with cinnamon, the way they did when she had nightmares as a girl.

By the time they arrive, Betty still hasn't taken her eyes from Mr. Paxon's hat seam, so everything should be all right. She thanks Mr. Paxon and lets herself inside. The hotel is silent, the big room is empty and the upstairs landing smells of wine.

"Mother?" she calls.

She pushes open the bedroom door. There is a noise coming from inside; an old fisherman's shanty, it sounds like. The door opens fully and there is Mother, lying diagonally across the bed, singing and shivering and wearing only her thin summer nightdress.

"He loves me, he loves me not," she is singing to the fisherman's tune as rain taps on the window. "He loves me, he loves me, he loves me."

"Mother," gasps Betty.

She pulls a crocheted blanket from the top shelf and drapes it over Mother. She pauses for a moment, wondering what to say.

She wants to tell Mother what happened. She would like to describe the patch of sand stained rust red and the tender way the piano man placed his purple jacket over the dead girl's face and her gray feet poked out. But she looks again at Mother and slips out of the bedroom, shutting the door quietly behind her.

Downstairs, she opens the larder door. The jars and tins and herb pots are blurred and wobbling, and she realizes that she is crying.

She shuts herself in the larder, sits on the floor, her knees drawn to her chin, and she weeps.

The men amble back eventually. The front door opens and closes, opens and closes, and she holds her breath, hoping that no one will find her in the larder. When they are upstairs, she opens the bread tin, but only crusts, studded with furry white mold, are left. She licks her finger, presses it into the tub of cinnamon, and tastes it. Her nerves still don't settle.

She steps out into the kitchen, wondering where to sleep, and spots a pile of half-dry towels on the table. She arranges herself a bed on the floor and stuffs one in the crack under the back door to block out the icy slug of draft and the screams of wind, but the raven girl's wails echo in her head as she falls into a restless sleep.

The next morning, it happens again: Mother's eyes lose their shine and she looks gray all over. She stands for ten minutes, then crumbles back into bed. There isn't time for Betty to think about the killer or the raven girl or the dead girl, or even Mother; only a pile of breakfasts that need cooking. She pastes on a smile, just like Mother's, and starts work.

x

ONE WEEK LATER, BETTY ambles along the water's edge, enjoying her last gulps of salty air before she must go back indoors. She twists her wrist in little jerks, making the string shopping bag in her hand spin upside down. The parsnips and carrots don't fall out; somehow they cheat physics, making her laugh.

She is still laughing when she notices Gallagher striding across the cove. She stops, self-conscious, and thinks she might slip away, but he looks up, and their eyes meet. He, too, pauses, as though wondering whether to run away, but he walks toward her.

"Lovely day," she says a little too brightly.

Funny how the sun can still shine after terrible things happen, she would like to add. Gallagher nods. He looks out to sea, but his brain seems elsewhere.

"You're not working today?"

He shrugs.

"The others left at seven," she continues for want of anything clever to say.

He still doesn't speak, and she feels trapped in this electric silence.

"Cat got your tongue?" she says lightly.

"Something like that."

"My friend Mary says the best thing about me is my ears."

"Is that so?"

"Yes, they're very good listeners."

She hopes it will make him laugh and blow away the awkwardness, but he still frowns.

"I'll remember that," he says eventually, and she wishes she hadn't spoken at all. She sounded young and silly.

"I always think, if it's a bright day, that you might be able to see Morlaix on the other side of the water," she says in a serious tone. She hopes she has pronounced it correctly. She had read the name in an atlas left behind by a guest who wore a monocle and a single tarnished cuff link and disappeared one day, without paying his bill. But Gallagher still doesn't respond. She checks her wristwatch. It is almost time to go back to the hotel and peel the vegetables for supper.

"Fancy a dip?" she tries.

"In this weather?"

She lowers her head to hide her disappointment and unbuckles her sandals. The shingle is cold under her feet. A tinny whistle of wind and then she is in the shallows, wetting her toes and jumping back from the sharp bite of the water. She doesn't turn back to see whether Gallagher is watching. He might think she is showing off. She tries to enjoy it and not think about him watching; she will be back at a chopping board soon.

Every day has been the same since the dance: scrubbing potatoes, washing bed linen, cleaning crockery, shining the doorstep, and repairing, cooking, greeting, all in a big circle as if her life were on a loop, while Mother lies in bed sobbing. She should never have left Mother alone.

Time up: Betty turns away from the sea, shakes the water off her feet, and picks up her sandals. Gallagher watches, but his face looks different, as though his softer twin has replaced him.

"Wasn't there supposed to be a day trip to Torquay yesterday?" he says. "For locals."

"Hardly anyone went what with . . . you know, everything that's happened. They organized it before."

"Didn't you want to go?"

"I stayed behind to help Mother."

He looks thoughtful. Betty works her gritty foot into the garish raspberry slingbacks that Mother bought her last summer. They have buckled straps and bits of toe cut out. Peep toe, Mother had called them. The straps cut into her skin, and sand grates her foot. She can't quite push in her heel.

"How about we take our own outing, just as soon as your mother's back on her feet?" says Gallagher.

Betty looks up, startled.

"Because I'm thinking of going for a spin to St. Ives next week," he continues, in a voice that doesn't sound as robust as usual. "You should come."

"I don't imagine she'll be well enough."

"But if she is."

Why me, she would like to know.

"I'm not sure," she says instead.

"Forgive my bluntness, but . . ." He pauses. "Everyone deserves a break, Betty."

She loves the way he says her name; long and deep and precise. She looks down so Gallagher won't see her red face and tries to squeeze her foot back into her sandal, but it has grown, or the sandal has shrunk. Gallagher crouches, too, and their heads almost bang together. He reaches down and holds her ankle, clasping the sandal with his other hand. His fingers are cold and his breath is warm on her wet shin. Betty blushes deeper as he buckles it.

The second shoe now; he guides it on and stands upright again. Her legs wobble, but she pretends to feel nothing. Gallagher goes pink, but it is probably just because he was bent over and the blood has rushed to his head.

"I should go home," she mutters.

He nods. She nods at the promenade and he nods again. Betty giggles shyly, thinking them a pair of puppets with loosened neck joints and bobbing heads.

"What's funny?" he asks, searching her face.

"Nothing. Just the bobbing."

"I see." But he still looks uncertain. "You'd better get yourself to the hotel." He pauses. "Take care, won't you?"

Betty smiles to herself as she walks back across the sand in his upside-down footprints.

x

Tinny music pumps out of Hotel Eden and fills up Newl Grove. Betty peers through the nets into the big room. Mother is mid-pirouette, her skirt fanned out like a ballerina's tutu and her arms raised above her head. Betty looks away. She should be pleased that Mother is out of bed again but a cold, hard lump sits in her stomach.

She unlocks the front door and steps into the hall. The music is even louder indoors. She walks into the big room, just as Mother trips over the coal bucket. Black dust spits out, speckling the rug. Mother waves.

"Come on, dance with me, Betty boo boo," she screams over the song, kicking the rug out of the way. "I got a girl named Sue. She's the gal that I love best. You know he loves me, yes indeed."

Mother grasps Betty's hand and spins her in a circle as she sings. Betty lets herself join in; after this song, she'll calm her down. Mother tips back her head and screeches with laughter.

"Oh, tutti frutti, tutti frutti. Tutti frutti, aw rooty."

They twirl until the room looks like a spinning top. Betty closes her eyes and inhales the rush of air, laced with Mother's perfume and wine. There is a loud smash as Mother's hip catches the spout of the teapot and sends it crashing to the floor. Mother dances over the broken pottery with her bare feet. The song ends abruptly, and the carpet is covered with red footprints.

"Mother, your feet!"

"Everything's fine," breezes Mother. "Did you hear it? What a song!"

She limps into the kitchen, leaving more bloody footprints, while Betty roots in the dresser for a bandage and pin.

"You're bleeding," Betty calls after her.

"Wonderful how much life a bit of music can bring to a dull, dead place."

Betty hurries into the kitchen. It smells of burnt mutton pie. Mother collapses onto a chair and Betty kneels at her feet. There is a small tear in her heel and blood still seeps out.

"You're a sweetheart," coos Mother.

Betty dabs it with antiseptic and winds around the bandage while Mother sways, as though the music were still playing.

"I wanted to talk to you," says Betty carefully. "It's about Mr. Forbes."

"We're having a very special supper tonight, with very special guests," trills Mother.

She picks up a gin bottle from the table and pours it over a teacup, but it is empty.

"Please, Mother, it's Mr. Forbes. I'm not supposed to know this, but I do—and you should, too, before everyone else finds out."

"Bloody vultures, who's drunk all my gin?" She bangs the bottle on the table.

"The police think it's him."

Mother looks down at Betty. She smiles in a slow, strange way as though her brain hasn't caught up with her ears.

"They think that Maureen loved him," whispers Betty. "She was carrying his child and that's why he killed her. Because he changed his mind or was angry or something."

"Enough!"

Mother bangs the gin bottle on the empty table to coax out the last drop. It smashes. Shards of glass rain over the table and the floor and Betty.

"Are you going to clear up that mess or must I sort out every problem we have?" shrieks Mother.

Betty shakes off the glass and reaches around to pin the bandage.

"Let me finish this first. It'll be all right."

Mother sighs loudly and drops her head to her hands, muttering something to herself that is too slurred to make sense of. Betty focuses on the bandage and feels Mother's calf to make sure it sits evenly. On the back of Mother's leg, just below her knee, is a bump. Betty cranes her neck around to look. It is an angry claw mark, as if a human-size cat or animal with sharpened talons has clung on and gouged out a trench.

"What's that?" she says, alarmed. "Who hurt you?"

"An old war wound," says Mother, but it looks fresh.

"It needs antiseptic."

"Stop fussing."

"All right," she says, and fastens the pin. "But Mr. Forbes—"

"I won't hear another word about the filthy pair of them," says Mother. Then she beams in a plastic sort of way. "The Paxons will be here for supper soon. You'd better go and make yourself pretty for George."

Betty's chest sinks, but she nods and hurries upstairs to their bedroom. Mother will slot back into her old self soon, she is sure of it. It always works out that way and has done ever since her eleventh birthday when she had come home from tea at her friend Margaret's house and watched Mother's tears plop into her birthday trifle.

Mother had used her hands to scoop out the sherry jelly from beneath the custard and whippy trifle cream. She had swallowed every last drop of the sherry jelly while Betty watched.

"You greedy bitch," Mother had snarled when she finished as Betty wiped slops from her chin and lips. "You ate it all, not me. You'll be chubby as well as plain."

The trifle slops and Mother's spit had stained Betty's birthday dress, but she hadn't minded. It was the black snowman talking, as she used to call Mother's bad spells, not Mother herself. She had helped Mother to bed.

"Don't play with that Margaret girl again," Mother had muttered, peeking from beneath the duvet. "You don't need anyone but me, do you?"

"No, Mother," she had said, and Mother had smiled.

"We're best of friends, aren't we?"

"Yes, Mother."

She had smiled back, but Mother was already asleep.

It is easier now. All Betty must do is hold her tongue, show Mother that she loves her, and keep things bubbling along, then Mother will wake up one morning, all bright. She will stroke Betty's hair instead of the other way around, and, wordlessly, she will take over the reins again.

x

THE DOORBELL RINGS AT half past one. Mother's heels clack through the hall. The front door opens, and voices drift up the stairs. Betty tiptoes across the landing.

"The wind's blowing a gale," Mrs. Paxon is saying in a tight voice. "What weather for summer."

She shakes her head, and the long strip of foxtail around her neck jiggles.

"What a beautiful fox," exclaims Mother. "Now, where's Mr. Paxon? Parking the car?"

"There's a problem with the engine, all very last-minute, and he can't come, after all. Men troubles, you know," says Mrs. Paxon. She notices Betty's feet on the stairs and looks up. "There you are, Betty. Haven't you grown?"

Not since I saw you last week, Betty wants to reply. George loiters in the hall, trying not to meet her eye. Mother looks out into the street.

"Perhaps he'll fix the car in time for sweet. Should we wait?" says Mother hopefully.

"No, no, he's not coming. Very generous of you to have George and me, though."

For a split second Mother's face darkens. She ushers them into the big room and removes a set of cutlery and place mat. Betty takes a place, and George sits opposite. She tucks her legs under her chair, not to touch his. Mother returns from the kitchen with plates of steaming pie, the pastry charred black.

"Well, isn't this a sight?" says Mrs. Paxon with a bitten lip.

"It was no bother. It's your favorite, isn't it, George? And your father's, too," says Mother.

Betty frowns. She doesn't remember telling Mother that.

"I'll have to package up a piece for him," she continues. "Men and their motorcars, eh."

George fidgets with his fork handle.

"I suppose you're quite used to serving people," says Mrs. Paxon.

Betty wants to kick her shin under the table, but Mother smiles.

"Oh, you know how it is. We muddle along. And Betty's learning fast, too. Aren't you?" There is a pause. "So how is Mr. Paxon?"

Mrs. Paxon doesn't reply. They eat in silence, nothing but the clink of silver on Mr. Eden's Royal Doulton china. Someone hiccups. Mother looks sheepish.

"Excuse me."

George sniggers, but Mrs. Paxon keeps her eyes low. No one speaks and Betty can hear stifled hiccups pulse through Mother's chews. She smiles at Mother, but Mother glares back.

"I hear your school marks are exemplary, George," says Mother after a mouthful of water. "Tell me—and Betty—what good things you will do with that fine brain of yours."

George opens his mouth, but Mrs. Paxon speaks first. "He's taking over the reins of the family business."

"Isn't that exciting?" squeals Mother.

"He's very keen," says Mrs. Paxon, looking sharply at him.

"And what will Mr. Paxon do, then? A talented man like him."

"They'll be partners. George has a long way to go. Don't you, George?"

George's eyes glue onto his plate. He slices his carrot into tiny bits with the edge of his fork.

"I need a hand with the custard," says Mother in a curt way, and nods at Betty.

Betty is about to reply that they have barely begun their pies, but Mother has scraped back her chair and is halfway to the kitchen. Betty murmurs an apology to Mrs. Paxon and follows. Mother storms into the backyard and slams the kitchen door behind them both.

"You're making me look like a fool," spits Mother.

"What? I don't understand."

"George! Can't you even string together a sentence to say to him?"

"I don't know what to—"

"Because this is it, you silly girl. Your future hangs at that table, and if you don't grasp onto him right now, you'll lose it. And then where will we be? Still slaving in this hotel twenty years from now, that's where!"

"I'm trying."

"You're not. Before you know it, you'll be thirty-six years old with no home and no man wanting to even look at you sideways. If you hadn't . . . If your father hadn't got himself killed and left me lumped, things wouldn't be this way. You don't know what I do for you, Betty. And for us. You really don't."

There is a tapping at the kitchen window. "Everything all right?" mouths Mrs. Paxon.

Mother looks up. She blinks hard and pastes on her widest smile.

"Coming," she tinkles, knocking into Betty on her way back inside.

Betty follows. They sit back down, and Mother kicks her shin under the table.

"George," begins Betty. They all look at her. "How was the outing to Torquay?"

"It was all right," he says, still avoiding her eye.

"Did you see Agatha Christie on your travels?" Mother gives her an encouraging nod.

"That madwoman writer?" splutters Mrs. Paxon. "Wasn't she sent to a lunatic asylum?"

"Because her second husband left her," says Mother smugly.

"*The Mousetrap* was marvelous," pipes up George.

"Then she should have clung onto her husband a little tighter, instead of writing those silly books," Mrs. Paxon retorts, and sets down her knife and fork, her mutton barely touched.

Mother smiles in a funny sort of way, then conceals it with her hands.

"Gray's father took us to watch it at the Ambassadors in London last summer," continues George.

Another silence falls over the table. Betty roots around for something to say.

"That's very interesting, George," she manages stiffly. "I've never been to London."

"George, you'll like this," says Mother, when they have all finished. "We borrowed that music player over there from Mr. Eden. Why doesn't Betty show you how to play it?"

George pushes back his chair, and Betty follows him to the dresser, while Mother pours two thimbles of sweet wine and hiccups again. Betty lifts the needle and drops it halfway through the record. A tune bleats out. George looks bored.

"Don't you like Little Richard?"

"We have one of these things at home. Two, actually."

She blushes. She can feel Mother's eyes on her, and she can't stand it any longer.

"Excuse me," she mutters, squeezing past him and hurrying to the hall.

"Tell me about this Mr. Eden who owns the place," Mrs. Paxon is saying to Mother as Betty makes her way up the stairs.

"He's on a cruise with his wife, Evelyn," Mother is saying distractedly. "It's quite the cruise liner, so I'm told. Popular with the royal family and—"

Betty closes the bathroom door, and their voices fade away. It is cold inside; someone has left the window open. She presses her forehead to the wall tiles with tiny pink roses and green vines creeping over them. The coolness is a relief against her headache. She can't go back downstairs. She has never liked George and now that he has gone off her, too, Mother will soon find out. Betty sighs, just as the door jerks open, and Gallagher appears.

"Sorry," he blusters, looking away and backing out. "Sorry, it wasn't locked and I didn't know anyone was—"

He is about to close the door behind him when he stops. "Is every-thing all right?"

"It's fine . . . I just came in here for some peace."

He peers back around the door and opens his lips, pausing before he speaks.

"Your mother shouldn't speak to you like that."

"You were listening?"

"My window was open. . . . It was difficult not to."

"You shouldn't even be in the hotel at this time of day," she snaps. "What are you doing, creeping about and eavesdropping; you don't know anything about me or Mother, so why don't you just—" She stops, appalled.

He steps inside the bathroom and closes the door behind him.

"I'm sorry," she whispers.

He crosses the bathroom to her and wraps his arms around her shoul-ders so her head buries in his chest. It is familiar and comforting. She cries in deep chesty heaves, relieved, but horrified at herself, too.

Minutes pass. She pulls away from him and wipes her face with the pink hand towel from the peg. When she looks up, he is crouching, and level with her.

"Tell me what I can do to help," he says gently.

"Just take me away from it all for a day."

"Where?"

"Anywhere."

He gives a single sharp nod. She looks down, not meeting his eye. Her hands, she realizes, are shaking.

"The morning after tomorrow," he says. "Half past eight by the farm. We'll meet then."

He kisses her lightly on the forehead and walks out of the bath-room.

x

THE MORNING AFTER TOMORROW arrives eventually. Betty wakes at seven o'clock. She had hoped that Mother would be asleep so she could leave a note and slip away unnoticed, but she finds her in the garden scrubbing the window nets. She has flung open every window so the curtains dance and Hotel Eden breathes again.

"I'm going to Spoole for the day to see Mary," mutters Betty. "But if there's too much to do, I can stay here."

There, she has said it. It is the first time she has properly lied to Mother. She waits to be caught out or for Mother to refuse because of the Cleaver. She half hopes that Mother will refuse.

"Of course I'll manage," says Mother. She points at a plate of doorstep-thick bread and syrupy jam on the windowsill. "Can't have you going all that way on an empty stomach."

Betty's insides knot up; she feels doubly bad now. She eats the drippy sandwich under the cool morning sun, not minding when the black currant jam spots the ground and an army of ants swarms around it.

"There's something I have to say," says Mother seriously, shaking soap suds from her hands. "I see how much you do for . . . this hotel. And I'm going to try harder, too."

"Don't get all soppy," Betty says, and chews her tongue to stop herself confessing where she is really going. "What are you clucking on about?"

She puffs out her cheeks like a chicken and flaps her arms like wings, the way Mother used to when she was young. You don't need friends when you have me, Mother used to say.

"Cluck, cluck, chicken," says Betty.

Mother laughs and copies, the way she always does when Betty pretends to be small again. It is when Mother is at her brightest.

"Cluck, cluck, hen."

They waddle in a circle around the small paved yard, clucking and flapping and laughing until Betty's chest hurts so much, it is ready to rip in two.

"Go on. Off with you. Let me get on with my washing," says Mother, wiping away happy tears.

She strokes Betty's hair. Betty beams. Mother is back.

x

BETTY ARRIVES AT TREVARTHEN Farm before Gallagher does, still bristling with guilt. She should have stayed with Mother. She will tell him that there was a mix-up, that she can't go with him after all, but his Austin rumbles up the track, his curls flapping about in the breeze, and he pulls over and leans across to open the passenger door for her.

"You came," he says, sounding relieved.

She nods and slides in, forgetting her planned speech and wishing she had checked that her teeth were clean of bread and jam. They weave their way out of St. Steele. The sun glares down on them, and Betty covers her part with a hand in case it burns. Gallagher glances sideways at her with a grin. We could be married, and on a Sunday run through the countryside, she tells herself.

When they have driven more than halfway and the sun is lost behind clouds, Betty's hands unclammy themselves and a sort of relief settles inside her. Rows of thatched cottages roll past. They pass a thread of bonfire smoke, a hunched-over woman with a prune-like face. She waves a red handkerchief and Betty waves back, proud of the car, proud to be sitting beside Gallagher.

After the thatched village, a herd of cows slope into the road, and Gallagher brakes. Dozens more cows pour out of the field. Gallagher cuts the engine and strums his fingers on the wheel.

"We haven't got all bloody day," he grunts.

Betty picks at the skin around her thumbnail. It is as though he is scolding her. This is her part of the country, so it is her fault.

"Christ almighty," he groans as two more cows amble out.

Betty unlocks her door and steps onto the road; she won't let a cow herd spoil their day.

"What are you doing? Don't." He reaches over to stop her, but she is already walking toward the cows. "They're dangerous."

"Dangerous, my foot."

She charges at them, mooing and shaking her fists. Two cows surge forward into the field. Others slowly follow. She glances back and sees Gallagher clutching his stomach. He seems to be laughing, but he stops when he sees her looking at him.

"Come on," she calls. "Help me."

"I'm not going near them. Look at their eyes."

"You're scared!"

"Don't be ridiculous."

"Then help me."

Gallagher steps out of the car. As his foot lowers toward the grass she spots something brown beneath it.

"Mind," she calls.

But it is too late. His shoe lands in a thick slop of cow pat.

"Stinking bloody countryside."

"Clean it on the nettles."

Gallagher picks a leaf and wipes the sole of his shiny Oxfords with it, muttering under his breath. The last of the cows disappear into the field, and Betty sits back in the car. She tries to ignore the strange pound of blood and the adrenaline that is stretching her veins.

"What am I doing?" grunts Gallagher, climbing back into the car. "Why am I here?"

The blood and adrenaline slow. Betty turns away her head so he won't see her disappointment. The rest of the drive passes in silence.

x

GALLAGHER PARKS AT THE railway station on the fringe of St. Ives and holds her elbow as he steers her through the labyrinth of streets. They reach a tiny front door that they have to duck to enter. A bell tings and a lady with a flowered apron and gray tufts of hair steps from the scullery to the wooden counter of cakes. Gallagher chooses a table next to the window.

"Cream tea or afternoon tea?" she calls from the counter.

"That'll do," he mutters.

The lady looks puzzled but says nothing. They take opposite chairs, and the lady brings them white floury bread with salty butter and apricot jam and the teas. She looks closely at Betty's face as she sets it down.

"Perhaps your daughter would like some cold water to cool her tea."

Neither of them answers. Next she carries out a two-tiered stand of wedged Victoria cake sprinkled with icing sugar and an oblong marzipan cake made of checkered pink-and-white sponge. Gallagher rests his hand on top of Betty's, which is flat on the table, while the lady lays out the spread. Betty almost jerks back, but she doesn't. His hand is cool and smooth, but it makes her very hot. The lady looks between them, and Gallagher only removes his hand again when she has gone. Betty drinks the tea fast, scalding her throat, while Gallagher looks out of the window at a war memorial surrounded by poppy wreaths.

"Thank you for bringing me," she says, between mouthfuls of bread.

She wants to ask him why he hardly speaks, why his lips are buttoned together and his posture is ramrod straight, and why he touched her hand in front of that lady, but she is in earshot, so Betty says nothing.

Gallagher's long cuffs have been turned up so she can see his slender fingers and neat, trimmed nails as they reach for the milk jug.

"Tell me something interesting about yourself," he says.

The lady brings a fresh pot of water and hovers next to Betty for longer than she needs to.

"Well, you know my name is Betty—Elizabeth Mary Broadbent in full. I'm fifteen years old, almost sixteen actually, and—"

"That's not what I meant," he hisses, glancing at the tea lady. She has disappointed him again in some way. There should be a rule book for boys and men: how to speak to them, what not to say.

"So?"

"Well, there's not a lot else to say, Mr. Gallagher," she whispers. "There's not a lot special or interesting about me."

"Don't call me Mr. Gallagher. You make me feel like my father."

"All right, then," she says, realizing that she doesn't know his Christian name, but she can't ask what it is when the cake lady is listening. She thinks for a second. "I've lived at Hotel Eden since I was three; I suppose that's unusual."

"And before that?"

"We stayed with Uncle Harold and my aunt Beryl, Mother's sister. I don't remember her very well. We had to move out, and I've not seen them since."

"Why did you have to move out?"

"Uncle Harold said Mother was a bad egg. It was strange; he went from liking her very much, maybe too much, to not even wanting to look at her. But luckily Mr. Eden offered Mother the manageress job at the hotel—he and Father were at war together . . . I don't know where, because Mother doesn't speak about it. All she would say is that Father died when I was in her stomach and Mr. Eden survived, so he feels indebted to us in some way."

"Bad egg?"

"Yes, you know. Someone who isn't good to have around."

"I know what a bad egg is, I meant why?"

She looks at him over her teacup, just as the bell dings and a family trickles into the tearoom. There is a mother, a father, and two small boys wearing matching shiny yellow raincoats. The tea lady doesn't notice them, she is staring at Betty. Betty ignores her and focuses on Gallagher's question.

"What is this, the Spanish Inquisition?" she says.

"How do you know what the Spanish Inquisition is?" he replies with a raised eyebrow.

"I know a great many things."

His face is all glowy, not at all like his expression at the dinner table in Hotel Eden.

"For example?"

"For example, I know Prime Minister Churchill had special dentures to correct his lisp. And I know that the gold ring you wear is a family ring, probably with your family crest on it. See, I can tell by your face that I'm right." He smiles and, emboldened, she continues: "And I'd also know how to make very good raspberry buns, if only I could find sweet raspberries that didn't make my tongue curl up."

He bites his lip, his expression clouds, and the loveliness of it all vanishes.

"So very young," he says.

She has said something wrong again. It is infuriating, but she sips on her tea and says nothing.

When they have finished, the tea lady puts a sheet of penciled paper on the table without smiling. It lists how much everything costs. Betty sets down her birthday half crown.

"Don't be soft," he says, putting down his own coins.

He presses the half crown back into her hand. His skin is warm now and the only thing that separates them is the hot metal of the coin. He lingers there for longer than he needs to, then scrapes back his chair and walks out. She follows him, passing closely by the family that has just entered. As she looks at them, she realizes that she dislikes being in this tearoom. She doesn't fit in here; she has never belonged somewhere as normal but lovely as this and she still doesn't, not even with a great man like Gallagher sharing her table.

They start down a narrow street with shops on either side and walk with their hips almost touching. Gallagher's strides are twice as long as hers and she struggles to keep up. She has seen grown women tuck their arms into the crooks of men's elbows and she would like to do the same, but he might tell her not to. That would be worse than never having tried at all.

She stops to inspect a row of oily herrings outside a fishmonger's, then they turn onto a promenade strewn with seine nets and crab cages and docked boats that clank against the harbor wall like wind chimes. Fishiness and salt fill Betty's nose. Something changes Gallagher's mind, and he steers her down a quiet alleyway of cottages to a windier beach with a green archipelago that juts into the sea. On top of it is the shell of a brown chapel. It is a short walk to the chapel, and Gallagher leads. He lights a cigarette. The wind picks up and Betty rubs her ears to warm them.

"Can you blow a bit of that nice warm smoke into my ear?" she says. "You tickle me pink."

But he doesn't look very pink, just bitten white with cold.

When they reach the church wall, Gallagher is panting.

"Good job you weren't in the war with lungs like those," she says.

He doesn't smile.

"I was only teasing."

"Yes."

"Were you in the war?"

He doesn't answer. They perch on the church wall and watch the frothy waves.

"We were talking about you back at the tearoom," he says. "Tell me what you enjoy."

"Being questioned," she says with a smile, but he frowns and she feels silly again.

The wind hiccups and her skirt billows up. She pats it down, bunching the fabric under her thighs. When she looks back at him, he is staring into her face.

"I mean, what do you enjoy doing?"

"Just normal things."

"Such as?"

"Spending time with Mother. Painting sometimes. Taking photographs and being by the sea—I love walking by the sea." She thinks harder. "I don't know what else. No one's ever asked me before."

"I don't suppose they have."

"I like taking photographs most of all," she says again, and when he still doesn't respond, she pulls her camera from her cloth bag.

He glances down at it.

"That's a beauty," he says, the same way he did of his car, and she is pleased.

"Do you have one?"

"Not one as smart as yours."

"I'd like to take a picture," she murmurs.

"You must. What a view."

"I meant of you."

"What on earth for?" he says, but he notices her blush and speaks more kindly. "Go on, then, but quickly now. I'm not looking my best, as my grandmother would have said."

"I think you are," she says shyly, and stands in front of him, pointing the camera.

She doesn't look at him properly through the viewfinder; it burns to look at him head-on. She presses the button fast without checking the angle of the light or how central he is. She is relieved when they are side by side again, her camera back inside her bag.

"What do you like?" she asks, her chest thumping.

A seagull flies low. Waves beat on the sand, and somewhere distant, a car honks its horn. Minutes pass.

"I thought I used to know," he says eventually. "I don't remember what I thought exactly. All I know now is that it's not that. I suppose that doesn't make a word of sense."

"It makes perfect sense," she says, still trying to unscramble it. "Do you have a family?"

She sounds stupid; of course everyone has a family.

"Just a father, he was a private physician for many years. I rarely see him. He lives in Paris. He has . . . strong ideas about my . . . my work."

"Private? It must have been someone very important to have had one of those."

"Chamberlain," and he looks away, embarrassed. There is a pause. "We write, Father and I. Well, I write him letters, he writes me lectures."

"But that's wonderful. He must have seen amazing things if he went everywhere with the prime minister. You must have, too, when you were a boy."

"I was at boarding school, so I only went along in the summer. It's not as grand as it sounds."

"Oh?" There is a long pause. "Actually, one of the hotel guests told me that Prime Minister Chamberlain was a frightful bore. I don't know how he knew, but he sounded sure."

"You're a funny one," says Gallagher without laughing. "No, he was a nice chap. And Halifax, too, back when he was the viceroy. He was at Eton with Father, brought me back a stuffed tiger from India once. Vile thing."

Betty doesn't hear the rest. You're a funny one, that's what he said. He thinks I'm funny. She wants to say something kind in return, but his words have steamed on and left behind that little sentence.

"Can I ask you a question?" she says nervously.

"This sounds ominous."

"I want to know why you like . . ." She stops and starts again. "Why did you agree to spend today with me?"

He lets out that barking laugh of his. "Because of that."

"Because of what?" She glances back over her shoulder.

"Because you're bold, just as you were to have asked me that question."

She reddens and looks down at her fingers. She should never have asked. He probably thinks she was fishing.

"It's not a bad thing. Don't be ashamed," he continues. "It means you're unafraid . . . Though perhaps you should be afraid sometimes."

His face darkens.

"You'd make a good reporter," he continues after a pause. "You'd cut straight to the truth."

"I'll never leave St. Steele."

"That's a waste."

She frowns.

"I couldn't leave Mother. And I wouldn't want to. In theory perhaps, but I couldn't. She needs me too much."

"You talk as though you're her mother."

"Mary always says I was born fifty. And she says that, even now, I age two years for everyone else's one."

"That's one bit of sense this Mary has spoken, then."

"Don't be cruel," she says, but she grins.

"But honestly, when I see you and listen to you . . . there's something so wonderfully, I don't know, so unpolluted . . ." He stumbles over his words.

"Well, it won't be unpolluted when the new road into St. Steele is built. The workmen begin in December, and Mother says the fumes will be unbearable."

"Don't do that," he says.

She looks away.

"You knew what I meant," he continues. "You're clever and you're—"

"Your job seems marvelous," she says to steer the talk away from her. "Driving to new places, writing about the people you meet there."

"I didn't choose it. I chose not to have the life I was supposed to have."

"Life as a doctor?"

"Or, God forbid, a politician. No, I did this because it's the worst fate Father could have imagined for me—my pathetic little rebellion. Pah, even that's a failure."

"Surely there are worse professions."

"Than mixing with men like those? Debasing myself, that's what he calls it."

"But—"

"My mother died when I was born and he sees me as some sort of precious incarnate. Nothing I could do would ever make him hate me, Lord knows I've tried. He wraps me in cotton—" Gallagher stops. "I've never told anyone this, but . . ." He clears his throat. "My father's well-placed, as I told you, and when conscription came, I was never called. I went to volunteer, but they sent me away and said that something in my medical report meant I couldn't serve. They wouldn't tell me what. He did that to me. My own father."

It takes her a moment to catch what he means. She swallows hard and tries to think of something suitable to say.

"How can you be a man when your peers, your cousins, your neigh-bors, everyone you know, is out there fighting for his country and you can't because your father has falsified your medical records?"

"He must have done it to protect you."

"Do you know the worst thing? I was relieved. Actually relieved."

"Couldn't you have done something? Told the truth, or changed your papers back?"

"You despise me now, too."

"I don't," she says, horrified. "I couldn't ever despise you." But she can't work out what to think. "You didn't force him to do it."

"Well they despise me, the whole family. They suspected, and then my cousin, the golden boy, died serving. . . . I know what they think—it should have been John. So now all I have is him: my loathsome father."

"You don't really hate him."

"I might as well tattoo a white feather onto my forehead."

There is a long pause. She would like to hug him, but she doesn't dare.

"Come on, then, let's be off," he says.

He jumps to his feet abruptly, as though nothing unusual has been said. Betty stays seated.

"Perhaps we could have another few minutes," she says.

He looks down, his curls flop over his eyebrows, and his fists ram into his coat pockets. If she really were brave, she would wrap her arms around him and unlock his fists and bury her face in his neck, just to see how he smells. Instead, she smooths her skirt and sits nervously.

"I suppose another five minutes won't harm," he grunts, but instead of sitting down he paces toward the flat top of the hill.

"He probably did it because he loved you so much," she calls after him, hoping he will sit with her again if they continue talking.

He stops walking and glares back at her.

"How would you know?"

His anger has a button; she doesn't know how she manages to press it so often.

"I know you only get one father," she calls back.

"You haven't met mine," he says, sounding like a boy.

"Still, remember that, and make the most of him," she says, growing pink at her boldness. "Mine died."

She won't remind Gallagher that he died at war.

"I don't want sympathy or anything," she continues. "Just remember you only get one."

Gallagher shakes his head. His jaw softens, and he looks at her as though she has told him something amazing, when, really, all she has said is the obvious.

"You're a wonderful little oddity, I hope you know that. You really are something."

"Will you do something for me?" she asks, emboldened, and he looks uneasy.

"This sounds serious."

"It's not difficult. I only want you to not reset yourself again."

"You make me sound like a broken wireless," he says with a tense half laugh.

"Please don't joke."

"All right. What is it you want from me, Betty?"

"Only that you don't reset us again. I don't know how else to put it, but you seem to start from scratch whenever we see each other. As if we haven't really met before." She stops and frowns. "It made sense in my head."

"I won't do it again."

"If you know what I mean, why do you—"

"I promise," he interrupts.

"But why did you always ignore me?"

He doesn't answer, but he looks closely at her. Little black hairs prick through his chin pores. Sweet cake breath lands on her mouth from his. The seagulls grow silent and the sea quietens and their faces move closer until they touch. Their lips meet.

Seconds pass. To Betty, it seems longer. Like hours, days even. She isn't certain whether she draws back first, or who began it at all, or how his lips tasted. Only that they are separate again but that they really kissed.

She has to bite hard on her bottom lip and think of Joan's poor dead cat Beatrice (run over by the milk float), to stop herself from grinning, but Gallagher jumps to his feet and paces away from her. Betty reaches out and touches the bit of wall, still warm from where he sat. When he turns, his hands are hidden in his coat pockets and his face is stony.

"We're going."

He nods in the direction of town. He walks, she follows, and then they are hurrying through the streets, almost running back to his car. Gallagher closes the door without looking at her, and he drives back toward St. Steele faster than he ought.

Half an hour passes before Betty speaks.

"You said you wouldn't do this."

She can't tell whether he heard her over the road and the engine, but he pulls over and parks on the verge of the empty country lane. Through the windshield, a stream dribbles along between the road and the field. The sky is salmon pink.

"It was wrong of me," he says in his formal voice. "Today shouldn't have happened."

"But I'm glad it did."

He thumps his fist against the driver's door.

"Don't, Betty."

She stares out of the window over his shoulder, burning to shout something that will change his mind. A trail of ducks waddles along the stream, led by a drake with emerald feathers. If this all weren't so serious, Betty might point them out. They might get out of the car and watch the ducks toddle toward the tar-colored fields.

"But I am glad," she insists, forgetting her nerves.

"No, I'll hurt you."

There is a long pause.

"Is that why you ignore me?" she presses. "Because you think you'll hurt me?"

"It's not right. That woman in the tearoom was bad enough."

"So you don't dislike me?"

"Of course I don't dislike you. I wouldn't be in this bloody car if I disliked you. Or watching terrible, terrible films with you. I don't know what I'm doing. I'm thirty years old and I'm—I'm not the sort of person you just make friends with, Betty."

"You didn't enjoy the pictures?" she says, pretending to sound cross.

He half smiles, as she had hoped, and reaches forward to touch her cheek but jerks back again, as if possessed and fighting with his two halves.

"No," he scolds himself. "But . . ."

She can't find sensible words, so she swivels in her seat and reaches forward to kiss him, fast before her courage fades. Their noses bang together, and Betty winces. She is about to draw back in shame and let him drive on, when his head tilts diagonally and his lips find hers. Then they are kissing again, but with their lips parted this time.

Betty hopes she is doing it right. His lips are warm. They fit with hers. Gallagher opens his mouth and works harder into the kiss. Hot air passes into her mouth, and she is careful not to breathe in, not to choke on it. She tries to inhale, but her nose is blocked up. She splutters.

"I'm sorry," he says, pulling back.

"Don't be sorry. I'm just not very good at it."

"Shush," he says softly.

He rubs a lock of her hair between his fingers and searches her face. Betty moves forward again, and this time, their noses don't bang and their teeth don't clank. They kiss and they kiss, and when they finish, her lips sting in a good way. He places her hand on the gear stick, beneath his own hand. Then he drives back to St. Steele slowly, so very slowly.

8

Fifty years later

The building is easy to find. Mary asks for directions from the railway station guard, and she reaches it five minutes later. It is stucco fronted and broad and seems to have once been a mansion with servants' quarters. Today it is flanked by a gravel drive crammed with eight cars, sleek ones that Jerry would whistle through his teeth at. Number six, it says in gold stickers on a glass panel above the beetle-black front door.

She stands in front of it for a long time, looking at the window sills that smell of new paint and biting her fingernails down to stumps. He is inside, probably just a few steps away. She wonders what he is doing and wearing, how his face has altered with age, and whether he will recognize her.

She has known he was here for little more than a year: she had stumbled upon him as she was skimming the readers' page of the *Surrey Comet*. One of the letter writers' surnames had grabbed her and made her shiver, the way that surname always did.

She had read the letter with vague interest: the writer was disgusted that the council had backtracked on a policy to grant parking permits to relatives of people living in Surrey nursing homes, and he went on to calculate how much he had spent over the last year on parking outside Eugenie Heights, the care home of his dear father, John, the famous war correspondent.

Mary was glad that she was home alone when she read that, as she choked on her tea. It was as though she had lost another small part of him, though she knew deep down that she had never had him at all.

By the time Mary had finished rereading it, her mind was knotted up. To untangle it, she had sifted the dirty socks from the laundry bin, rinsed them, and pegged them on the washing line with neat two-inch gaps between each. As she clipped on the pegs and measured each space with her thumb, she had let herself wonder how many children he had, who he had married, and why he became a war correspondent of all things, when he had once told her that war terrified him.

When the washing line was full, she had looked up the address of Eugenie Heights in the telephone directory and written it down next to his Christian name—his full name would have been too much. It would have brought him to life again. She had slipped the scrap of paper into her old diary, where she thought Jerry would never look.

x

MARY STEPS TOWARD THE front door. She is gathering the courage to knock when she notices her reflection in the bay window; a shapeless figure with a flat bun. She turns away ashamed—she should at least tidy herself up for him—and she hurries back to the station entrance.

There is no bathroom, so she uses the glass front of the chocolate vending machine as a mirror and runs her fingers through her hair before repinning her chignon. She dabs her wrist with a spot of perfume, too, but it feels like a betrayal to Jerry, so she tries to rub it off.

She walks back to the building slowly. The door is locked. There is a silver intercom with one button. She presses it before she has time to change her mind.

"Dr. Braintree?" says a snappy voice through the speaker.

"No, Mary Sugden," she replies, confused.

"Sorry, visiting hours are over. Medical professionals only."

Mary checks her watch. "But it's only three o'clock."

"Are you a relative?"

"No . . . but I just need ten minutes."

"Our residents are with their doctors on Wednesday afternoons. Come back tomorrow morning after nine."

"But it's important."

"Management is very strict on it."

Mary flops onto the steps defeated, just as her cell phone begins to vibrate. She fishes it out of her pocket. Jerry's name flashes on the screen. Two rings, three rings . . . She still doesn't answer. How can she talk to him as his wife when she is here? She presses the reject button, a cruel word, and tries to ignore the spear of guilt.

She sits on the cold steps for hours, until the streetlamp switches on and until the wooden sign on the driveway is only just readable if she squints. It says, Eugenie Heights is a privately owned nursing home offering luxury residential care for older people living with dementia-related conditions.

X

ONE HOUR PASSES. MARY's fingers are bloody. She has picked them to bits with nerves. She perches on the edge of the bed, her coat still buttoned to her chin, and she looks out through the porthole window on the fourth story of the guest house. Lightning stabs the terraces, and cars hiss along the wet road. Her phone buzzes again; it is Jerry's seventh call. She rejects this one, too.

In the bathroom, she rinses the blood off her hands and unwraps a small toothbrush from its plastic packet. She brushes her teeth hard. Her cell phone vibrates again. She pauses, looks at it, then slips on her shoes and makes her way out of the bedroom, leaving the phone behind.

The dining room in the basement of the guest house is empty. A fluorescent light hums overhead. Pink napkins and pink paper menus cover the tables. The dinner courses are fixed. Prawn cocktail. Chicken à l'orange. Jam roly-poly. Mary sits at the corner table and looks around for a waitress, wondering whether this is the sort of food she will be served at the hospital, whether they will feed her at all. No one comes to take her order, so she walks up to the reception desk and asks for a glass of wine. They are out of red and white, but there is enough rosé for a small glass. Mary swallows it fast. Still no one comes to take her order. She isn't hungry, anyway.

It was never like this on holidays with Jerry. They never ate in hotels, as he always compiled a list of recommended restaurants. He wrote daytime itineraries, too, and lined up interesting attractions for them to visit. He knew she needed structure, even though it didn't come easily to her.

Sometimes they fell behind schedule because she took so long doing things—not that she spent hours applying lipstick or mascara, just an inordinate amount of time drifting between rooms, picking up a skirt here, a bottle of moisturizer there and setting them down elsewhere as if her brain had frozen. Jerry never complained. He just seemed afraid to ask why she was that way.

Their honeymoon to the Isle of Man: Jerry always said that was a good holiday—one of their best. Mary picks over the exact days of it in her mind. Actually, it wasn't good. She recalls an argument about her clerical job and how he had suggested that she slow down to get ready.

"Get ready for what?" she had shrieked.

It was the first time she had raised her voice around him, and she had felt her neck veins jut out like spines on rhubarb. He had looked at her, baffled, yet she knew exactly what he was going to say next, just as she knew what her answer would be. That conversation had been scripted in her head years earlier, between her and whichever man took her on.

"To have a baby of course," he had said.

"Never."

She had said it once and firm and, so she wouldn't have to look at his face, she had taken out her gold tube of lipstick and drawn on her lips. She waited for him to hate her or hit her, that would have been easier, but he only picked up his itinerary.

"The Manx Woollen Mill," he had said. "Shall we go before it shuts?"

He unlocked their rental car and drove steadily to the wool loom. She watched a woman with thin fingers pick over the threads, weaving them into one another. Something about it had made her want to cry. But it was soothing, too. She would have liked to have stayed there with the wool loom woman and the plaited threads, but Jerry had checked his watch and said the restaurant reservation wouldn't wait for them.

Over dinner, he drank bloodred wine from a carafe, and she watched him over a candle flame. Her heart should have swelled when she looked at him, but if it did, she didn't feel it. He finished supper quickly, drank his wine dregs in one, and left an inordinately large tip, then they tripped back to the guest house along the promenade, their feet in step and his arm draped around her shoulder, the way newlyweds should walk. But his arm was too heavy; it pressed down on her, though she didn't like to say so. You should be grateful for a good man like him, she reminded herself.

He had laid out her nightdress, the long cream one with the belted waist that his mother had bought her for the honeymoon. She pulled off the tag and changed into it behind an open wardrobe door because it still didn't feel right to show herself to him. She lay down cautiously. He lay over her and she observed, once again, that he had a pleasant face, good symmetrical features and a genuine smile. Then she turned back to look at the long shadows on the ceiling while his fingers worked into the knot of her belt and undid each of the silly pearl buttons. He kissed her lips, and she could tell he was trying to be gentle, but it was still like a sheet of sandpaper rubbing across her face.

His chest pressed on hers: his heart hammered as though it were ready to leap out, while hers stayed measured and dull.

"I love you," he might have said in his usual way.

She can't remember exactly, because at that second, her inner self seemed to leave her body, float to the ceiling, and watch it all from above. When she looked down at the couple on the bed, she saw a living man and a still waxwork of a woman with dead eyes. The only thing that showed she was alive was the faint pink of her lips.

The man exhaled loudly, flushed crimson, and rolled off her again, while the waxwork lay still, her arms straight as though someone had put her on a board and starched her, then ironed her flat.

"You're so beautiful," he had whispered.

"I'm sorry."

"You've nothing to apologize for," he had said, and he kissed her cheek. "I can't believe my luck when I look at you and realize you're mine. . . . Sometimes I wonder when my luck'll run out."

Jerry worked his way back into his checkered pajamas and switched off the lamp.

When he was asleep, Mary pulled the nightdress around her and slipped into the doorless bathroom. She tried to be quiet, but the whoosh of the tap, the brush of toilet paper, and the rustle as she folded it were all dangerously loud. She propped one leg on the toilet seat and used a pink washcloth to scrub herself clean.

She rinsed it and wiped again, faster, more desperate. She stepped into the bath, scooped tap water in her cupped hands, and threw it upward between her legs. She wiped again with a cloth, then toilet paper. The paper was hard and rough as she cleaned away every last bit. Only then did she turn and catch Jerry's half-open eye.

That was the first time she had heard him cry, but she pretended she hadn't. She dried herself and crept back to bed without a word. His back faced her, but his whole body trembled and the mattress shook with his silent, swallowed sobs.

When she woke the next morning, he had written another list. He drove them to a farm, to a jam shop, and they walked along the promenade in the cold, eating vanilla ice cream. Jerry had smiled and wrapped his arm gently around her waist.

"Where next, Mrs. Sugden?"

She had laughed a little at that.

x

MARY AMBLES OUT OF the dining room and back up to the bedroom. She is nervous, she realizes with surprise. This is the first time in decades that she will sleep without Jerry beside her. She is overwhelmed with the heat of the room, and she opens the top button of her blouse. It makes no difference, so she unbuttons them all and unfastens her bra. She catches sight of herself in the wardrobe mirror; milky torsoed with a dimpled stomach and tiny breasts that sag. She pushes closed the wardrobe door, disgusted.

Thirteen hours until nine. The phone rings again. She ignores it and roots through the bedroom cupboards instead. There is a packet of toothpicks in one, two sheets of notepaper in a drawer, and a Gideon Bible in the one above it; she bangs it shut. She should answer the phone; this isn't fair to Jerry. She must at least tell him that she is safe. She takes a deep breath and reaches to pick it up, but the buzzing stops.

She tries to call back, but her phone has run out of credit, so she uses the hotel room landline instead. He knows it is her, even before she speaks.

"Hello? Mary? Can you hear me?"

She swallows.

"Hello."

"Are you all right?"

She presses the phone harder to her ear.

"I'm fine. I just had to— I'm fine."

"You had to what? What's going on?"

"I'll be back soon."

"Where are you?"

"I-I'm not far."

"What happened? I was so worried."

She opens her mouth, but nothing comes out. The phone is slippery in her hand.

"I've called a dozen times. I thought—"

"I just didn't hear it ring," she cuts in.

"We're all worried about you."

They have spoken about her, then; all thought what a bad wife, bad mother, bad grandmother she is, but all too good-hearted to admit it aloud. She knows, though. They all know.

"Please come home. No, tell me where you are and I'll bring you home."

She hopes he won't cry. She couldn't stand that.

"I only called back to say I'm fine and I'm sorry, but that I . . . I need a few days to collect my thoughts."

"About what? What thoughts? We can talk about it now, whatever it is." There is a long pause. "Please, Mary!"

He sounds shrill. She resents Shrill Jerry. Shrill Jerry fills her with guilt. It means that she is hurting him or being unkind, when he never is. Shrill Jerry is why she conceded and had Cath; her gift to him and her penance, no matter how dearly she loves Cath now.

"I'll see you soon. I'll explain then."

"Explain what? What am I supposed to do until then?"

"There's a shepherd's pie in the freezer. The bottom shelf."

"No, I didn't mean that. I mean— Don't hang up."

"I'm sorry. I'll see you soon."

"Are you with someone?"

She pauses. She can hear the click of plastic at the end of the line. He will be standing in the hall, twisting the curly telephone cord around his thumb until the blood stops and his skin whitens, the way he does when he is upset or frustrated, usually with a call center worker.

"It's a man, isn't it? Are you with a man?"

She pictures Jerry's face. He will be in pain. She knows pain. She could make it better. I'm just visiting an old acquaintance. I met him when I was a girl— No, there would be too much to explain.

"Yes," she squeaks. "I'm here to see a man."

There is another long pause.

"Who's John?" says Jerry eventually, a tremor in his voice. "Are you with him?"

The phone is hot, so hot, it could burn a hole through her hand. How do you know about John, she wants to scream.

Instead she puts down the receiver and unplugs it at the wall. Mary turns off her cell phone, too. She throws it onto the bed, surprised at her own force. She pushes back her hair and tips up her head to the ceiling, which is puckered with mildew. She must have said his name in her sleep, how else could Jerry know about him? She kicks the base of the bed and stubs her toe. She didn't want this; Jerry was never supposed to be hurt. She lies diagonally across the bed. It seems lavish, so she straightens out and presses her hands over her eyes but she can still see blue lights and swirling stars. Her hands are heavy, as though someone else is pushing down on them. She rests them by her sides and keeps her eyes closed.

Soon she is lost in the underwater chasm between sleep and consciousness. Photographs swim in and out of her head: Jerry with oiled hair and a sharp white side part. Nigel Forbes's mug shot. Jerry hunched over his typewriter wearing his tortoiseshell glasses, while she wheels a trolley of papers past his desk. Jerry removing the glasses and smiling shyly at her across the office, then slipping a note onto her trolley with one word. "Lunch?" Jerry again, this time standing over her hospital bed. He wears a blue paper gown and stares at her splayed legs and feet tied in high stirrups. His face is twisted, as though a big hand has taken it and crumpled it into a ball, while she screams and a nurse ushers him out of the room to a waiting area with the other fathers-to-be. He had pleaded to stay and told her afterward that he had been able to feel her labor pains, as if she had clawed his hand every time Cath's head tried to push out, though they were a whole corridor apart. She had told him not to be so ridiculous. He hadn't a clue of pain.

"A beautiful firstborn," the nurse had said.

"It's not my firstborn," mumbled Mary, still heady from the gas and air.

No one responded. Maybe Jerry hadn't heard. His face was buried in Cath's tiny cheek.

Mary wipes her eyes and opens them. She is awake now. Only she isn't in bed. She is sitting on the closed toilet lid. She is peeing. Urine seeps between her buttocks, drizzles down her legs, and patters onto the mat. She tries to stop midstream but she can't, so she stands and wrenches up the toilet lid.

By the time she is sitting on the toilet seat, she has finished peeing. The toilet seat and mat are soaked, and her leg is drenched. She rolls off her sodden trousers and underpants and steps straight into the shower. Then she remembers that she hasn't any spare clothes for tomorrow.

Mary drags her trousers into the shower with her and rubs the entire contents of a small bottle of green shower gel into them. It takes thirty minutes to dry them with a hair dryer. The linen is stiff as cardboard when she has finished. She flops onto the edge of the bed and sighs. Still only ten o'clock.

x

THE PAVEMENT IS WASHED with early-morning sun when Mary walks back to Eugenie Heights. Her trousers, still stiff with shower gel, rub against her. She arrives sooner than she expected, still twenty minutes too early, but she pushes the buzzer, anyway. No one answers. She presses it again, and the door clicks open.

"Hello?" she says into the intercom.

No one replies, and she steps tentatively inside. The nurse's booth beside the front door is empty. There is a bell on the desk. She should ring it, but who would she say she is? Mary takes in the carpet, the console table with a crystal vase, and a dish of polished artificial fruit. The staircase is lined with framed portraits of old aristocrats, politicians, and a long-dead prime minister.

That moment, an alarm pierces the stillness. Mary isn't sure whether to move: if they all evacuate, he might turn down the stairs and see her standing there, her mouth agape like a fish. What would he think of her? She shouldn't care what he thinks, she reminds herself. This is just about the truth.

Three nurses wearing plastic aprons steam into the hall. They talk hurriedly as they pass Mary, seeming not to notice her, and they turn off into another room. There is no smell of burning, and the fire alarm stops as abruptly as it began. The only sound is the disappearing click of the nurses' shoes.

She should come back in twenty minutes but her feet don't listen. She finds herself flitting along the empty corridor, running her hand across a ridge in the wallpaper, peering into a bedroom with bright white bedsheets pulled taut. She could be invisible. If another nurse appears, Mary is sure she would walk straight through her.

She ghosts her way up the stairs, past the marble busts that Jerry wouldn't notice, were he here. Jerry prefers modern things. Poor Jerry, irritating Jerry, but loving Jerry. How disloyal of her to think of him in this way and when she is here.

Her feet are silent on the stair carpet as she drifts upward, past the first floor, second floor, third floor. She climbs to the top story and watches over the banister as the tulips in the entrance hall shrink to tiny yellow spots. On the top floor is a short corridor with oriental urns along the carpet and, at either side, two closed doors. At the far end of the corridor, a third door is ajar. Mary can't make out what's inside, only a rectangular slit of room that dazzles with light.

She steps closer to the door. Next to it is a small brass plaque engraved with a name. She reads it and gasps.

Turn back.

No, knock.

You can't go in.

You need the truth.

You shouldn't be here at all.

It really is him.

She steps forward, forward, another step forward until she is an arm's length from the door. She is about to grasp the handle when it flings open.

"Oh," says a nurse. "Are you looking for someone?"

Mary nods. It takes her a moment to find her voice.

"I've found him," she says quietly.

"Who are you looking for?"

"Mr.—" Mary clears her throat and corrects herself; she is no longer a schoolgirl. She concentrates on keeping her voice steady and not letting it leap up a note as it touches his name—his actual name. The nurse checks the small silver clock clipped to her pocket.

"Have they sent you up already?" she says, a touch irritated. "Give me a minute to finish getting him ready, then you can go on through."

Mary half wants to turn around and run back down the stairs; his brain must have disintegrated entirely for the nurse to be speaking about him as though he is a child. But she nods instead and watches the nurse disappear back into the room.

Through the open door, Mary can make out a wide window and a pair of venetian blinds pulled open. There is a folded *Daily Telegraph* on the carpet, the arm and wing of a tan armchair just beyond it, and, at the bottom of the bed, a pair of long narrow feet mummified in a woven white blanket. She reddens, her hands grow clammy, and she turns her back on the doorway. Be polite, be formal, do what you came here for; ask him the questions and leave as soon as you have the truth. This is not a reunion.

Eventually, the nurse pokes her head around the door and clears her throat.

"You can come in now," she says.

"I don't know if I should—"

"It's all right; he's decent." She disappears back inside. "How about a nice jug of fresh water, John? That'll perk you up."

A door creaks, the nurse's feet pad from carpet to linoleum, and a tap gushes. Water clinks on glass. Mary walks slowly into his room, keeping her eyes low. It smells of cough syrup and pollen from a vase of drooping lilies sitting on a table; unbefitting of him. She stops at the foot of his bed and draws in a deep breath.

"Hello," she says quietly. "Hello Mr. Gallagher."

Then she dares to look at him.

9

When Betty wakes, a hoarse whistle has replaced her voice. Mother tucks a thermometer into her mouth.

"You need bed rest, my girl," she trills. "No more swanning off to Spoole for you."

Betty curls her toes beneath the blankets. This must be God's punishment to her for lying—and for kissing. She replays the kiss in her mind and decides that, next to that, flu is no punishment at all. She tries to pull herself upright, but her legs are too weak. They crumple, and she flops onto the floor.

"No, no, no," clucks Mother, walking into the bedroom.

She grasps Betty's armpits and hauls her fully onto the bed with such ease that Betty could be a toddler.

"No talking or working, just lots of rest. Nurse Dolores at your service," and she curtsies, making Betty smile.

Another day slogs on. Betty listens out for Gallagher. In her mind, she traces the contours of his jaw and his frame and his long pianist fingers. She drifts to sleep eventually, and her dream is eaten up with his face. His Adam's apple sticks out of his neck like a swallowed horse chestnut, and his pallor is gray.

A second dream figure appears, masked and pungent with ash fumes. It holds a bundle that drips with something red and stringy and clotting. Betty's dream self walks closer until she is within touching distance of the bundle. She realizes that it is a baby, half-dead and hacked to bits. She doesn't cry out but takes another step forward and watches, transfixed, as the baby transforms into a miniature beast that smells of burned meat. Betty gasps: he is a tiny version of Gallagher himself. She sits upright in bed and looks around. Just a dream. Mother snores beside her, curled up like a fetus, her presence a comfort in its way. Betty drifts to sleep again.

When she wakes next, sunshine streams through the curtains, and George's voice drifts upstairs from the hall.

"What's the matter with her?" he is saying in a voice that chills Betty, despite the sun.

She wraps her blankets tight around her.

"A nasty bout of flu," says Mother. "I thought Mary'd have dropped in, but I suppose she's a working woman now. Has she even asked after poor Betty?"

There is a pause.

"Is Betty about? There's something I need to tell her," says George uncomfortably.

"She's not looking her best. How about you come back on Friday and I'll make a nice spread for both of your teas," replies Mother. "Tell your father I said hello, too."

George says something muffled. The front door closes, and Mother's hands clasp together.

x

THREE MORE DAYS PASS and, with each, Betty grows stronger. Mother brings vegetable broth with lumps of butter to replenish her salts, and

Betty winces as she drinks it. She has heard Gallagher's voice only once in these days. He had been on the landing with another man who sounded like Sam or one of the older reporters.

The older reporter had said curtly, "Can I pass?" at the same moment Gallagher said, "Excuse me." There had been a shuffle of feet and a creak of floorboards, and Betty had imagined them circling around each other, the way male lions do. There were boots on the stairs, the click of a door, then the heavy press of silence again. But his voice still rings in her head: crisp and rounded but throaty, as though he has swallowed a sack of gravel.

When Betty gets her first strains of energy back, Mother carries the Dansette upstairs and plays a Bobby Darin song. She dances along to it, weaving around the bed, but the song ends with her sitting on the mat, nursing a stubbed toe.

"Off to serve the suppers," she sighs, and kisses Betty's forehead.

There is a familiar sharpness to Mother's breath. As she sweeps back downstairs, Betty covers her face with her hands. That smell. She drags herself from bed and pulls on her belted pink skirt.

"I'm fine," she argues when Mother tries to frog-march her back upstairs. "Really, I'm so bored cooped up in the bedroom like a little chicken."

"Cluck, cluck, hen," says Mother, flapping out her elbows like wings.

Betty smiles weakly and scans the kitchen for bottles, but she can't see any.

X

AT DINNER, REGGIE SITS at the head of the table, his hair oiled to one side.

"Feeling better, duckie?" he calls to Betty.

"Let's hope what her mother has isn't contagious," mumbles Sam.

"You'll not talk about our landlady dearest like that," snaps Reggie.

They all go quiet. Betty sets down the water jug and glances at Gallagher. He is squashed between two other reporters, his elbows tightly at his sides, his eyes fixed on his place mat and his curls still wet from washing. He doesn't look at her, and she is nervous suddenly.

"So, all's quiet on the western front," says Tony. "Any ideas what we're going to headline with next, chaps? Or how long our Cleaver is going to lie low?"

"You've been too quiet for my liking," says Reggie, turning to Gallagher. "Your turn to come up with a new angle for the team to follow, I think."

There is a pause.

"Then I'll disappoint you," says Gallagher, his lips barely moving.

"Will you, now?" sneers Reggie.

"We're not a team."

Betty returns from the kitchen with the corned beef stews, and all eyes around the table are still fixed on Gallagher. She reaches over his shoulder to set down his dish—she would like to whisper something comforting in his ear—but the dish tilts and a slop of hot stew lands in his lap. He jumps up; his shoulder hits the dish and it ricochets backward, landing flat against her front. Corned beef and dumpling slide down her blouse.

"Look what you've done, you great oaf," shouts Reggie, and Betty looks aghast. "Not you, Betty love. Him. That big lummox."

Gallagher's jaw twitches. He pushes back his chair and storms upstairs. Betty runs into the kitchen, still clutching the dish and mess to her front. Mother whirls around to see and claps a hand over her mouth.

"We'll have to get you a bib, you mucky pup," she splutters, laughing.

"Reggie shouted at Mr. Gallagher."

"Don't worry about him. He's a big boy."

"But it's my fault."

"Scoot upstairs and get yourself changed; I'll fix him another plateful," says Mother, turning back to whipping the egg whites. "Oh, and before I forget," she adds casually. "I'm going for a spin tomorrow night, now you're well."

"With who?"

Mother taps her finger to the side of her nose.

"Not with Reggie?"

"Ha, no," says Mother, grinning. "With someone I like very, very much."

"Who's that?"

Mother shakes her head, once and firm.

"It's not Mr. Forbes, is it?" says Betty carefully.

Mother turns to her. Her eyes are black. Her fists are balled up and pressed tightly to her sides. Betty is so stunned, she steps backward and bumps into the kitchen table. She has never seen that face.

"I hope you have a nice time," she murmurs.

Mother smiles, and her face is back as it should be. Betty wonders whether she imagined it.

She keeps her head down as she passes through the big room. Upstairs, she is about to step into her bedroom when another door opens and Gallagher steps out onto the landing.

"I'm sorry about the stew," she says, and turns to face him. He waves his hand to dismiss it.

"Mother'll get you fresh," she adds.

He nods and looks down at his shiny toe caps.

"I was ill," she says.

"I heard."

Then why didn't you knock or send a note, she wants to know, but she won't ask aloud.

"I enjoyed St. Ives so much," she says slowly. "And now we're back."

He reaches out and touches her cheek. A long tingle creeps up her spine. She waits for him to kiss her again, but he drops his hand.

"Maybe we could go for another drive," she tries.

"What happened wasn't right."

"But—"

"No buts," he cuts in firmly. "It's wrong. Imagine what your mother would say."

"I don't care about my mother."

"You don't mean that. And either way, I mean it. I should never have—"

"Why not?"

He sighs and stares hard at her. He must have found someone else; someone prettier and cleverer. Tears prick her eyes, but she won't cry in front of him. She would like to grab his hands and kiss each finger and let him drive her away again. To America, for all she cares, as long as it is just them.

"You said you wouldn't reset," she mutters.

Gallagher watches her. He opens his mouth and closes it again. Cutlery scrapes on china downstairs. Mother chatters away in a high voice, and someone laughs.

"You'll find a nice young man," he says gently.

"I don't care about nice young men."

"You're special, Betty. I intend to leave you that way."

She gulps. So this is what he has been thinking these days that they have been apart. Foolish of her to imagine he would say anything else.

"You will meet someone. And you'll forget you ever met me."

He strides past her and back downstairs. The front door opens and clicks shut.

x

THIS, THEN, IS WHAT sleepwalking feels like. The afternoon drags on, and so does the night. She doesn't sleep. Eventually it is the next morning, the next afternoon. She could be walking in a bubble, slow and gray and airless, while everyone else busies on as though nothing has changed.

Betty is still suffocating when Joan arrives with a can of hair spray and a pocket of rags to set Mother's hair in curls for her special night out. Mother slicks on smudgy mascara, and Joan helps to tie her sash before they waltz off downstairs. Mother squeals her goodbyes and clicks to the end of the street while Betty watches through the window, hoping to catch a glimpse of the man she is meeting, but Mother turns the corner and disappears.

The reporters are all at the Lamb and Flagg, and the hotel is empty but for Joan. Betty wonders whether Gallagher is with them at the pub, but she can't imagine it. She creeps onto the landing and presses an ear to his bedroom door. Silence. She holds her breath.

"Aren't you coming downstairs to make me a nice cup of tea?" calls Joan from the hall.

Betty jumps. "Coming."

Joan is settled on Mother's bruised armchair, lighting up a cigarette.

"There's a darling, I'll have two sugars," she says when she sees Betty.

When Betty returns with the tea, Joan is leafing through Mother's knitting patterns, her cigarette ash dropping onto the paper. Betty hasn't the energy to ask her to stop.

"Fetch me some nice jam sponge to go with that, will you, Betty love. Just a smidgeon. Thinking about my hips, but I do love your mother's baking. . . . Now, what do you think of that Reggie? Not exactly a looker, is he?"

Betty says nothing. She trudges back to the kitchen and slices the cake. She eats a slab standing up and carries out a smaller piece for Joan, who will ask for seconds anyway.

"Is it Reggie she's seeing tonight?" Joan continues.

Betty shrugs.

"Didn't she tell you either?" presses Joan. "She can keep a secret, can our Dolores."

Joan eats her cake, smokes two cigarettes, and tucks one of Mother's knitting patterns into her handbag. Betty reads six newspaper articles, all with Gallagher's name at the top. Joan's eyelids begin to droop.

"Mother asked you to stay here and look after me, didn't she?" says Betty.

"Is that what you think?"

"Joan?"

"Fine, she did," says Joan, slurping the last of her tea. "You've had flu or something, haven't you? She wanted me to keep an eye on you. It's only because she loves you."

"I'm fine. You should go home to Richard. He'll be wanting his supper."

"You're sure?" says Joan, already on her feet.

She clasps Betty in an awkward hug. Betty walks her outside and waits on the doorstep as Joan lets herself into her own house, just next door.

Betty is about to step back into the hall and shut out the dark road when she notices a streak of white on the doorframe. Closer, she sees that it is lumpy seagull mess dried onto the wood. She goes to the kitchen for a scouring pad, returns, and begins scrubbing.

She has turned over the scourer and is working it into the wood when she hears a pair of feet on the pavement. Someone is panting. She should go back indoors and double lock the front door, but she freezes.

Her hand is frozen, and the scouring pad is still pressed to the doorframe. Suddenly a shadowy figure appears behind her. She can't make out the figure's face, only a hat, a long coat, and two man hands hustling her into the hall.

"Get away," she cries, but it comes out as a gurgle.

Betty trips over her own feet and drops the pad. She can smell wet wool and something earthy and metallic. She wants to scream, but her lips and lungs don't connect with her brain. Her back is against the wall now and the figure stands over her. Betty tries to push him away, but it is like pushing at a lamppost. His hat is tilted down, and his dark collar is pulled high. Two hands reach out and push closed the front door. They are smeared red. Something glints.

"Stop," she calls, but she sounds feeble, even to her own ears.

In the weak light, Betty sees what glinted. A ring. A familiar solitaire.

"Mr. Gallagher?"

"It's me," he whispers at the same time.

She is half-relieved for a second, until he takes off his hat and she sees the spray of red on his jaw.

"Don't look at me, Betty."

"What have you done?"

She sees his face differently now. His eyes are bloodshot and unnaturally wide, his coat is sodden, and red fingerprints smear his face. She still wants to scream, but instead she guides him to the kitchen.

"We found her—" His voice cracks.

Betty clutches the edge of the sink to steady herself.

"Mother?"

He shakes his head, and she relaxes a fraction. Gallagher begins to cry and crumples to the floor.

"A girl. We had to carry her to the ambulance . . . Napier and I . . . Met on the beach to tell me something . . . And the blood still came . . ."

He heaves in a deep breath. She digs her fingers into the hard sink.

"Who?" she breathes.

"Napier didn't recognize her. . . . A fishing hook . . . Blood spurting . . ."

He sobs in a dry, guttural sort of way while she stands over him, frozen solid, letting his tears wet her feet. His arms wrap around her ankles, and his shoulders tremble as he presses his face into her shins.

"Her eyes were bulging and—"

"Stop it," she says.

He looks up at her face, still kneeling and hugging her ankles.

"You think it was me, don't you?" he splutters. "Dear God, you actually think I could hurt someone."

Betty looks at him harder. She thinks she might unpeel his arms from where they've grasped her. She might tie him to the kitchen table somehow so she is safe, then run outside. She would bang on Joan's door or find a policeman, and she would stand under the streetlamp until they cart him off—until everyone is safe again. Mother would come home then. They would toast bread with sugar and cinnamon to calm her.

"Shh, it's all right," says Betty instead.

She crouches on the floor, level with Gallagher, and she hugs him while he shivers. His hands are frozen. She rubs them inside her own to thaw them.

Blood has smeared her ankles, but she doesn't wash it away. She holds him for a long time, until the temperature in the kitchen plummets and the metallic smell sets in her nose, then she guides him up to his room and tucks him into bed. She sponges his face and hands with water from the basin in the corner, while he lies still. When she has dried him gently and unlaced his sandy shoes, she kneels at his bedside and strokes his hair in a jerky, uncertain way.

"You do believe me, don't you?" he says, looking hard into her eyes.

She gulps.

"Yes . . . yes I do," she says, and she keeps stroking his hair until she loses him to sleep.

Part Two

10

Betty's footsteps echo in the empty street. She walks faster as she nears Mr. Forbes's butcher's shop, shivering though the sun is high and bright. She tells herself that she is only hurrying because she is late to meet Gallagher, and she glances into the shop window as she passes. The lights are switched off, and the silver display trays are empty but for a cow shoulder, buzzing with bluebottles, that hangs from a meat hook.

Betty almost feels sorry for Mr. Forbes; he couldn't have hurt those five girls. If he was a killer, surely he would have bashed up Mother when she beat at his door every night, shouting that she loved him and why didn't he love her, too? Betty could see that Mr. Forbes still loved his dead wife, even though the newspapermen had started to print cruel stories about him.

Just this week Reggie wrote an article that said a year before his wife died, Mr. Forbes had come home drunk from the Lamb and Flagg and beat her black-and-blue for no reason at all. Her face was covered with so many bruises, they joined up, so a source in the article said. Betty had asked Reggie the name of the source, but he had only tapped the side of his nose.

"B-Betty," calls a man's voice, and she jumps, almost dropping her shopping.

She looks back and sees Mr. Forbes himself peering out of his shop doorway. He wears striped pajama bottoms and a grubby white vest. She walks faster and grips her bag tighter, mentally counting the number of new bedsheets inside it. Four, yes, she bought the correct number. She will drop them off at the hotel, then leave straightaway to meet Gallagher.

"P-p-please," he cries after her. "Just a quick word."

"I need to get home," she calls over her shoulder.

She looks back fleetingly at him and sees that his face is pale, almost yellow, with blue shadows beneath his eyes. She can't tell whether he has been punched or if he is exhausted. Perhaps both.

"Ask Dolores to help me. It wasn't me. She knows me. If she c-c-c-could just tell the p-police what I'm really like. P-please!"

Betty is stunned; she has never heard him speak so much, let alone shout. He usually looks stiff and awkward, his posture straight as a pencil and his words sparing, the way he must have been taught in the army. Betty walks faster, almost trotting.

"I've no one left," he yelps. "No one b-b-b-believes me. I've men and boys knocking at my door all night threatening me. But it w-wasn't me. Tell Dolores. Tell someone!"

What do you want me to do about it? Betty wants to shout, full of anger suddenly. You didn't see Mother lying on your abattoir floor, sobbing that she loved you. You didn't help carry her home barefoot.

"They set me up," he shouts after her, his voice thinner.

You tucked down your head when you saw us in the street afterward, and in church you acted as though we were strangers, then stopped going altogether. You're the reason she's in a bad way again.

"Someone stole three knives from my shop. And now those stories in the p-p-papers . . . I didn't lay a finger on my wife, God bless her soul. Nor those girls."

She tightens her knuckles around the bag handle. Three men turn onto the street at that moment, and he stops shouting. She is relieved, though she doesn't recognize the men. They aren't staying at Hotel Eden, but they wear city suits like the other reporters.

She glances back at Mr. Forbes one last time. He is on his knees, half on the pavement, half inside his shop. His head is tucked in his hands, and she can see his crown beneath his thinning hair, though he is barely thirty-five years old. She nods an acknowledgment at the men, and when they have passed, she runs back to Hotel Eden.

x

IN THE KITCHEN, BETTY runs cold water over her wrists to calm herself; she can't let Gallagher see her in this state.

"What's wrong?" says Mother, creeping up behind her. "You were gone forever."

Betty tries to smile. Mother's hair is set in perfect curls, her lipstick is bright, and her eyes are flicked with black liner. She looks stronger than Betty has seen her for a long time.

"I saw Mr. Forbes," she says tentatively. "He asked after you."

Mother turns away and takes down her apron from the peg.

"He said he didn't do it. He said he'd been framed," she continues. "He didn't seem well. . . . He wants you to tell Inspector Napier what he's really like. That he wouldn't hurt anyone."

"Off for another of your secret afternoon jaunts today?"

"Mother, didn't you hear me? He's in trouble. You loved him once."

"Loved him? That murdering wife-beater?" she splutters. She ties her apron string in a brisk bow. "He's a rotten one. He deserves it all."

"Did he hurt you?" whispers Betty, but Mother raises a palm, and the conversation is over.

Betty dries her hands and unpacks the bedsheets from the shopping bag.

"I'm going for a walk," she says without meeting Mother's eye.

"Give my love to George," says Mother in a gooey voice.

"George? I'm not seeing George."

"Things are working out finally, aren't they? For all of us."

"I'm just going for a walk in the clearing."

"Whatever you say," giggles Mother, inspecting the new sheets.

Betty gathers her sandals and book with a frown, but it is her best time of day, so she mustn't let anything spoil it.

x

AFTERNOON SUN PIERCES THE canopy of oaks and elms, and the grass is mottled with patches of light. The clearing is empty; Gallagher is even later than her. Betty finds a warm spot beneath the lone willow that droops into the pond, and she sits there, squinting between the trees for a glimpse of him. As she waits, she counts their afternoons together; this will be their nineteenth.

"Best view in all of England," booms a voice.

Betty turns around. Gallagher's fedora is perched on his head, his crisp white shirtsleeves are rolled up to his elbows, and he is grinning as he strides toward her.

"You're here," she breathes, exhilarated, the way she always is when she sees him.

"Of course I'm here."

He reaches down and kisses the top of her head, then sits apart from her, careful not to touch her. He takes off his hat, dusts it lightly, and rests it on the grass. They say nothing more, but the silence isn't awkward. Her forehead is still moist from his kiss.

There is a breath of wind, and dozens of tiny leaves dance through the air, landing on the surface of the lake. The air smells of stagnant water. Betty idly plucks a fuzzy gray dandelion. She closes her eyes and blows it. He watches.

"One o'clock." Another blow. "Two o'clock." Half of the spores fly off. "You try," she says, holding out the last of it.

He shakes his head, smiling all the same, and from his jacket pocket he pulls out a cigarette tin. He strikes a match and lights the cigarette tip. She watches as he sucks and breathes out circles of smoke, angling his head away from her, though she likes the smell of it now.

"I'd like to try one," she says.

"One day."

"Why not today?"

"Ask me a different question."

"Fine." She thinks for a second. "Why do you let Reggie speak to you the way he does?"

Gallagher drags on the cigarette. "You're very inquisitive today."

She can't think of a reply. His voice is already prickly and she doesn't want to spoil their thin slice of time together, so she picks around for a different topic.

"What do you think of the Mr. Forbes situation?" she asks eventually.

He smudges the tip of his cigarette on the grass and turns to her.

"Honestly? I'm foxed."

Betty nods in agreement.

"He's a loner, a touch odd, perhaps. But a killer? I'm not convinced."

They look in opposite directions. Gallagher takes a long slurp of a new cigarette. She wants to tell him everything, it is bursting out of her, but she begins in a mousy voice.

"I saw him today on my walk back from Spoole."

Gallagher sits upright and turns to her. "If he touched a hair on your head."

"Of course he didn't," she says, and he relaxes. "He just seemed so desperate. I almost wanted to help him."

"You can't help everyone all the time. Anyway, you barely know him." She bites her lip. Yes, she trusts him.

"I know him better than I let on," she says slowly. "If I tell you, please don't put this in the newspaper. Swear it?"

He nods, looking concerned.

"He gave us free mutton and eggs and things last winter," she begins carefully. "And Mother started to love him. She loves any man who's kind to her but . . . they had a romance thing," she stammers. "It was just after Mrs. Forbes died. He must have liked Mother, too. At first, anyway."

She waits for Gallagher to say something, but he only puffs on his cigarette and nods.

"But then he said he'd made a mistake and that they shouldn't meet up anymore. I was furious with him—I'd never seen Mother so low. She kept saying that he was just having a bad day and he would change his mind. I didn't have a clue how to help her."

"You never stop helping her."

Betty ignores him. "I never really understood him. He was so cold and stiff and he had this terrible stutter when he was upset, but he seemed sad, too. Not angry, just deep-down sad. Mother said it was from the awful things he'd seen when he was serving in France."

"But you never really know a person. Look at what he did to his poor wife."

"That's the thing. I read Reggie's article, but I can't picture him beating Mrs. Forbes. Do you know the name of his source?"

Gallagher shakes his head.

"Do you think I should go to the police?" she continues. "Maybe I should say that he wasn't violent to Mother, and, if he was a killer, then he would have been. Wouldn't he?"

Gallagher turns over his hat in his hand and scans the pond, frowning.

"But then Mother would be dragged into it all," she says. "If she was questioned by the police and it was all dredged up again, her nerves wouldn't stand it."

"Look, if Forbes is innocent, he'll be exonerated," says Gallagher. "I honestly believe that. They haven't even charged him; it's just rumor. And as for worrying about your mother . . . put yourself first for once. She's certainly moved on."

"What do you mean, moved on? Why are you always so hard on her?"

His voice softens.

"Nothing. I didn't mean anything."

"Yes you did. Tell me."

"Forget I said it."

"I can't now."

"I only meant that she's not short of male company, and that she's probably put that business with Forbes behind her. Just the other night, I saw her on a drive with a man. Now, it's not my place to say who, but the point is, you can't keep looking after her like this."

"She's all I have."

"Yes, but what do you want? Let someone do something for you for once. Let me do something for you. Especially after my performance the other night . . ."

She frowns. They haven't spoken about the evening he found the dead girl. After their first two afternoons at the pond, the conversation had oiled itself along, and she was glad not to mention it. Now she doesn't know what to say.

"You don't need to do anything for me; you were in shock."

"Yes, it was a shock—I think it was something to do with my mother. You know, she died when I was born, so when I saw that young girl—"

"There's no need to explain," she says, though she hopes he will continue. It makes her feel special knowing about his secret thoughts, his past.

"All the same. Let me or someone else do something for you for once."

"Just being here is enough," she murmurs, and blushes.

Gallagher reaches for another cigarette. He holds out the tin and, surprised, she takes one. He puts it between his lips, lights it, and hands it to her. She slots it between her lips uncertainly, but she doesn't breathe in, in case it makes her sick, the way Miss Hollinghurst said cigarettes would. It hangs there limply and tastes fuggy, like a mouthful of hot dustbin rubbish, but she is certain that she looks sophisticated and at least five years older. He half smiles.

"That's enough for one day," he says, taking it out of her mouth.

He wraps her in a tight hug, his chin resting on the top of her head. They stay locked together for a long time.

"I'm going to protect you from now on, my Betty," he whispers into her hair.

"But what if I don't need looking after? What if I'm a tough old nut all by myself?"

He hugs her tighter. In the murky light of his neck where her head is pressed, she can make out a curl of his black chest hair and the pulse in his throat. It makes her insides ticklish.

"Lie down with me," she whispers.

His hug slackens. He draws back, holding her shoulders away from him and searching her face, his eyes narrowed. She looks down at the grass, hot and fidgety and shocked that the words left her lips.

"You know I can't do that," he says eventually.

He releases her shoulders, and she lies on her front so he can't see her face. She digs her knees into the turf. If only it would crack open and let her disappear, now that he has refused her.

They are silent again. Her blush doesn't lift, and his wristwatch ticks louder. But then the smell of cigarette smoke overpowers the grass, and something firm presses into the dip of her lower back. It is an arm. Her body turns to jelly. A nose nuzzles her ear and the woody smell of his aftershave mixes with the smoke and grass.

"Don't be upset. I hate seeing you upset," he whispers.

She can sense his body: he lies on his side, an arm propping up his head as he looks at her. His other arm drapes over her waist and lower back. She reaches forward and kisses his lips. His head tips sideways and their faces slot together again.

Betty is the first to run out of breath, and she comes out of the kiss for air. He rolls her over gently so she is flat on her back and he is above her, nose to nose, his shadow covering her. She watches the daggers of cloud slice up the sky, until his head moves directly over hers and she can't see them anymore. He kisses her again, harder than he ever has before, pushing his tongue into her mouth. His hands work down her hips. The tickly feeling in her stomach expands. It is almost itchy, and it makes her want to cry or laugh; she isn't sure which first.

"You meant that?" he whispers, his mouth pressed to her ear.

"Yes."

"You're sure?"

"Stop asking."

He goes back to kissing her, at the same time resting his body lightly on top of hers. It gets hot, too hot then. She tries to relax, to show that she is happy, but a sharp bit of bark or maybe a twig needles into her back, while something jams into her lower front. The top half of her body seems to divide off. It is floaty and separate from the sickly pain everywhere below. He kisses her cheeks, her neck, her chin, then returns to her lips, but even that doesn't plug the pain. His hand finds hers. It is hot and smooth. She clutches his fingers as he moves over her. A drop of his sweat lands on her lip.

She can't speak or tell him that it hurts because it will spoil it: this, which is all she has wanted for weeks. She breathes in his neck and would like to bottle his smell, but at that moment the pain gouges even deeper, and Betty has to bite the inside of her cheek to stop herself from crying out.

She isn't certain what happens next. Perhaps she has fainted or fallen into a strange trippy sleep for a fraction of a minute, but when she opens her eyes, the weight of him is off her, their hands are apart, and he is offering her a blue cotton handkerchief with white diagonal stripes. A wobbly smile covers her face as she takes the handkerchief. The pain has almost disappeared and something serene has replaced it, as though she could step onto the pond and walk across its surface.

Gallagher turns away his head. She wipes the top of her leg under her skirt and rearranges her hem over her shins. When she holds out the handkerchief to return it to him, it is stained red. Embarrassed, she balls it up in her hand and checks he hasn't noticed. He hasn't; his back still faces her. She watches the square slope of his shoulders and the circles of gray smoke float up from his cigarette. A dull ache tugs down between her legs now that she is standing, but she doesn't mind. Not now that they are sweethearts.

But when Gallagher turns around, his eyes are hard slits. Something is wrong. She reaches forward to hold his hand, but he jerks back. He is about to speak when he spots something over her shoulder. She looks around, but no one is there. When she turns back to Gallagher, he is running in the opposite direction.

"John!" she cries.

He doesn't turn around; he only runs faster.

x

BETTY SLUMPS ONTO THE grass, confused. She thought she had fathomed him. He hadn't reset himself once since finding the girl, not until now. She tries to recall what she might have said wrong, but she hardly spoke at all. What upsets her most is that he hasn't walked her to the edge of the wood, the way he has done every other afternoon. "To make sure you get home safely," he always said.

Minutes pass, and there are footsteps. She looks up just as Gallagher reappears. He is panting, and his hands are shaking. She stands and smiles for him, but his face is twisted in a frown; he looks furious.

"You're back," she says, beaming.

He picks up his hat from the grass, pulls it low over his eyebrows, and looks around to make sure that they are still alone, though there is never usually anyone else in the clearing but them and the birds and the fish.

"Promise me you'll never tell a soul," he says in a hard, hushed voice, his eyes boring into hers.

"Of course I won't."

He grips the tops of her arms, his fingers digging into her. "I mean it. You don't understand the trouble I'd be in. I should never have let myself."

"Don't let's go through all that again."

"Betty, you don't realize how serious this is. You're fifteen. My father's reputation . . . I'd be locked up."

"I won't tell," she says quietly.

"I'd be in prison for ten, fifteen years. Do you know what they do to men like me in prison—men with my background?"

"Prison?" she says, horrified. "But you've done nothing wrong. I—"

She wants to say I love you but she can't; not here, and not in this way.

"I love being with you," she finishes.

"This isn't a game. It would end me. I'd be dead, one way or another. Men have hanged for less."

"Hanged?"

"You're not to tell your mother, nor that girl Mary—you must tell no one that you were with me, or even that you were here. Do you understand?"

"I've said I won't. I promise. But I don't understand why anyone could . . . hang for something so—"

"Stop! I need to think. I need to work out what to do."

"Okay, I'll stop. Just please don't be upset."

He lets go of her and squeezes the bridge of his nose, shutting his eyes and shaking his head.

"I'm sorry," he says. "This is exactly what I didn't want."

"Can't we just make the most of what's left of our afternoon?"

"I've been trying so hard not to let this happen. And now . . ."

"We'll be all right."

"I'm so, so sorry, my Betty."

He gives her a long, sad look. Her insides run cold.

"If you'll just sit down with me again," she tries. "We can pretend that nothing happened, if that's what you want. We could talk about your work, or films, or . . ."

But he shakes his head. He reaches forward and kisses her forehead, so lightly, she can barely feel his lips at all, then he turns on his heel and stalks off between the trees.

Betty lolls under the willow and turns over the afternoon in her mind. Gallagher will return to his old self tomorrow, she is certain of it. He called her his Betty, after all.

She pulls bunches of grass from the earth, and her insides burn up with embarrassment as she recalls how she moved her lips at a foolish angle and dribbled saliva on him. They burn up in a different way as she relives the heavy press of his body on her own, but the loveliness of it all is punctuated by that word: *hanged*.

She wishes that she had asked him exactly what he meant, or that she could dissect it all with Mary, but she won't. She will keep her promise to him forever. She will tell no one, no matter what.

When Betty pulls herself from her trance, there is a new throbbing pain just below her waist and something is rustling in the trees, louder than the wind on the leaves. She looks around for Gallagher, but the daylight has faded, the clearing is bathed in pale orange light, and her eyes can't quite adjust. Her skin prickles with nerves.

"John?" she calls into the emptiness.

But she pictures Mr. Forbes prowling for victims, his cleaver raised above his head. She sits very still, holding her breath and reminding herself that he is harmless.

Something mews. It sounds like a cat, only more rasping. The noise gets louder. There is a whisk of brown feathers and an almighty crack of branches. Then it is in front of her: a buzzard swooping low over the pond. It grazes the surface of the water with its wings and sweeps up again, disappearing between the trees.

Betty feels silly. She laughs aloud to prove to herself that she isn't scared, but her legs wobble as she stands. She is dusting herself down and picking a sticky burr off her skirt when there is another noise in the bushes. It sounds different, louder, like a person. Gallagher must have come back for her, after all.

She squints and spots a shape between the trees. She squints harder and the shape untangles itself and becomes two people, so far away, they look like dollhouse miniatures. The girl is clearest. She has long hair to her waist, and she wears a floaty dress. Her hair falls over her face, and she is weeping with laughter. A man stands beside her. He wraps her up in his arms and pushes his lips to her neck. The girl says something—Betty can't make out what—but the singsong voice is familiar. It is the voice that reads Bible stories to the children every Sunday morning; Miss Hollinghurst.

Betty is about to call out her name, but something stops her because the man is still kissing her neck and the laughs are getting louder. Their arms knot around each other and the man strokes her hair. There is something sneaky about watching them. If someone happened upon her with Gallagher, wouldn't she want them to slink away quietly? Better that than making all three of them embarrassed. She takes one last look at the man and tries to make him out, but it is difficult because his back is facing her. His suit is brown and he wears a hat. A familiar fedora. The tall, proud way he stands is familiar, too. Betty gives a little cry.

She turns and hurries out of the clearing, her cheeks flaming. Branches snap under her feet and she runs faster, praying they won't spot her. The shadow of another figure, or perhaps an animal, prowls between the trees. Betty doesn't register it. She runs back to Newl Grove without stopping, uncertain how she will look either of them in the eye again.

x

BETTY SLIPS INTO THE hotel through the back door, careful to tiptoe, but when she turns around, she almost screams with fright. Joan and Jennifer are staring at her. *They know what you've done.* She holds her breath, but Jennifer goes back to chopping up a grapefruit and Joan plops down onto a chair next to the foldaway kitchen table, an empty wine bottle, and two glasses in front of her. One is scarred with Mother's lipstick.

"Where's Mother?" she says, not able to meet Joan's eye.

"Out looking for you," says Joan, tartly. "So's my Richard. And Paxon's boy came knocking, so I sent him after you as well."

"George? Why did he—"

"What do you think you're doing, staying out all hours? You know how dangerous it is. Really, Betty."

"It's not even eight o'clock yet."

Joan purses her lips.

"Mother didn't mind me going out," adds Betty.

"Yes, I've had words with her about that. Do you know the lengths everyone's going to, to keep this village safe? There's my Richard volunteering to patrol the streets, there's the new Neighborhood Watch roster, not to mention all of those policemen on lookout. And there you are, gallivanting off and putting yourself in harm's way."

"I'll go after her."

"No, you stay here, madam."

"But Mother's on her own."

What if she saw me with Gallagher, she wants to add. Her eyes fill with hot, stingy tears at the thought. But she tells herself that if Mother saw anything, she wouldn't have stayed quiet.

"And get your bottom upstairs and clean yourself up before your mother sees you like that," calls Joan over her shoulder, rummaging in the cookie jar. "You look like you've been dragged through a hedge backward, upside down and goodness knows how else."

"I'm sorry," murmurs Betty, glad that Joan isn't looking at her.

She is certain her face is so transparent, Joan would see straight through it and know.

"Save your apologies for your mother when she's home."

Betty is relieved to be upstairs, away from Joan's beady eye. She tip-toes across the landing and stops at Gallagher's bedroom door. A rush of confidence fills her: she will tell him that she loves him. He will kiss her and say the same back. They will agree to meet by the pond again tomorrow afternoon; and the next afternoon; and the next; and he will never again talk about awful things like being hanged.

She gives two brisk knocks and steps back. A hot burning fills her chest. She thinks she hears a creak of floorboards inside the bedroom, but she can't be certain. There is no answer, so she knocks again. Still nothing. The creaking noise stops.

"It's me," she whispers into the crack of the door.

But the hotel is silent except for Jennifer and Joan clattering and chopping downstairs.

The hot burning rises to her throat. She wants to pound on his door until he answers, then shake him until he slots back to his old self again. She should chase after Mother, too, instead of letting her wander the dangerous streets alone when it is nearly dark, but instead she ambles into the bedroom.

On the bedside table, she spots Mother's pot of sleeping tablets. She swallows two with a swig of last night's stagnant water and forces herself to lie down, but she still can't rest: how will she explain to Mother where she has been? How long until the tugging pain between her legs eases? What will she say to Miss Hollinghurst in church on Sunday? And to Gallagher tomorrow? Why did he run off? Could he really be sent to prison for that, for an act of love? Or was it an act of love? She swallows a third sleeping tablet and squeezes closed her eyes.

x

WHEN BETTY WAKES, THE bedroom is bright with morning sun and her wristwatch reads twenty past eight. She curses herself for sleeping so late and leaps out of bed, still wearing yesterday's clothes. Only when she is halfway downstairs, Gallagher's face already sitting in her mind, does she register that Mother's side of the bed was untouched. The sheet, she recalls, was still tucked taut into the mattress, but there is no time to worry because at that moment she sees that the hotel is in chaos.

Men stampede between the rooms. The front door opens and slams, opens and slams. Betty stands at the foot of the stairs, cups her hands around her lips, and shouts into the din: "If you'll all sit down, I'll serve the breakfasts in five minutes." There is a chorus of tuts and groans. More men leave. She looks around for Gallagher, but she can't see him and there isn't time to ask after him. She hurries into the kitchen and almost cries out. Strings of beef fat are slung over the countertops and grapefruit peelings litter the oilcloth. A pan of dingy gray water sits on the stove with bits of carrot and parsnip skin inside it. Something is rustling in the larder.

"Mother?"

The larder door opens, and Tony shuffles out with bulging hamster cheeks and fists full of stale bread.

"I was hungry," he says guiltily.

"Guests aren't allowed in here," she snaps. "Have you seen my mother?"

He shakes his head, still chewing.

"Who served the dinners last night?"

"That mousy girl," he says between chews. "And some old blonde with a smoker's cough."

Betty sighs. She rolls up her cuffs, sets the kettle on the stove, and pours milk into a clean-looking jug.

"Make yourself useful and take this in with you," she says, pushing the jug into Tony's hand. A rush of confidence fills her. "And please could you tell Mr. Gallagher I'd like to speak to him . . . about his bill. If you see Mother, send her through to me, too."

When the bread and butter and jams and teas are all on the table, and Betty has taken orders for boiled eggs, and Reggie has given her a wink that she pretends not to notice, she scans the room for Gallagher again. He must have left early. Perhaps Mother did, too.

She tries to forget about them. A reporter who she only vaguely recognizes is pressing his finger into Mr. Eden's best sugar caddy and licking it. She swats away his hand, and he pretends to look frightened of her. The others see. They all laugh, and Betty joins in.

The pan of eggs boils away, and Betty clears up the kitchen mess, listening lazily to the chatter in the big room.

"You know he's gone?" says Reggie. "Packed up his prissy little suitcase and left before morning."

Her ears prick up. She stops fishing the grapefruit skins from the sink, but, before anyone else can speak, there is a crash at the front door and feet thunder into the big room. Betty hurries in, the same moment Richard appears. His face is red and spluttery. He removes his hat.

"There's been another," he cries. "They've found a body."

The table falls silent.

"Christ alive," breathes Tony. "I thought they were holding Forbes at the station."

Richard shakes his head.

"They let him go yesterday morning."

"Imbeciles," cries Reggie.

"It's a local this time. Lovely girl. Just turned twenty-one. Wouldn't have harmed a flea."

"Why weren't they watching Forbes?" says Sam, getting to his feet.

"They were. We all were," says Richard. "He must have snuck out somehow."

The reporters scribble in their notebooks, and Reggie writes on a scrap of paper napkin.

"Girl's name?" he barks at Richard.

"Patricia Hollinghurst. She was a Sunday school teacher, poor lamb."

"Miss Hollinghurst?" mutters Betty. "But I saw her—"

"Let's go, boys," booms Reggie at the same time.

"And where's Mother?" says Betty, but no one hears.

Chairs are scraped back, and they all dash for the door, leaving behind half-drunk cups of tea and bits of bread. No one notices that Betty's legs have dissolved under her. She catches the edge of the dresser to keep herself upright.

"I saw her with—" she breathes. "Not him. It can't be him."

The front door slams, and the hotel rings with silence.

✕

BETTY IS STILL CLINGING to the corner of the dresser when the door opens again ten minutes later. Mother staggers in, tripping over her own feet. Her hair hangs in wet ropes, tangled with seaweed, and she is naked but for an unfamiliar white dressing gown, belted loosely around her waist.

"Make your mother a hot sweet sherry," she slurs.

Betty feels sick. "Where are your clothes? Where've you been?"

Mother staggers toward her, tripping over the hem of the dressing gown.

"That's no way to greet your dear old mother," she cries, clinging to the edge of a dining chair. "Especially when I've been out all night, working for us, securing our future."

Betty bubbles with rage.

"Our future? Miss Hollinghurst's dead," she cries, tears streaming down her face. "I thought you'd been hurt, too."

Mother looks blankly at her, as though she doesn't know who Miss Hollinghurst is.

"He could have killed you! Why are you like this? Why can't you just be normal and happy, or pretend to be happy the way everyone else does?" Betty wipes her face with her fist and stares at the dressing gown. "And who does that belong to?"

"I found it on a washing line," says Mother simply, her head tilted to one side. It makes her look very young. "He said he doesn't love me."

"She's dead, Mother. She was killed. By the pond. Miss Hollinghurst. It was lovely Miss Hollinghurst."

I saw her there, she wants to add. I saw her there and I know who killed her. But she can't say any of it—not when Mother will ask why she was by the pond and with whom. She would never be able to look Mother in the eye again, and, worse, she would be forced to break her promise to Gallagher. He would end up in prison or hanged or killed by some other horrible means, just as he said. She must speak to him before she says anything more to anyone, even Mother. She buries her head in her hands and sobs.

When she looks up again, she is alone. She searches for Mother in the kitchen, but it is empty and reeks of stale fat. Upstairs, she finds Mother collapsed on the bathroom floor, the stolen dressing gown hanging off her and vomit puddling the floor. Betty glares at her. She should pick her up; she should sponge her mouth and carry her to bed. She should give her a glass of cool water and soothe her until she falls asleep, the way she usually does.

"Water," gasps Mother.

Betty shakes her head. She walks back downstairs and tries to block out the bangs and scrapes upstairs as Mother crawls her way into the bedroom. She hums so she can't hear or think about anything at all, and she scrubs every inch of the kitchen. When it is dazzling and sharp with the smell of bleach, she takes a key from the peg next to the back door and walks upstairs slowly. She can hear Mother snoring through the closed bedroom door. She stops on the landing outside Gallagher's bedroom. Her breaths come fast, and her chest is tight. She will tell him what she saw; he will know what to do.

She knocks gently, but there is no answer, just as she somehow knew there wouldn't be. She turns the key, but the door is already unlocked. She pushes down the handle.

Please be in there.

It creaks open.

Please smile up at me and say you love me, then tell me what to do about all of this.

She walks inside.

I don't mind if you're angry with me for sneaking into your room. Just be inside.

But the room is empty. The air hangs with old smoke. Betty touches the tapestry blanket spread neatly over the bed, and she knows he hasn't slept in it. The brown suitcase has vanished from the alcove beside the window, and there are no shoes on the floor.

She opens the wardrobe, but that is empty, too. Betty falls to her knees and searches under the bed for a sign of him, but there is only a stray cushion and a ball of gray hair, not even his hair. She cries out, clamping a hand over her mouth as she does in case Mother hears. There is nothing left of him in the whole room but a handful of cigarette stubs in the glass ashtray.

She notices the envelope then. It is tucked beneath the ashtray, and the flap is unsealed. She grasps it with trembling hands. Inside is a wad of banknotes, nothing more. She turns over the envelope and sees his writing, looped and orderly:

"For Mrs. Broadbent. To settle my bill."

Betty picks up the longest cigarette, a nub covered with gray ash. She dusts it off, her hands still shaking. It is cool—it has long been stubbed out—but the tip is still damp with his saliva. She droops it between her lips.

11

September 1956

The bedroom is hot and the curtains are still drawn, though it is past three. The day smells of sour breath and perspiration. Betty sits on the edge of her unmade bed, counting on her fingers. She loses count and starts again. Yes, almost three whole weeks have passed since Miss Hollinghurst died and Gallagher left. She counts again: six days since Mother's sad spell ended and she rose from bed to take back the reins of Hotel Eden.

Betty goes back to listening. There is little else to occupy her now that her workload has thinned, so she passes long hours in her bedroom, tracking the noises inside the hotel and on the street below and counting the days until Gallagher will return to help her fathom what to do. Today, though, the world seems to have stopped. It is silent with nothing to examine but the symphony of floorboards and clanking water pipes.

The hours crawl along until, finally, there is a new noise. A pair of feet pad up the stairs, and a second pair shuffle onto the landing. Mother's voice calls out:

"Why not move into Mr. Gallagher's old room? No sense in leaving it empty."

Betty opens her bedroom door, just as Sam appears on the landing with a brown leather suitcase. He lugs it across to Gallagher's bedroom.

As Sam pauses to catch his breath, he notices Betty staring at him, and he smiles. She frowns back; Gallagher will return soon and he will be angry to find his bedroom taken over. Sam's smile fades. Betty shuts herself inside her bedroom again. She hates Sam for stealing that room and hates Mother for letting him, but most of all she hates Miss Hollinghurst for being in the woods at all and for making her carry around all she knows. The knowledge makes her so heavy; Gallagher's words have buried themselves into her skull, weighing it down, making her whole body droop and flag.

Three times in these last few days, Betty has lugged her body out of this bedroom, hulked it down the stairs, and put her hand on the front door handle, planning to step out into the street and make her way to Inspector Napier's house. She would knock on his door and there, on his doorstep, she would tell him exactly who she saw in the woods with Miss Hollinghurst the night she died. She would feel light again, she would have done the right thing. But each time she presses down on the door handle, something makes her glance sideways at the coat pegs: the pegs where Gallagher's hat and coat hung during the seventy-four days he lived at Hotel Eden.

His words fill her head next, dragging her down further, rattling around her skull, pinging between her ears. I'd be dead one way or another. Men have hanged for less. And then her own: I promise. I'll never tell another soul. Instinctively, she clutches her neck.

Even when she pulls herself back upstairs and shuts herself in her bedroom, the words still fill up her brain. Maybe if she has one more nap, she will wake up and know what to do.

Betty heaves in a deep breath and is gathering the energy to climb into bed when the bedroom door opens.

"You'll go gray if you don't get out of this bedroom," says Mother, glaring at her over an armful of clean laundry. "And then what boy will look at you?"

Betty starts to cry. Mother shakes her head and looks disappointed.

"You need to try harder, Betty. Lord knows I try to help us. Do you want to find yourself dried-up and alone like me?"

"You're not alone," she says, but Mother has already swept off.

x

LATER THAT NIGHT, WHEN Mother is in the bathroom rubbing cold cream into her cheeks, Betty shuts the bedroom door, kneels by the bed, and prays to God. She has never done that before, except in church when someone else speaks the words and all she must do is parrot amen.

"Please, God, let me have a bit of peace," she whispers.

A door handle rattles somewhere in the hotel, and she drops her hands; if Mother sees her praying, she will know something is wrong. But the rattle seems to be coming from the far end of the landing, so Betty takes up her prayer position again.

"Just one moment of peace in my head, God. If you'd empty it for a minute, then I might be able to work out a way of telling Inspector Napier what I saw and still keeping Mr. Gallagher safe . . ."

She stops. God will know about Gallagher—God will know what they did.

"I know I don't deserve help," she continues. "But sometimes I think my head will explode over the walls . . . Then I'll have to clean that up, too. That sounds stupid, but it's so full, it hurts. Please, will you empty it, just for one day or even one minute?"

It is easier to speak to God than she realized. The toilet flushes and a pipe creaks, but Betty doesn't care. She prays on.

"There are so many faces in my head, God, it's as if they're haunting me. I don't want to see them anymore, but they never leave me from the second I wake up. Sometimes they come in my sleep, too. I can see Mr. Forbes on his knees, shouting after me. I can see Mr. Gallagher watching me from the breakfast table. I can even smell his cigarettes."

God will know that she smoked, too.

"And Miss Hollinghurst. That's why I haven't been to church since. I can't stand it, Father. I want to tell someone that I saw her, and that I saw . . . him. And that he was kissing her. But I don't understand why you would kiss someone and then kill them."

She gulps.

"Or why you would kiss someone and then leave them. Do you?"

She takes another deep breath.

"Of course you do; you know everything. Maybe you're punishing me by giving me this knowledge. Yes, you're probably testing me and wondering what I'll do with it. But what if I told someone and the whole village turned on him, just as they turned on Mr. Forbes? And then what if I'd got it all wrong and it was some other man altogether? After all, I didn't see his face, just his hat and suit?"

She lowers her voice.

"Please, God. Clear my head, tell me what to do, and help me keep Mr. Gallagher safe. I need to help Mr. Forbes somehow, but I can't risk telling anyone in case Mr. Gallagher"—she can't say the word *hangs* aloud—"ends up dead, like he said he would. But I can't let a killer walk around, either. I don't know what to do next—I can't work it out by myself."

The door handle lowers. Betty opens her eyes and pretends to tuck in a loose sheet as Mother walks in.

Mother falls asleep quickly, her snores come thick and fast, but three hours later Betty is still awake. Her pillow is hard and damp with sweat. At two, she creeps out of bed, down the stairs, and through the empty rooms, her head still overflowing. She needs to contain herself somehow, so she shuts herself in the larder.

In the dark, she can see Gallagher's lips as clearly as when he lay by the pond. He fades, and the image is replaced with the beach during the dance. She can see the raven-haired girl screaming on the dance floor and the ivory figure on the beach, the sand around her bled crimson. She can see Miss Hollinghurst being kissed roughly, and Mr. Forbes wearing his pajamas in the street, clutching that shoulder of cow studded with bluebottles. The picture changes to Gallagher again. He is clinging to her ankles and sobbing; his hat is drenched with blood, and a thick red burn mark—as if from a dry rope—encircles his neck. Betty claws her fingers into her cheeks and screws up her eyes.

"YOU DIDN'T TELL ME WHAT TO DO, GOD! YOU'RE NOT REALLY THERE, ARE YOU?"

It hits her. Gallagher will know what to do; she must find a way of reaching him.

x

THE NEXT MORNING, WHEN Mother is making the breakfasts, Betty locks herself inside their bedroom to write the letter. Rain lashes the windows and the wind growls, shaking the hotel's bones. The mirror above the dressing table rocks slightly, and Betty catches a glimpse of herself; her eyes are purple and puffy, and her hair is matted with grease. She looks down at the paper instead.

Dear Mr. Gallagher, it says.

She presses the nib into the page, and though her hands shake, she forces herself to continue.

I desperately need your help. Mr. Forbes is about to be sent to prison or, worse, the noose, and I'm the only person who can help him. I told you before that I suspected him innocent, but I now know he absolutely is because I saw Miss Hollinghurst by the pond just after you left, the same afternoon she was killed there. She was with the man I believe is the real killer. You might remember him—

She writes faster, blotting the paper with tears and ink. Then she pushes it into an envelope and writes his name and address—the one printed inside the newspaper—on the front: Mr. John Gallagher, News Department, Daily Telegraph Offices, Fleet Street, London.

She unlocks the bedroom door and runs to the postbox at the end of Newl Grove. It is the first time she has left the hotel in days, and she is slapped awake by the wind and wet autumn air. She kisses the envelope, not caring if anyone sees her, and posts it.

There is a strange sinking feeling as she walks home in the rain, but at least her head is clearer. Gallagher will tell her what to do. All she must do is wait and hope, and pray that no more girls are found in the meantime.

That night she sleeps easily for the first time since he left her. It is still dark when Mother nudges her awake. Betty can just make out her flat curls and red eyes. She looks as though she has cried all night.

"A cup of tea, my darling?" she says in a hoarse voice.

"What's happened? What's wrong?" says Betty, sitting up.

"I just wanted to make my girl a cup of tea."

"But it's the middle of the night."

"He doesn't want me."

"Who doesn't want you? Did you go somewhere last night?"

Mother clasps her hands and presses them to her heart, as if to hold it together. She crawls into bed and wraps Betty in a stifling hug, the way she did when Betty was small. Her hair is appley with cider, and her chest wheezes.

"Tell me what's the matter," whispers Betty.

"What would I do without you, my boo boo?"

Betty wants to ask Mother where she has been, who has upset her, and who doesn't want her, but she forces herself not to. It might trigger another bad spell. They are cycling too quickly these days.

"You won't have to do anything without me," she whispers. "Because I'll always be here for you, whatever happens."

Mother nods like a small child. Then she is asleep while Betty lies awake, staring at the ceiling and counting down the hours until Gallagher will help—until she will see him again.

×

ONE WEEK PASSES, AND Betty hears nothing from him. She doesn't leave Hotel Eden once, though St. Steele seems safer now that the killer is unmasked in her mind. She sits by the bedroom window and looks out for him. Every few minutes, she sneaks a glance at the road that cuts into the village over the brow of the hill, half expecting to see Gallagher's topless car steaming over it, but each time the road is empty and her chest sinks.

The breakfast cutlery clatters downstairs, and the men chatter away. Finally, the front door opens and they all trickle out for the day. When the door shuts again, Betty creeps downstairs. Mother is washing dishes at the sink and singing. Betty grabs the newspapers from the breakfast tables and tiptoes back upstairs. She leafs through them all, tearing out stories with the word *Cornish Cleaver* in the headline and trawling for Gallagher's name. It hasn't appeared since he left; a different man writes about the Cornish Cleaver for the *Daily Telegraph* now. His name is Charles Entwistle. Betty hates him.

She tucks the cuttings inside an orange folder and is sliding it back into her hiding place under the bed when there is a knock at the bedroom door.

"I'm busy."

"Only me," says Mary nervously, pushing open the door. "Your mother let me in."

Betty pulls Mother's bed jacket around her, flustered to have been caught in her nightdress.

"What's that smell? Are you ill?" says Mary, pursing her lips and looking around. "You really should open a window."

"What do you want?"

There is a long pause, and when she looks up, Mary is crying prim ladylike tears. She walks around the bed and holds Betty in a wooden hug. Mary smells of lavender. It matches her lavender skirt suit. None of it is quite right, as though Mary is wearing her aunt's clothes and play-acting a role.

"What's the matter, Mary?" Betty says. Even her voice sounds exhausted.

"I don't know how to tell you this. You'll hate me. Promise you won't hate me."

Mary plants herself on the edge of the bed, dabbing her eyes with a small lilac handkerchief.

"It's just that . . . I should have said something sooner, but you haven't made it easy for me because you haven't been out with us, so—"

"Spit it out," says Betty, more gruffly than she intended.

"Have you lost your manners as well as your hygiene these last few months since I saw you?"

"I saw you just the other week," says Betty, confused. "At the dance." Mary frowns.

"That was two months ago. What's wrong with you? Anyway, it's George and I," continues Mary. "We're in love."

She shrugs in a nonchalant way, but she looks at Betty expectantly. Betty stares back aghast.

"But you can't," splutters Betty. She thinks for a moment. "What about Gray?"

"He's moving to Devon," says Mary with a coy smile.

"You can't," she repeats.

"George said you'd mind terribly, but I didn't think so. Because you told me you didn't like him. And you haven't been out with us all for ages. So you haven't any right to mind."

"Don't," says Betty, filled with panic.

She reaches out and holds Mary's arms gently. Mary widens her glassy blue eyes and tosses her curls over one shoulder.

"Get your jealous hands off me," she says tartly. "I'm in love. You can't help who you fall in love with. And you, Betty Broadbent, don't get dibs on every boy in Cornwall."

"I don't want him. I just—promise me you won't go anywhere on your own with him or to his home. Please!"

"Don't be jealous."

"I'm not jealous. Just don't pick George. You have to trust me."

"You are jealous. I knew it," squeals Mary.

She steams on while Betty's panic thickens. She would like to tell Mary everything but she can't; she can't tell anyone until she has spoken to Gallagher. *Hanged*: the word replays over and over, cutting over Mary's voice and tangling itself up with her own words. She can't risk saying anything more in case that slips out, too.

"I can't help it if he thinks I'm prettier than you," Mary is saying. "And I'm not dumping you as a friend, because you're not even there to dump. You're never around."

"Mary, you can't . . . He . . . I— You're right. I still like George!"

"I thought as much," says Mary, and her smile widens. "But he likes me now. And if you make me choose between you both—George said you'd do that—then it's no contest."

"But it's not safe."

Mary glares at her.

"It's probably spending so much time with your mother that's making you so weird."

"It's dangerous, please trust me. Just stay away from him until the killer's been caught. We shouldn't be going out at all. . . . Just stay away from St. Steele until then."

"Like I said, I choose George. I love him, and if you can't accept it, you can lump it."

"I wish I could tell you the truth . . . I will, but I can't yet."

"The only truth is, I'd rather one George Paxon than one hundred friends like you."

Mary lets out an exultant little sigh and slams the bedroom door behind her. Betty flops onto the bed and covers her face with a pillow. Minutes later the door opens again. Mother appears, her face red and eyes bulging.

"Why must you spoil everything?" she seethes. "For weeks I've been running the whole bloody hotel on my own while you do God knows what. And now this."

"What?"

"I did everything I could to fix you up with that boy, even invited his god-awful mother to supper. They would have been our ticket out of this . . . this life."

"I didn't like him, anyway," says Betty in a small voice.

"Didn't like him?" sneers Mother. "Like him? I swear, Betty, my hand is itching."

She raises it and makes to hit Betty's face but, instead, she smacks the dressing table and marches out of the bedroom.

X

HOTEL EDEN SHRINKS AROUND Betty. The walls slide inward, and she has to beat them to keep them at bay. Eventually, she can stand it no longer. When Mother is in the larder, she slips out of the open back door and runs to the clearing. Ribbons of police tape flap about in the breeze. She is careful not to look at the bit of scrubby grass where Miss Hollinghurst was stabbed. More than twenty times, wrote Charles Entwistle.

She looks for the blue handkerchief that Gallagher gave her that last afternoon they spent together—she must have dropped it somewhere around here—but after an hour of crawling around on her knees, she still can't find it. She sits under the willow tree waiting for the buzzard. When that doesn't come, either, she closes her eyes and prays again—but this time to Gallagher.

"Help me," she pleads. "You said you'd look after me, so where are you? I can't wait much longer. What if another girl is killed? What if it's Mary this time? What if it all slips out and I end up telling someone what I saw, putting you in danger? Why won't you come back?"

The sky is inky with twilight when she makes her way out of the clearing and marches to the Lamb and Flagg at the far side of St. Steele. She has never seen the inside of a public house before, but she marches inside and squints through the cigarette smog until she sees Inspector Napier.

He is standing in the corner with another police inspector whom she vaguely recognizes. They are talking to two scruffily dressed men. A uniformed policeman ambles over to them and cracks a joke, waving his hand in the air to illustrate something. When he says the word *ghost*, the others all collapse laughing. Betty walks to their table, ignoring the funny looks from the other men. She opens her mouth, but she isn't sure how to interject. Inspector Napier notices her first.

"Betty," he slurs. "What a surprise."

"I'm sorry to disturb you," she says.

"This isn't the place for young ladies," sneers the other inspector.

"I wanted a word with Inspector Napier," she stammers, not knowing how to siphon him away from the others.

"And here I am," he says, raising his glass.

"I wanted to speak to you about the murders," she says.

"Yes, yes, one bit of evidence short of an arrest," says Inspector Napier in a tired way, shaking his head. "Otherwise that animal Forbes would be behind bars right now. You're about the twentieth person to have asked me that today."

"No, I meant I have some information for you," she begins, just as the saloon doors to the lavatory swing open.

A figure strides out and approaches the table. His head is tilted down, so she can't see his face, but she recognizes him instantly and she is chilled with fear. She runs out of the Lamb and Flagg all the way home. As she flies into the hall, she bumps into Mother.

"Where've you been?" Mother calls after her, following her upstairs.

"Nowhere."

"There's no such place as nowhere."

"I saw Inspector Napier," says Betty, softening and turning to face her. "He says he's one bit of evidence short of arresting Mr. Forbes."

Mother nods, but her face pales.

"It's all right," says Betty gently. "I know you loved him. But you've always got me."

x

THE NEXT MORNING, BETTY can't pull herself from bed. Mother shakes her awake at eleven.

"We're going to Spoole," she says. "No arguing. You need new stockings."

"I don't want to go anywhere. Has the postman been?"

"You're coming, and that's final. Make sure you look decent in case we see George. There's still time."

"But is there a letter for me?"

Mother gives her a confused look and shakes her head. Her lipstick is red, and she is wearing an orange wool skirt that makes her look like a film star. Her eyes are bright, maybe too bright.

They don't talk on the bus to Spoole. Betty stares out the window, trying to think about Mary, but there isn't room for another worry. They head to the greengrocer's first, and Mother makes a show of picking out the fattest runner beans, while Betty keeps her eyes on the street in case he jumps out.

At the fishmonger's, Mother talks in a loud voice to a slippery silver fish that she calls Mr. Mackerel. It makes the elderly fishmonger laugh. When they have paid for their kippers and mackerel, Mother leans across the counter and presses a kiss onto his face, while Betty stands guard at the door. She ignores the round of red lipstick on the fishmonger's lips as she mumbles goodbye.

"Oh, Richard went to the darkrooms, so I gave him your camera to develop," says Mother when they are out on the street. "Your pictures are in a packet on the dresser."

"Why didn't you tell me?" cries Betty.

Two elderly ladies with shopping bags stop to look at her. Mother only raises her penciled eyebrows and does a funny eye roll.

Mother seems to drag out every last second in Spoole, while Betty pictures Gallagher standing before the camera, his lips in a straight line and the St. Ives wind tousling his curls. She wants to see the photograph now, this second, but Mother is squinting over her new horn-rimmed glasses at a dozen pairs of stockings. She rubs each of the fabrics between her fingers before she decides on a pair for herself and a second pair for Betty.

They start walking back toward the bus stop finally, but Mother changes her mind and dives into another shop to try on the dress in the window. It is made of cerise satin with a tight bodice and a ring of rhinestones around the waist. Mother doesn't even ask the price.

The shop is too small, too hot, the carpet dusty. There is a small velvet armchair in the corner that she sits on while Mother wriggles into the dress behind a moth-nibbled curtain. Through a gap at the curtain edge, Betty catches a glimpse of Mother's bony back. She is about to turn away her eyes when she notices an angry scar cutting down from Mother's right shoulder to her left hip. Betty stares at it, horrified and nervous somehow, until Mother pulls up the bodice and the scar disappears again. Only then does Betty realize that Mother is talking to herself in the faintest of voices.

"He'd like it," she seems to be saying. "Yes, he'd love it. No good on our farm, though. A farmer's wife in satin?"

She lets out a soft laugh.

Betty looks at Mother carefully as they wait for the bus home.

"What happened to your back?"

Mother says nothing, as if she hasn't heard. The bus draws up and they file on.

"Your back, Mother? Did someone hurt you?"

"None of your business."

Betty clings onto the packet of new tights in her lap all the way home, while Mother chatters to Mrs. Thompson as though the scar isn't there and Gallagher hasn't left and Miss Hollinghurst and the other girls are still breathing.

X

NEWL GROVE IS CROWDED when they turn the corner. Even from the bus stop, she can see a group of men standing outside Hotel Eden. One of them is beating at the door. Mother's face is gripped with terror. She drops her bags on the street and runs ahead, her heels slipping off and clattering on the pavement. Betty stoops to pick up the bags and struggles after her.

Inspector Napier emerges from the bunch of men. He says something in Mother's ear, and she glowers back at Betty. Reggie says something else, and Mother's face softens but only slightly. She unlocks the door to Hotel Eden, and the reporters push their way inside, so only Inspector Napier and Mother are left out in the street by the time Betty reaches them.

"You wanted to speak to me?" says Inspector Napier to Betty.

"He says you wanted to tell him something," snaps Mother, a razor edge to her voice. "And that you went inside the Lamb and Flagg last night."

Something crashes inside the hotel, and a door slams.

"What happened?" says Betty. "What are they all doing?"

"So? What did you want to say to the inspector?" says Mother, her voice still icy.

"But has something bad happened? Is Mary all right?"

"No, it's all good news. We've finally charged Forbes," says Napier. "One of his knives turned up in the woods this morning."

"He's locked up?" she says in a small voice.

"He's being moved to custody in Plymouth as we speak. It's all over." Mother is still looking at Betty's face.

"So?" she says. "What did you want to say?"

"I can't remember."

"Your mother's right to be worried," says Napier kindly. "A public house isn't the place for a nice young lady."

"I just wanted to find out how the investigation was going," says Betty quietly.

She can still picture that rope mark seared into Gallagher's neck; it is thick and jagged and reddish purple. Forbes has burrowed into her mind, too. He wears that grubby vest and kneels on the doorstep outside his shop, sobbing and stammering, but she bites down on her tongue to stop herself from saying more.

"So it really is over?" says Mother.

Betty carries the packet of photographs upstairs to her bedroom. Feet trample about downstairs, and coins clink as the men settle their bills and leave Hotel Eden for Plymouth, where Inspector Napier says Mr. Forbes will be held until his trial. Betty tries to block them all out. It will be all right; they will soon realize he is innocent. Forbes will be released long before a trial can start, and all will be well.

Her fingers brush the paper packet. She should wait until no one else is about in case she is disturbed, but her fingers are already at the seal. There is a tearing sound, and then her hand is rifling through, scattering photographs onto the floor until there he is.

She has sliced off his right ear and he doesn't smile, but his eyes bore into the camera as though he can see through to its core and out the other side to the photographer herself. His gaze is so penetrating, she looks away from it and traces her fingers over the paper, over his curls, over his jaw and over his suit, all starched and mushroom colored.

But when she looks at his eyes again, anger sets in. Why haven't you replied to my letter, she wants to know. Why did you leave me? Why have you abandoned Mr. Forbes, too? What sort of man are you?

x

THE BEDROOM DOOR SMASHES open after midnight, and Mother staggers in, a bottle of gin in one hand, and a half-drunk brandy in the other.

"Finally, those sweaty, little good-for-nothings have gone," she shrieks.

"Did they leave a tip?"

"Did they, heck. Tight-fisted, arrogant swines."

She mutters something under her breath. She tips back her head and swigs gin, brandy, gin again. She wipes her mouth with the back of her hand. The gin bottle falls to the carpet, and the drink sloshes out.

"Have a swig," she says, holding out the other bottle to Betty.

Betty shakes her head. She kneels and scoops up the gin, blotting the spillage with her handkerchief.

"Have some. You're your mother's daughter, aren't you? You love me, don't you?"

"Yes," she says tearfully.

"Then drink. We're having a party, aren't we?"

"I don't want to."

"So you don't love me?"

"Please, Mother."

"You don't, do you? You don't know what I do for you."

"I don't like you like this. Stop it. Please."

"Drink!"

And Mother grabs her hand, scratching her with her long fingernails. She pushes the brandy into Betty's hand and closes her fingers around it.

"Unless you don't love me."

Betty sips and splutters, her eyes watering and throat heaving.

"Good girl," says Mother, stroking her head. "All over. Just you and me now, my Betty boo boo."

12

Betty glances one last time at Mother, asleep and dribbling over her pillow.

"I'm going to see Mary in Spoole," she whispers; the lies slip out easily now. "I'll be back tonight. Or tomorrow."

Mother doesn't stir. Betty picks up her lunch box and tiptoes out into the moonlit street.

The railway station is six miles from St. Steele. She walks quickly, blowing her white winter breath in curls and zigzag shapes to distract herself. Her feet are sore by the time she arrives at the platform, and she wishes she had worn sensible shoes. But then she looks down at her red sandals and her good skirt, and she is pleased that she dressed in her Sunday best for Gallagher.

She checks the station clock; she is far too early. As she waits, she counts her pocketful of coins, all birthday money from Mr. Eden that she has saved over the years. She rubs her special half crown—the one that Gallagher touched—and she hopes it will bring good luck. There hasn't been much of that for a long time.

The train toots as it rolls up. Betty clambers aboard, and the guard blows his whistle. She pulls down the window and leans out, holding on to the leather strap to steady herself. From this angle, she can see the steam belching up to the sky as the train slides away from St. Steele, from Cornwall.

Betty makes her way toward her seat. The train jerks, and she topples into the corridor wall, smacking her lunch box into her stomach. She winces and her eyes water, but she pushes on. There are six passengers in her carriage, all silent with their heads tilted down, except for an elderly man who is crunching loudly on a celery stalk. Sick rises up Betty's throat again, just as it did yesterday morning when she disinfected the kitchen floor, then vomited over it. She sits very still, looking at a grubby spot on the carriage wall until the nausea subsides.

Another hour and her stomach settles. She shells a cold boiled egg to busy her hands and nibbles on it, though it is too early for lunch. She turns to the bread with fish paste next, and is about to bite into a green apple when a man with brass buttons on his coat comes to punch her ticket. She waits for the click and is relieved when he moves on without speaking to her. Her voice might have given her away; she is certain that fifteen-year-olds aren't allowed to travel this far unaccompanied, though Joan once said that Betty looks at least nineteen.

When he has moved into the next carriage, Betty closes her eyes and lets herself picture Gallagher finally. She wonders how surprised he will be when he sees her and what he will say when she appears in his office, whether he will kiss her and apologize for leaving St. Steele so abruptly or take her to a tea shop first to discuss what they should do about Mr. Forbes. This is a serious visit, she reminds herself, and a worm of worry edges in. He left you, says the worm, he didn't come back for you or respond to your letter. But maybe he never received her letter; busy London postmen must lose things all the time.

Betty tries not to think about that anymore; it is dangerous to let her worries fritter about. All she knows is, now that Mr. Forbes is in court, she can't wait a minute longer. She must find a way of stopping the trial and telling Inspector Napier who was really with Miss Hollinghurst in the woods that night but without letting any harm come to Gallagher. And the only way of doing that is by making him agree to her plan.

She will tell Gallagher that, finally, she understands why he ran off so abruptly that last afternoon they spent together. He must have seen Miss Hollinghurst in the woods with that man—with the real killer—and Gallagher must have assumed that they saw him, too. "So, there's only one solution," she will say. They will be sitting on opposite sides of the table in a London tea shop, perhaps with his hand resting on hers again. "We should go to Inspector Napier together and tell him who we saw with Miss Hollinghurst, but we should also admit what we did together in the woods that day." Gallagher might look shocked at that, but she will push on. "That way, if he saw us together, he won't be able to use it to discredit us because Inspector Napier will already know."

The word *hanged* has stitched itself into the seam of her brain, but she won't say it aloud, not even to repeat it back to him. "And no harm would come to you if, before we confessed to Inspector Napier, we got marr . . ." She rearranges the words in her mind, still blushing. "What we did wouldn't be a crime if I was your wife."

She watches through the window as the green fades to gray, and the trees and bushes and bits of blue sky become chimneys and brick towers and low-hung pillows of smog. The sickness returns then, and she runs to the lavatory to vomit. Back in the carriage, she focuses on the horizon to steady herself. It is a clever plan, she thinks with a blush, as she replays it again in her mind.

X

THE TRAIN PULLS UP at Paddington eventually. Betty freezes when she sees the platform. She has never seen so many people in one space. There are one hundred of them at least, all seeming to know exactly where they are rushing. She would like to hide in the lavatory until the train slides safely back to Cornwall, but then she thinks of Miss Hollinghurst and Mr. Forbes.

"Safe journey," says the guard, opening the door, and Betty steps into the crush.

Paddington Railway Station looks bigger than St. Steele itself. Betty stares up at the glass ceiling arches flecked with pigeons. The noise is deafening: a din of horns and voices. Betty tries to catch the eye of a kind-looking lady wearing a pea-green hat.

"Excuse me," she calls after her. "Could you point me in the right direction, please?"

But the lady hurries off, her two tiny corgis scuttling behind her. Betty turns to a girl of her own age.

"Can you help me?" she tries, but the girl soldiers past.

A tornado of strangers circles around her. Betty is about to sit on the floor, to hide her head in her hands and wish herself back to St. Steele, when a man nods at her. He wears a white apron and carries a tray piled with floury buns.

"Ham baps," he shouts. "Get your ham baps here."

"I'm lost," says Betty, trying not to look at the fleshy pink meat lopping out of the buns in case her queasiness returns.

"Where're you after, sweetheart?" he says, and holds out a bun. "You know you want one. Made them myself, I did."

Betty hands him a coin and takes one, trying not to smell or look at it. She asks for directions to Fleet Street.

"You'll want the tube, my love," he says.

"But if I were to walk?" she replies, too ashamed to ask what the tube is.

He looks down at her shoes, the raspberry-colored slingbacks that Gallagher buckled for her once.

"Walking'll take you a good few hours, m'darling. And I wouldn't fancy your chances of finding it on those pretty little trotters."

"But if I did walk?"

"You'll want to come out of the station through that door over there, and keep going till you reach the big old park. Can't miss that, you can't," he begins.

Betty repeats the place-names in her head until he finishes and disappears into the crowd shouting "ham baps" again. She scribbles what she remembers on an old sweet paper from her pocket and begins walking, dropping the bap into a bin.

The walk is long, and her sandals pinch. She absorbs the streets, astonished that so many rushing bodies and taxicabs and buildings can fit into them. On Oxford Street, she pauses to catch her breath and admire a flower stall. A woman wearing a long camel coat walks away carrying an armful of yellow roses. Betty thinks of Mother, spread like a starfish over the bedcovers, and how she would brighten if she saw a vase of roses. But then a blister bulbs its way onto her heel, and her mood sours again.

Betty asks a policeman for directions, and he points her toward steps that lead down to a dark tunnel filled with hot, fast bodies. A guard helps her buy a ticket and shows her to the correct platform, where she finds a dirty-looking underground train. The seats are taken, so Betty holds on to a metal post and tries to weave her body in time with the carriage, the way she did when she rode ponies years ago with Mother and a strange man who stayed at the hotel for months, not letting Mother out of his sight, then disappeared one day as suddenly as he had appeared. The carriage snakes through tunnels, swerving at peculiar angles, and the lights flicker. The train stops, and she bashes into a post. No one notices. She would hate to live in London and always feel this topsy-turvy. She is glad when she comes up above the surface and gulps the sooty air again. This must be how coal miners feel every afternoon, she thinks.

She stops for more directions; she passes a pub filled with lots of men puffing pipes and wearing identical suits; a fresh blister appears; she walks past three more pubs; and finally she is there. The *Daily Telegraph*.

It has six pillars that look very grand indeed, even though they could do with a good scrub, and above them is a huge clock that must be very tricky to wind. It is more impressive than every other building on the street, but it is also the meanest, hardest, and most angry-looking building she has ever seen. Something about it makes her not want to stand too close, so she watches the entrance from the other side of the street.

Only when she is propped up against a lamppost with her lunch box at her feet and her focus fixed on the doors does it hit her: she has made it. She is impatient suddenly. She half considers walking inside and asking for him, then she looks down at her weeping blisters and scuffed-up sandals. They would laugh her straight back out of the building again. She leans harder into the lamppost, her breath quickening as she thinks again of her plan. What if he laughs at her?

Two hours later, he still hasn't appeared. She doesn't take her eyes from the door, not even when she leans down to douse her blisters with a handkerchief. A steady stream of men walk out with umbrellas. Rain switches on and off. Betty hardly notices that her hair is soaked and her toes are numb.

Three hours of waiting and the streetlamps flicker on. The seats in the back of the shiny black taxis fill up. She checks her watch. She can't miss the sleeper train home, or she will have to stand on the street all night. Her eyes leave the door for a minute to watch a police car shoot along the street, and when she looks back, three men are making their way out of the building and down the steps. The middle one makes Betty look twice. She recognizes the long folds of his black coat and his tilted-down hat.

"Mr. Gallagher," she shouts.

The car engines drown out her cry, and the man doesn't hear.

"John Gallagher!"

She picks up her lunch box, steps into the gutter, and is about to run toward him, but a taxi honks its horn. She leaps back, just missing it, and looks at the man again. He is still there, but his face has turned sideways so she can see his profile, and, from the curved hoof shape of his nose, she realizes that it is not Gallagher at all. She can't wait out here any longer. She hurries toward the entrance of the *Daily Telegraph* and runs up the steps.

At the reception desk, a woman with a black pixie crop and a jeweled blouse looks up.

"Can I help you?" she says sharply.

Betty feels very small. Her polka-dot skirt is garish among all of these dull colors, and her hand-me-down coat from Joan swamps her.

"I'm here to see Mr. Gallagher," she mutters.

"Who? Speak up."

"Mr. John Gallagher; he's a reporter here."

The receptionist rummages through a wad of papers.

"He's not on my list."

"But I need to speak to him."

She is ready to cry. The receptionist turns over another paper and frowns, touching the tip of her small pointed nose.

"Ah," she says. "I can see now. He used to work here, but he doesn't anymore."

"Doesn't work here?" Betty squeaks, gripping the reception desk.

"That's right."

"But he can't have gone," she begins shrilly, then stops herself. "When did he leave?"

The receptionist stares at her.

"I can't disclose that information."

Betty opens her lunch box and pulls out the folded-up photograph of him, scarred with creases and fingerprints. She holds it up.

"It's definitely this Mr. Gallagher?"

The receptionist gives Betty another funny look, but she nods at the photograph.

"Yes, I remember him," she says curtly.

"I wrote him a letter and sent it to this address about a month ago. Do you know whether he received it?"

"Do you really think I keep track of every letter that passes through this place?"

"It was important."

The receptionist sighs, but her expression softens.

"It says here that they're forwarding letters to his home address, and that he's currently overseas. That's all I know."

"Overseas?" she croaks. So he really has left her. "Please, could you tell me his home address?"

"I can't give you that, either."

Betty holds the edge of the reception desk, exhausted. The receptionist looks at her as though she has landed there from the moon, but Betty is too tired to mind what anyone thinks of her anymore. If the reception desk weren't covered with folders and pens and paper clips, she might clamber onto it and lie there. Gallagher would come back eventually. He would scoop her up and protect her, the way he said he would. They would marry and tell the police everything; Mr.

Forbes would be free, St. Steele would be safe again, and all would be right.

"Is there anything else?" says the receptionist.

"If you see him, could you tell him that I came here, please? My name's Betty Broadbent."

The receptionist writes it on the corner of her pad.

"Would you please make sure he knows. It's very important," she adds, but the receptionist has already torn out the sheet and pushed it onto a wire tray on her desk.

Betty staggers into the street and collapses onto the pavement. Just five minutes' rest. Then she must keep going.

13

November 1956

At the brow of the hill, John Gallagher slows the car. From here the road snakes down into St. Steele, and he has to clutch the steering wheel and pause for a moment before he can continue.

He had forgotten what the village looked like—perhaps a deliberate slip, for he had never imagined that he would return, but now that he is back, the streets are so familiar, he might never have been away at all. Farmhouses are still stumped on the outskirts, and in the center are three rows of tiny terraces. Their rooftops still crawl with lichen, but a layer of frost clings to the village now.

He presses the accelerator and drops down the hill, scanning the streets and the sand for her. The village is dead, but he thinks nothing of it. He concentrates on allowing his lungs to fill and empty, fill and empty, because if he doesn't, his mind will whir and he is sure that it will explode.

On Newl Grove, he pulls over and looks in the rearview mirror. He rubs the skin beneath his eyes, smooths down his springy curls, and notices with embarrassment that his hands are shaking. He has never understood how so small a girl has that effect on him, when no woman ever has before.

He is still surprised that she crept into his thoughts every day he was in France, a comfort somehow, but even then he imagined that he would never see her again. It had been enough to close his eyes and picture her as she was the last time he saw her: she had been holding his handkerchief and looking sadly at him, a tiny fragile thing, a sparrow of a girl, with leaves caught in her hair and a thin dress that rustled in the wind.

As he had looked at her then, he had inwardly scolded himself for being so weak. He had been finding a way to explain that he should never have touched her, but he had heard the movement in the trees. He was certain that he had seen the flash of a blue dress and a stream of golden hair, and he was sickened with panic that someone had seen them together.

He had turned and chased through the woods, searching for whoever it was. His lungs burned, his chest pounded, and his slippery-soled shoes skidded on the wet leaves, but he kept running. Half of his brain told him that it was just his imagination or perhaps his conscience, while the other half sizzled: whoever saw them together was probably on their way to tell the police right now. No one would understand. He would be branded a rapist and locked in prison, or hanged, even. He would be written about in the newspapers—Reggie would like that. And Father, what would he say?

He had finally given up looking that afternoon and retraced his steps back to Betty. She was still standing where he had left her. She looked even tinier, but his insides had steeled over and he had made her recite that awful promise over and over, until he was satisfied that she could never break it. Then he had charged back to the hotel and thrown his sparse belongings into a bag before he could change his mind.

He had circled each roundabout three times on the drive back to London, but he still didn't turn around. She would be confused, hate him even, but better that than let either of them become more attached. It was always going to end badly, a pair like them.

He had reached London eventually and parked outside his office, where he scrawled a vague resignation letter on the back of a paper napkin. He loathed all of it: the reporters, the editors, the whipping up of stories from misery and trifles. Even reporting on murder grew repetitive. He didn't wait to see his editor but drove directly to the port and crossed the loading bridge at sunrise.

The ferry ride was long and choppy. Once on the other side of the water, he sped to Paris, to his father's apartment. The closer he got, the more he hungered for his father's comfort, but, in the back of his mind, he braced himself for the terse lecture and the cold handshake that duly came.

Yes, he had almost accepted that he would never see her again, but then he had returned home from Paris yesterday and found her letter, months old, buried in a pile of unopened post on his doormat. It stood out because the lettering was spidery and had been written by what was clearly a wobbly hand. He was exhausted from the drive, but after reading it, he necked a whiskey, fired up the still-warm engine of his car, and sped to St. Steele. He had to help.

As he drove, he pieced together what to say to her: he decided to be honest, to admit that he left her out of cowardice but never imagined how painfully he would miss her. She would be angry and upset at him, as she should be, but she would forgive him eventually.

She will forgive him, won't she?

She must, he reassured himself.

And after he kisses her, they will peel themselves apart to visit Inspector Napier, confessing their own affair before Betty tells him that she saw Miss Hollinghurst by the pond before she was killed. When Forbes is free and the killer is in prison, perhaps Napier will offer Gallagher leniency for the underage matter, especially when he sees how deeply he cares for Betty and how close she is to sixteen.

X

GALLAGHER LOCKS THE CAR, and the twist of the key echoes in the street. His hard soles click across the cobbles. The door to Hotel Eden is locked. He raps once, twice, and when there is still no answer, he hammers on it.

"Betty."

Nothing. He pushes open the letter box and calls into it.

"Mrs. Broadbent."

Still nothing.

"Just give me five minutes!"

He puts his eyes where his lips were and sees that the hall is a shell. The framed pictures have been taken down, and the wallpaper is spotted with faded rectangular patches. There are no coats or hats on the pegs, and the mats have been taken up. The curtains are drawn so he can't see into the front room, but when he steps back, he notices a small handwritten sign propped against the window. It says, For Sale.

Gallagher runs to the next house along and bangs on the door. The owner, a peroxide-haired woman with fingertips stained yellow, whom he recalls is a friend of Betty's mother, opens it without smiling and without her usual slash of violent red lipstick.

"Has the hotel closed down?" he cries.

She tries to shut the door, but he jams his foot in the gap.

"Where are they?" he says.

She glares at him.

"You might remember me," he continues. "It's Joan, isn't it? I was staying there."

"I don't care who the bloody hell you are or what you want. Get off my doorstep!"

"I just want to know where they are . . . as a friend. I don't work for a newspaper anymore."

Joan leans out and looks up and down the street, so close to him, he can smell the carbolic soap on her hands.

"Nice try, sonny, but you're not getting a word from me. Or any of us. And tell the others not to bother coming back, either."

"I'm sorry?"

"We've made a pact—the whole village has—not to speak to you lot anymore."

"I'm just looking for Betty. Or Mrs. Broadbent."

Joan turns gray.

"What's wrong? What happened?" he says, his mouth dry.

Joan stares at him for a minute longer, her face still ghostly. Then she composes herself.

"You call yourselves men, but what you are is filthy animals, scrounging here at a time like this and trying to trick comments out of me."

Drops of spit fly out of her mouth. One lands on his cheek.

"Can't you let her rest in peace, or is that too much to ask?"

"Rest in peace?" he croaks. "What are you talking about? Someone else has died?"

"I've said enough."

"Look, I know her, she wrote to me." He waves Betty's letter. "You can tell me."

"Who wrote to you?" says Joan, narrowing her eyes. "Who did you say you are again?"

"John Gallagher. I'm a friend of Betty's. Please, it's important."

"Friend," she sneers.

"I love her," he bursts out.

Joan arches an eyebrow and looks him up and down, her mouth shriveled. He can't tell which of them is more stunned. He wishes he could hook the words and reel them back into his mouth. Joan shoves at the door, but his foot still blocks it.

"Don't close it," he says. "Just tell me where she is and I'll go. She needs my help. Please!"

"The only one who can help her where she's gone is the good Lord himself. Now get off my doorstep, or I'll call my Richard."

His toe is stubbed out of the way, and the door slams. He smacks the door knocker with his balled-up fist.

"What happened to her?" he shouts through the letter box. "She is safe, isn't she?"

But the doors off the hall are shut and the house is silent, as though Joan had never been there at all.

Gallagher knocks on six more houses, ten more, in all twenty-three. No one is home, or they pretend not to be. The cobbler's shop is shut up, and so is the Lamb and Flagg. A sign on the door says, Closed for mourning. Open tomorrow.

He ambles to the cove, but that is dead, too. He drops to his knees.

x

AN HOUR EBBS AWAY. The sun sags and the sand chills. His knees have locked, but he doesn't try to move them; there is nowhere to go, anyway. If he stares at the shore and concentrates hard enough, he can almost picture her standing beside him, just as she did on that July afternoon that he bumped into her here.

She had been swinging a mesh bag of carrots and parsnips and pacing the sand when he saw her. He had wanted to avoid her; the dance was still fresh in his mind, and though he had decided that any feelings he had for her had been one-sided, he had also promised himself that he would stay away from her. She was so young. He had turned to leave, but she spotted him and half smiled. He nodded back, and grudgingly, manners drew him to her.

Something strange had happened then, as he strode across the sand in her direction. She had stopped laughing. Her bag had stopped swinging, too. Her feet had planted themselves in the sand, and her back went so rigid that her posture almost mirrored his. He was puzzled. A bit of him had wanted to ask her why she had changed for him and what it was about him that had sucked the zest out of her, too, but before he could, she had said something about paddling—going for a dip, she called it— and her freer self was back, or almost back.

He had watched her paddle in the shallows and laugh as the waves bit her toes. He would have loved to have stood in the water with her, to have laughed, too, but laughter never came easily to him. It sounded unnatural on his lips. Even his schoolmaster had once remarked that when John Gallagher emerged from the womb, he probably offered the midwife a brisk handshake instead of a cry. The other boys had laughed at that; he had envied them.

He was still rooted there when Betty returned from the shore. No doubt she would think him odd for standing so stiffly and for wearing his shoes on the sand. In a funny way, her opinion of him made him jittery. She was so peculiar yet secure in her bubble of the world, but she was sharp, too, and, in her head, more mature than even he. She made him laugh inwardly and often, but she also made him think harder than anyone else ever had, and without even trying.

He had watched her struggle with those flimsy red sandals and let himself bend down to help. He had grazed her ankle with his thumb as he fastened the buckle and burned with shame at how it made him want her. She's fifteen, he had scolded himself. But he had longed to remove the shoe again, and her dress, and run his fingers in her hair, and hold her there, on that strip of beach.

When both sandals were back on her feet, when she had refused his invitation for a day trip and when she had skipped off across the sand, he had promised himself to never invite her anywhere again, certainly never to touch her. Father was right: he was a weak son, a weak man.

Gallagher unlaces his shoes. He pulls off his socks, too. The sand is cold and filmy against the soles of his feet. He staggers to the shore, his knees still locked, and he paddles in the icy shallows, the same way she did. His feet sting with cold. He tries to laugh, the way she had, but it sounds pathetic: a defeated sort of roar.

Eventually, he makes his way back to the car and slumps over the steering wheel, unsure what to do next.

"Where are you, my Betty?" he whispers, and brushes his fingers over her letter that still lies on the front seat next to him.

He knows it by heart—he had reread it at every fuel stop and every traffic jam and red light on the drive here—but he looks at it again:

8 September 1956

Dear Mr. Gallagher,

I desperately need your help. Mr. Forbes is about to be sent to prison or, worse, the noose, and I'm the only person who can help him. I told you before that I suspected him innocent, but I now know he absolutely is because I saw Miss Hollinghurst by the pond just after you left, the same afternoon she was killed there. She was with the man I believe is the real killer. You might remember him—his name is George Paxon. He's the biscuit factory owner and the father of the boy (also called George) who mistook you for a police

inspector at the dance. He is well respected in the villages and has
always seemed a good and honest man, which makes it all the more
confusing. I suspect they had a love affair that soured.

I know that I should tell Inspector Napier what I saw, but
the moment I do, he will ask why I was in the woods at all, with
whom, and a hundred more questions that I could never answer
without breaking my promise to you. Though I would never want
to see you locked up or, God forbid, hanged (for what we did
should never be a crime), neither can I watch poor Mr. Forbes
suffer. So please allow me to unmake my promise to you and tell the
inspector the truth, no matter what the consequence for us. If you
don't permit it, I'll keep my promise and never tell a soul what we
did. But if that's what you choose, I can't help thinking how cruel
it will be to Mr. Forbes and how bleak it will be to spend our lives
saddled with this guilt.

I also understand that you must have had your reasons for
leaving so abruptly and if, after this is all over, you still never want
to hear from me again, I'll leave you in peace. But if you changed
your mind and found that you could perhaps love me, too, I would
be the happiest girl in all of Cornwall, and on God's great Earth.

Your Betty

Gallagher drops the letter onto the passenger seat. Suddenly he
knows exactly what he must do: he will hunt down that monster Paxon
himself and find out from him where Betty is. He will force him to confess or drag him to the police station himself; Forbes will be released and
Betty will be safe, never mind the consequences for him. He guns the
engine and roars out of Newl Grove, onto the New Road toward Spoole.
The road is narrow and empty. The fields on either side blur past,

and the rain chips down. He passes the correct turning and smacks on the brakes too late. The tires scream. He slams the gear stick into reverse and backs down the street, turning sharply into a lane. At the end is a cluster of hedges and behind them, the two tall narrow chimneys of the biscuit factory.

The building itself is brick, blocky, and unremarkable with ribs of scaffolding around it. Gallagher parks by the front door and leaps out of the car, forgetting his keys. The door is unlocked, and he storms in.

The forecourt is deserted; it is too silent. The hairs on his arms stand on end. He strides between the rows of workbenches covered with silver machines, clamps, and strips of wax paper. In the center is an enormous open furnace. It spits and cackles.

"Paxon," he cries. "I know what you did."

His own voice bounces off the walls and pipes. At the far end of the factory floor is a door, leading to an airless corridor. It is dim but for the flickering shadow of the furnace. It smells of engine oil and sugar and ash. A row of offices juts off the corridor, sectioned behind a long pane of frosted glass.

"George Paxon," he calls again. "Come out here and face me."

Gallagher steams along the corridor, squinting through the windows. The offices are all dark, but for the last one with a dim yellow light inside. A figure is moving around a desk. He is stooped over. His body shudders as he half carries and half drags a bulky object to the center of the room.

Gallagher takes a sharp breath inward and flings open the door.

Part Three

14

Fifty years later

"Hello," says Mary quietly. "Hello, Mr. Gallagher." Then she dares to look at him.

He is a corpse of the man she once knew. His nose has bulbed out with age but kept its crooked bridge, his eyebrows are bushier, and oaky age spots color his face, matching the ones on her hands. His eyes are closed, and were it not for the rise and fall of his chest, he could be dead.

"Can you hear me?"

His eyes flicker, but he doesn't move.

"It's me," murmurs Mary.

She is about to introduce herself, but she stops, uncertain what to say. That moment his eyes open. He stares at her with glassy black pupils. She holds her breath and waits.

"You don't remember me, do you?" she says in a pale voice.

How can you not remember me? she wants to say. His face seared itself onto her memory, as if with a hot iron, on that terrible day they first met. Even after he left, she caught whiffs of his cigarettes and burnt woody aftershave.

"It's not you. It's the medication," says the nurse, wobbling back into the room with a full jug and two damp glasses.

Mary flushes; she had forgotten about the nurse.

"The doctors have been adjusting his dosages since the heart attack," she continues. "Give him a few minutes and he'll be himself again." She turns to John and speaks louder, elongating every syllable. "Why don't you drink this and sit yourself up, then you can have a nice catch-up with your friend?"

Mary wishes that the nurse wouldn't speak to him so condescendingly, but she looks at him again and sees that he is still unmoving and expressionless, as though any feeling or thought or knowledge that he ever had has long been scraped out of him.

What was she thinking, coming here and expecting an old man who hardly knew her fifty years ago to remember her now? He probably met hundreds of girls like her, all silly and naive and his for the picking. How was he supposed to know what happened to her after he left?

"I've made a mistake," she says to the nurse, gripping her handbag. "I shouldn't be here."

"Oh, don't worry about being early," says the nurse. "I'll just finish up, then he's all yours."

"No, I really shouldn't have come."

She glances fleetingly at him as she makes for the door. His eyes are still locked onto her face. They burn her, just as they burned her back then.

"But you've come all this way. At least remind him of your name."

"It's . . . it's Mary Sugden," she mutters, hoping he won't hear.

But his head twists and his eyebrows stitch together and his lips open.

"I don't know any Mary Sugdens."

His voice is shaky, but his tone is firm. It doesn't match his body.

"Come on, now," soothes the nurse. "Don't be like this."

"No, it's all right," says Mary. "I'll go."

She is light-headed. She leans against the wall to steady herself before she pushes on to the door.

"I don't know any Mary Sugdens," booms John again. "But I know you, don't I?"

Mary freezes in the doorway.

"They get agitated sometimes. It's normal," explains the nurse.

"You're not called Mary!"

"Don't shout," says the nurse. "You're scaring your friend. Look."

Mary shakes with inward sobs, but no tears come; tears never come. They haven't since the day she was wrenched from St. Steele, the day she ran the well dry. She cried for them all that day: for Forbes and for Gallagher, for her old best friend and for her dead mother, for her giblet baby and for herself. That first night in Middlebury, she had cried until her mouth parched, until her head throbbed and her brain shrank. She has never managed a tear in the fifty years since.

"I understand," says the nurse. "It can be a shock to see them like this, but—"

"I don't know any Mary Sugdens and I never forget a name."

"Calm down, John. Your heart . . . I'll have to call Dr. Lavery if you don't."

"But I know your face. I never forget a face."

The moment he says it, his eyes widen and his lips form an O.

"It's Mary Sugden," says the nurse firmly. She turns back to Mary. "It's quite common—"

"Say your name," he interrupts, but his voice is gentler.

"You remember me?"

"Say your name," he says again.

Her throat has clogged up.

"I was your Betty," she chokes.

She covers her face with her hands, horrified at how she worded it and horrified at how his burning eyes still make her feel. For a single awful moment, she remembers how it was to be Betty.

"You must leave," says John Gallagher.

15

At first Betty doesn't notice the blood. She wakes with her knees bent under her. Her muscles are knotted, and warm fingers seem to creep up between her thighs, but when she rubs her eyes and looks around, she is alone.

The windows are beaded with condensation, and outside, a film reel of green blurs past; Paddington far behind now. Her teeth chatter with nerves and cold, and she has to bite down to stop them. Everything is calm for a moment, but then the creeping fingers return and something tugs downward between her legs. Once. Twice. Again.

Betty tries not to panic. She maneuvers her numb feet onto the floor using her hands, and stands shakily. She unbuttons her coat next and twists around her skirt to check whether something jagged has caught in the nylon, for there must be a simple explanation. That's when she sees the stain. It is dark and sticky and it blots the back of her skirt, the same way Mother's port discolors the hearth rug. Then the smell hits her. Cold, liquid metal.

She leans forward to examine the stain, but as she does, a sharp pain slices through her middle, as though an invisible man with an invisible knife is carving into her stomach sac and wrenching downward, but she is too startled to scream. She stands upright and the knifeman pauses for a moment, then returns with another hack. All she knows is that she can't stay here. She needs to find help or perhaps hide away until she is herself again, but for a long moment she is frozen. The lavatory, she decides eventually. If she finds a lavatory, everything will be all right.

She opens her lunch box and grabs an empty brown paper bag in case she is sick on the way. Bits of broken eggshell and an apple core fly out. She crunches over them as she hurries out of the carriage. The train twists at sharp angles, and Betty concertinas along the passageway, slamming against the walls. Every few steps, she glances behind her: Mr. Paxon must be here. He must have stabbed her in her sleep. She is his next victim.

She stumbles into the toilet compartment just as another blade of pain rips through her. She thinks she might vomit, but everything turns white for a minute, maybe for ten minutes.

When Betty comes to, her cheek is pressed to the floor, her knees are folded beneath her, and someone is knocking on her skull with a mallet. She lifts her head and looks around, but she is still alone. The knifeman has disappeared, too, but a dull ache has set in her spine. She wants Mother to tuck her up in bed and press the hot water jar to her back, but home is far from here. So is Mother.

The knocking returns then. It sounds like knuckles on wood. He is at the door, she realizes, horrified. Mr. Paxon is hunting her down.

"Get away," she screams at him.

"Are you having a picnic in there or something?" replies a woman with a cross voice.

Betty is washed with relief. "I'm sorry."

"Hurry up or I'll call the guard."

"Please don't. I'll just be a second."

Betty presses her palms to the floor and tries to hoist herself upright, but she is too weak.

"Actually could you give me five minutes?" she calls.

There is a sharp little sigh, then the woman clicks away. Betty tries again to push herself upright. She makes it onto her knees this time. She wiggles up her skirt to her waist and is about to pull down her knickers to check where the pain is coming from, but there is another strange sensation between her legs. Her bladder seems to leak. She is wetting herself, only it is warmer and sludgy. Something stabs at her insides at the same time. She wants to reach up inside herself and pull out the blade or whatever it is that is ripping her to shreds.

It subsides eventually and slowly, still shaking, Betty pulls down her knickers to her knees. The color hits her first. A tomato-colored puddle fills the gusset of her good, white underpants. Some of it has seeped onto the floor, too. It is a tiny red swimming pool, big enough for tadpoles, not quite for frogs. Betty feels sick. A great snake of it slithers up her tubes and out through her lips. Acid burns her tongue. She vomits a second time. Her stomach convulses, and a fist of pain sits in her pelvis, replacing the knife blades. The ache in her back deepens, too, as though someone is trying to split the base of her spine in two.

She looks again, properly this time. In the middle of her gusset is a clump, no bigger than her little finger. It is the shape of a broad bean, but, in texture, it is a raw chicken giblet. It wobbles with the train's vibrations. She stares at it, lumped there on the blood and a streak of something gray. Betty thinks she knows what it is. No, she is certain she does; only she hadn't known it was there. Not one of those in a girl like her.

Gallagher's face sits in her mind, or is it Mother's face?

Their noses merge and chins clash.

"I'm sorry," she cries out, just as the train brakes squeal.

The carriage slows—into a station, probably. She can't stay in this cubicle; the guard will come or the woman will return or, worse, the train will pass Liskeard and she will be stuck on here all the way to Penzance. She needs to concentrate.

She flushes the toilet and glances at the fleshy giblet. It is an ogre inside this tiny cubicle, and she isn't certain what to do with it. She uncrumples the brown paper bag and is about to drop it inside, then toss the bag into the waste bin, but something stops her. It isn't right to throw it away like rubbish. Instead she picks it up gingerly between her fingers and examines it, her teeth clenched. Stringy clots of blood hang off. It is squidgy with a sort-of shell husked around it. She looks at it one last time through blurred eyes and rests it in the bag alone. It looks tiny inside. She twists the top to seal it, preserve it.

It takes a while to clean the scarlet puddle from the floor. The tap is stiff and her hands ache, so she uses spit and handfuls of scratchy toilet paper as a cloth. It doesn't absorb well, so she kneads the patch in lethargic circles until it fades. She wipes out her soiled knickers next, lining them with toilet paper before she pulls them back up. She picks up her paper bag, takes a deep breath, and walks back to her bunk, her head tucked down, her coat drawn around her, and her thighs squeezed tightly together because the peeing feeling still comes.

What surprises her most is that the carriage looks exactly as she left it. Bits of eggshell still speckle the floor. There is still a condensation-frosted window, a hard sleeper bed with protruding springs, and her lunch box lying open on it. The train steams on regardless.

She would like to haul herself onto the topmost bunk and listen to the soothing hooves of rain on the roof, but she is too weak. She slumps onto the bottom bunk and draws the curtains, still clutching the paper bag. If Gallagher were here, he would know what to do. She tries to loathe him but she can't, so she clings onto the paper bag and draws it to her chest. Her eyes open and close, her grip on the neck of the bag slackens and tightens, and, through the fug of half sleep, she realizes that the bag is pulsing; she wonders whether it is just the judder of the train or whether there is still a minuscule heart inside it, trying hard to beat.

x

No one else leaves the train at Liskeard. Betty steps cautiously onto the platform, her lunch box in her right hand and the paper bag in her left. She waits for relief to settle in now that she is almost home, but she feels only exhaustion and, surrounding it, a vacuum of nothingness.

When the tracks stop hissing, she sets down her lunch box and settles herself under the hedge where no one will notice her if they pass, still clutching the paper bag to her chest to protect it from the dew. Betty isn't sure how long she sits there, but when she moves off again, the sky is a sharper blue, the bushes are dry, and the platform is still empty.

She makes her way to the road in a daze. Her bloodied thighs rub together and a different sort of pull draws down between her legs, uncomfortable but less urgent. Her head stays empty. It is as though someone has plucked out every feeling and left her with nothing but a map of the road that zigzags down to St. Steele.

From the highest point, she can make out a cliff that jags into the water and envelops the little cove. Beyond it is a small cluster of trees. She staggers slowly toward them; she couldn't walk faster if she tried. If Mr. Paxon rolled up here now and hauled her inside his car or stabbed her in the heart with a bait hook, she is sure that she wouldn't care. She would just be glad to be horizontal.

"The pond," she mumbles aloud, woozy and swaying. "I need the pond."

She kicks off her pinching sandals and leaves them on the roadside, walking barefoot the rest of the way. The earth is damp under her right foot and her left is pricked by the gravel road. She pictures the pond: she can see Gallagher lying on the grass, an arm propped under his ear, and she can see a version of herself, too. It is a younger, lighter version of herself. She is dipping her toe in the pond and laughing: a strange sound.

The walk drags on. Betty passes Hotel Eden but doesn't notice it. She focuses on nothing but her mental photograph of the pond and the willow until, finally, they are both in front of her. She touches the bark to make sure that it really is there, then she sits against it, the trunk supporting her back while the stagnant pond sleeps in front of her.

X

BETTY MUST HAVE FALLEN asleep because when she looks up next, dusk has settled in and the evening smells of mint. It reminds her of the mint that Mother planted in the scrubby patch of garden at the back of Hotel Eden years ago. It was so strong, it strangled the thyme and the lupines.

When Mother saw the dead herbs and flowers, she slashed up the mint in anger and piled the cuttings in the larder. They ate mint soup and mint sauce and mint-flavored casseroles for weeks after that. Mother even tucked mint into their sandwiches instead of cucumber, and arranged clumps of it on the dining tables in eggcups in place of flowers. The hotel stank of mint. It only stopped smelling when Mr. Eden made an unexpected inspection and told Mother gently that he was disappointed she had turned his hotel into a crematorium for dead weeds. Mother has grown nothing since.

Mother!

Betty leaps to her feet, forgetting her pain for a second. How could she have forgotten Mother? She will be panicking, probably, and furious that she has been abandoned for so long. She might think that Betty has been hurt. What if she has contacted Inspector Napier? He will demand to know where she has been; it might all spill out. Mother would find out about the giblet baby and, worse, about Gallagher.

Betty looks down at the brown paper bag. She opens it and drops two small smooth pebbles inside, without pausing to think about it. She twists closed the top and throws. There is a loud plop. The bag lands in the middle of the pond and sinks. Ripples ring out. Betty realizes that she is panting. She traces a small cross shape on the surface of the water and watches the last of the ripples, then she hugs her coat around her and staggers in the direction of home.

x

RAIN HAS WASHED AWAY the chalked hopscotch run. Strangled dandelions push up through the gravel, and soda cans rust in the gutter. Strange how she noticed none of this before she left. She shuffles barefooted along the lane that runs behind Newl Grove, sidestepping the cans and weeds. Her legs are crusty. The old blood has dried and new stuff trickles out. She presses her thighs together even tighter.

She reaches over the gate and lets herself into the back garden. A damp sock lies on the ground. Betty drapes it over the washing line and glances back over her shoulder. The lane is empty, but she senses that she is being watched.

She hurries to the back door and slots her key into the lock. She pauses to button up her coat so Mother won't see the mud and the blood and the stains. If Mother is upstairs, she will have time to swill her face in the kitchen sink and scrub her hands, too. She will make them both a cup of tea and apologize for disappearing for so long. She misses Mother, she realizes. She will be more patient with her from now on.

Betty takes a deep breath and twists the key, just as something blue catches her eye through the kitchen window. A man she doesn't recognize is standing by the sink, his hand reaching into the glassware cupboard. He spots her before she can hide and before she can stop the back door from swinging open. He takes his hand out of the cupboard and turns to face her.

"Guv, she's here," he calls.

Betty realizes with relief that his blue jacket is a policeman's uniform. An older policeman appears in the kitchen doorway, too. He bows his head slightly when he sees her, and her relief evaporates. They must know about Gallagher or the giblet baby, or both. Mother must know, too. She will be ashamed. Betty won't cry, though. Mothers don't cry.

16

Fifty years later

Simon is there when John Gallagher wakes from his afternoon nap. John can tell it is him by the low guttural breathing, and he knows that Simon is squashed into the winged armchair in front of the window because the leather squeaks as he repositions himself. John keeps his eyes shut, the way he always does when he first wakes, until he knows who exactly is in the room and what to expect from them. It gives him back a little power.

He rummages through his memory. It's September 23, he's sure of it. It must be roughly half past six, for the light that seeps through his papery eyelids is pink. He remembers that Simon's birthday is August 15, that his own age is eighty. He checks that his toes still flex and knuckles still bend. He excels at his mental checklist and spends a few seconds resenting Simon and the doctors for shutting him up here, when his memory works perfectly well. Then he opens his eyes.

"Why are you here?" he barks, his voice coarse with sleep. "You're not supposed to visit on Wednesdays."

"Afternoon, Dad," says Simon with a sigh. "Feeling yourself, then?"

"Don't call me Dad; it's common. So? Why are you here?"

It isn't that he is angry; he just wants Simon to know that his brain is still sharp enough to remember rules and days.

"I told you yesterday, I'm flying to Geneva in the morning and I need to wrap up this chapter so Sylvie can transcribe it when I'm away."

John turns it all over in his mind. He doesn't recall Simon telling him any of that. Maybe Simon forgot. He wonders how to chastise him.

"Don't call me Dad; it's common."

Simon winces.

"Don't you remember that you just said that?"

"Get cracking," says John, "I don't have all day."

He is embarrassed even as he says it. They both know his days hang empty, but it is habit.

"Appointment with *Countdown*?" teases Simon.

John glares at him, but Simon is concentrating on switching on the small brown voice recorder balanced on the arm of the chair. John turns back to the Tuttle Tapes documentary that Simon muted when he arrived, but Simon reaches forward and turns off the television at the power socket.

"All right. Last time we were up to the point where you met Mum, remember?"

"Of course I bloody remember. I'm not an imbecile."

But he is touched at the way Simon clasps his pen like a boy, not a middle-aged solicitor.

"So, how about we start with where you met her?" says Simon. "At the French Embassy Ball, wasn't it? November 1956, Mum's twenty-first birthday?"

"If you know the whole damned story, why bother asking?"

Simon pours water into the spare tumbler and gulps it down, the way he always does when John upsets him. Sometimes Simon can get through two jugs in a single visit.

"Can't we just get through today without any of this? I'm up to my eyes in prep for the Geneva meeting, I've mediation with Carole tonight, and the publishers are breathing down my neck for this, and—"

"Fine," says John. "Get on with it before I change my mind."

Simon pulls the ostrich-skin journal from the bedside cabinet and eases back into the armchair. John had wanted to laugh when he first saw the journal.

That's why you'll never make a proper writer, he had wanted to say. Then he had thought of his own metal cabinets containing rows of scarred reporting pads that smelled of dust and foreign tobacco and singed flesh, and he had said nothing.

"Tell me what you thought of Mum when you first saw her," says Simon.

"Probably something like . . . Bloody French, can't get away from them."

"Don't be like that."

"The book's supposed to be about my career, not this puff."

"It's supposed to be about you."

John curls his nose and glares at his son.

"No one would want to read about our shambles of a marriage."

"Was she very beautiful when she was young?" presses Simon.

"Not as beautiful as she believed," says John eventually.

Simon shakes his head, but he scribbles it down anyway.

"And what did you think when you first saw her?"

"Nothing."

"I can't write that."

"Then write nothing."

"We've been through this. It could help when"—and Simon lowers his voice—"the illness advances."

"What good will it do then? I'll be a cauliflower."

The word doesn't sound right. Simon looks perplexed, too. John closes his eyes.

He had thought that Simon would give up if he gave monosyllabic answers, but the months wound on, and sometimes, as he neared sleep or his mind blurred, he found himself dribbling out facts without intending to. It was dangerous. The voice recorder filled, the ugly ostrich journal thickened, and slowly, his memoirs pieced together.

"Do it for Max," says Simon softly. "So he can learn about his grandfather."

"Fine. I thought she was loose. See what young Maximus makes of that."

"Just give me something to put down . . . What did you speak about when you met?"

John shrugs and tries not to meet Simon's eye. The truth was he had grimaced when he first saw Jeanette, the French ambassador's daughter. She was cold and brash, her dress was made of sequins, and her bony body slunk around the dance floor from one man to the next.

"You always shrug her off like this," says Simon. "Maybe she wasn't perfect, but she was your wife for ten years. You at least owe her a paragraph."

"Nine years," says John firmly, but his chest thumps: it is coming. "Write whatever you want. You knew her best."

Then it arrives. A wave of shadow rolls across, and his mind fogs over. He closes his eyes and pushes it away, just for this hour with Simon. He tries to remember facts to keep it at bay: yes, he had met Jeanette two days after he had driven back home to London from Cornwall. It was a cold Sunday in November and he was still shaking at the memory of everything that had happened in the biscuit factory.

"Why won't you talk about my mother?" says a faraway voice.

He had sat in his study drinking whiskey all day, and only dragged himself to the Embassy Ball because the bottle had emptied and the shops were dry on Sundays. He had driven there recklessly, still thinking about St. Steele. Or perhaps that is just his memory glossing itself. Maybe he hardly thought of it, or her, at all; just of himself and his own burden.

"I did it for her. She could never know," he reminds himself.

"Did what? And for whom?" There is a pause. "Are you talking about my mother?"

"Get them away from her!"

John tries to grip onto his memories, but someone has spilled a tube of M&M's over them. At least, they look like M&M's. The memories are laid out like a cartoon strip of pictures but with little discs of garish color blocking out part of each, so nothing is fully there.

"Get what away? You want me to go away?" says Simon.

"Not you. I didn't mean you. The shadow."

"Were you just talking about my mother?"

"No, not Jeanette. But Jeanette should have married that Henry, no, Harry, fellow when she had the chance. I told her I'd never love her but that I'd support the child financially. I was very up-front," he blurts out before that disappears, too.

Simon is silent.

"Where's my lighter?" barks John.

"What are you talking about?"

"Give me my lighter; I want my lighter back."

"Dad, you haven't smoked since 1994."

Jeanette had appeared next to him as he was leaving. She had asked for his lighter and plucked a cigarette from his tin. She lit it and took a long drag, fixing her dead gray eyes on him in a way that she probably believed was suggestive.

"I should never have lent her that lighter."

"Your face looks funny, Dad. What's wrong?"

"Where are you going?" Jeanette had asked.

"Home," says John.

"You can't go home, Dad. We've been through this."

He had let her catch his hand as they walked into the road for a taxi.

A black Hackney had stopped. He had opened the door; she stepped inside first and laughed under her breath, though neither of them had spoken.

"Get out of my taxi. I need to go back to St. Steele."

"You're scaring me, Dad. Don't try to move. I've called the nurse."

They went back to her suite and that night he slept with her twice. Jeanette had called for more champagne afterward, while he locked himself in the bathroom, turned on the bath taps, and cried for one of the first times in his adult life.

"It hadn't changed anything," he whimpers. "I still couldn't forget her or Forbes or any of it."

Something is bleeping, and a red beacon flashes through his closed eyes.

"I've pulled the cord; they're on their way," someone is saying.

"But then Jeanette found me a month later and told me she was pregnant. Her father said I had to marry her."

"Just stay calm."

"I was tired of doing the wrong thing, so I did. I married her."

"I've pushed you too hard. I'm sorry, I shouldn't have."

"She named the boy Simon. He was a good boy. Slow, perhaps, but kindhearted."

There is a long pause.

"It's me, Dad. I'm Simon," says a voice that is scratchy with sobs.

John opens his eyes. He can't recall the man, though his gray irises are familiar. An alarm is beeping. Feet are humping up the stairs. The man is peering into his face.

"Stay calm. You'll be all right."

The man's name is Simon. He is his son. Of course he knows Simon.

"Why is your face wet, son?" he asks Simon.

"You remember me?" Simon sounds relieved.

"Of course I do. Did you think I'd had a bloody lobotomy? I asked why your face is—"

"Don't try to speak. The doctor's nearly here."

A nurse sweeps in, and Simon swims out of focus again.

"I thought he was having a stroke," Simon is saying.

Something pricks John's arm and he forgets to protest. The nurse is speaking in a hushed voice that is too soft to hear. His lips taste of aniseed; he hates aniseed. Something runny dribbles down his chin, but he is too tired to find out what.

"He was talking gobbledygook," Simon is saying as John drifts unconscious.

×

WHEN JOHN WAKES NEXT, his mind is foggy, but he fights it away and listens. There is a squeak of leather; Simon is still here, then. John's toes still wiggle, his fingers still flex. Mental checklist complete, he opens his eyes and looks around the dingy room.

"You shouldn't have stayed," he says thickly.

Simon looks at him with that concerned expression he can't abide.

"The nurse said it was probably just a panic attack."

"Panic attack, my eye. I'm shut up here with nothing to do but examine my own fingernails. What's there for me to panic about?"

"I don't think I should go to Geneva."

"Of course you'll go. I never missed a day of work in my life. A half day for my father's funeral, but I was straight back to Saigon that night."

Simon is grinding his jaw.

"The nurse says I should ease off the questioning for now."

"Go on, get out your book. I'm not a retard."

"Stop it," cries Simon. "You think you're invincible, but you're not."

He drops his head into his hands and rubs his temples. John waits. He notices that Simon has developed a bald patch; he watches it with a twinge of unease but says nothing.

"I just don't understand why you don't try harder with the book," says Simon after a while. "The doctors agreed it could help."

"Everyone has stories, son," says John, gentler. "Not everyone's warrants a book."

"But yours are fascinating, the stories you used to tell me . . ."

"Maybe to you, but everyone lives a life and collects a bank of them. Then you're gone, and they're gone, too, and everyone else is too busy building their own banks to give a damn." He pauses. "And if you really want the truth, mine are only a product of my job and . . . well, I hated it."

"You didn't hate it. You loved being sent away."

"I despised it. Do you want to write that? How it was a penance, and how I counted down every hour until I could let myself leave, but I never could because I'd never repaid my debts?"

"Debts?" says Simon, looking up. "What debts?"

×

SIMON LEAVES EVENTUALLY. THE night drags along and another morning carousels around. Someone drags open the curtains by their hems instead of the pulley, and the silence is ripped by the scrape of metal on metal. John's instinct is to scold, but he keeps his eyes shut and trains his ears on the culprit instead.

Her shoes have sticky soles. When she walks near his bed, he is hit by a noseful of Pears soap; that means she is the nondescript redheaded nurse, an octave less shrill than the others. He has no desire for small talk with her and no desire to greet the chain of blank hours that lie ahead, so he keeps his eyes closed.

They are still closed when the nurse wafts out into the corridor and speaks to a woman with a chalky and lilting voice, pleasant somehow. But he blocks her out, too, and slips back into the cocoon of darkness. Minutes pass.

"Hello," says that chalky voice, louder.

It jolts him awake.

"Hello, Mr. Gallagher."

He strains to hear every shallow slide of air between her lips and waits for her to say who she is, but she doesn't. He reassures himself that she is probably just a newly recruited nurse getting to grips with the rounds, but something is wrong. She is too silent and she stands too close to be a stranger. Something about her makes the hairs on the back of his arms and neck prick up. He is impatient; without preparing himself and without completing his mental checklist, he opens his eyes.

Sun pierces the window and the room dazzles so spectacularly, he wonders whether it is his room at all or whether he is dead. The woman, for there is a woman, stands with her back to the window, cloaked in her own shadow. She looks like a black angel. He thinks that she might be an old friend of Jeanette but dismisses the idea; Jeanette's friends were glossier, showier reflections of one another. He is gnarled with frustration. Who are you, he wants to know, but the nurse speaks. The black angel speaks next, maybe he speaks, too, then the nurse speaks again. She says something that makes the angel dip her head, pull her handbag high up her arm, and move toward the door.

The shadow falls from her body when she steps out of the glare, and he sees her face. She has silvery hair twisted elegantly behind her head, her cheekbones are sharp, and her lips are hot red, but the dimples in her cheeks make her look girlish. She is beautiful in an understated, untrying way. Even her walk is serene.

"But I know your face. I never forget a face," he says, and she turns to him head-on.

The blood has drained from her skin now, and she is almost translucent. He sees her properly then, and he almost cries out. He sees the girl Betty. Her face has hardly changed. Her eyes are still almonds, and her gaze is still searching.

He frowns and balls up his fists. No, not Betty. Never Betty. He is deluding himself, just as he did the night Jeanette died: he had been lying on his sofa while Simon cried next to him for his dead mother. He had been thinking about Simon's heart; how it was a sponge that absorbed every drop of warmth and kept absorbing, not like a grown man's heart should be. Not like Jeanette's sharp mirror heart, either. Nor his own, a shriveled bit of bark. He had opened his eyes for a split second, and he had seen Betty quite unexpectedly. She was an angel with wings and still fifteen.

He had jumped from the sofa and grasped at the ceiling, where she hovered, but he couldn't quite catch hold of her and he had watched powerlessly as she dissolved into the cornice.

"Say your name," he says, in case he is deluding himself again.

"You remember me?" says that voice; Betty's voice.

It is gentle and songlike from her silky throat.

"Say your name," he repeats, ashamed of his old-man's voice. He is ashamed of his pinched lips, too, and his dead eyes, and his body, lying in bed like one of those impassive marble tombs that he had once glanced at in a Tuscan crypt. That is how she must see him; redundant and cracked and lifeless.

"I was your Betty."

Her face disappears behind her hands. Don't hide away, he would like to shout, but he needs a moment to plan what to say next and how to explain. At the very least, he must tell her that, even now, the thought of her standing on the beach kicking up fountains of sea makes him—but what does it make him?

He had once pieced together the optimal sentence to recite if he met her again: I loved you, and that's why I came back for you, but I left again to protect you. He had decided that it would be dangerous to utter a word more, but now she is here, the words sit on his lips refusing to budge.

He notices the nurse then. She has stopped drying the glasses, and she stands watching them with one hip cocked forward and her mouth agape. He snaps with anger.

"You must leave."

The nurse doesn't move. Instead she turns to face Betty—no, Mary. She turns to the woman standing by the door with her hands still glued to her face, the way a child might if she wanted to wish herself away from a moment of fear or terror or perhaps unbearable elation.

"You must leave," says Gallagher again, pointing at the nurse with his index finger.

She frowns and opens her mouth wider, but she closes it again and marches off. Finally, they are alone, and John is relieved. But the relief is replaced with a knot of terror. She will want to know everything.

17

Joan elbows past the two policemen and hurries across the kitchen toward Betty, her face streaked with mascara.

"Sweetheart," she weeps, wrapping her wiry arms around Betty.

"It's all right, I'm home now . . . I'm sorry if I worried you all," says Betty.

She tries to unbury herself from the brittle hug, but Joan has her tight. She smells of lemons and something greasy.

"What is it, what's wrong?"

Joan lets go and collapses onto a chair beside the little foldaway kitchen table. A half-drunk glass of wine sits on it. Joan picks up the glass and presses its lipstick mark to her cheek.

"Where's Mother?"

"Sit down, my love," says the older policeman.

"Where's Inspector Napier?"

"In Plymouth. Sit down, please."

"Am I in trouble? I was only gone for one night."

The policeman shakes his head. Betty sits. She watches Joan roll the lipsticked glass over her cheek, as though trying to make it kiss her. Her eyes still stream. The older policeman clears his throat.

"I'm sorry Betty, but your mother passed away."

Everything goes gray.

x

BETTY ISN'T SITTING ON the kitchen chair anymore. Betty is a spider. She clings onto the bit of ceiling next to the mustard lampshade and she looks down, as spiders do. Directly below her is a head of curls that belongs to sobbing Joan. A slight girl with matted hair the color of chestnuts stands beside Joan. The girl doesn't move. She doesn't even breathe. Two identical police helmets hover next to her. Both helmets are removed at the same time. The curls bob faster, but the head of matted hair is perfectly still.

Mother's head will join them soon. She will switch on the record player and dance around the room, her yellow hair bobbing about. She will grab the policemen and twirl them around. She will sing "Oranges and Lemons."

x

BETTY STANDS ON THE floor again. Mother still isn't here. She will come, though. And when Mother says dance, Betty will dance. She will cartwheel, too, and jive, and she will pour Mother a glass of wine—a bottle of the stuff if Mother asks her to. She would pour it straight down Mother's throat, if only she would walk in right now.

"I don't understand," she croaks.

"In her sleep," says the older policeman.

"She choked," chips in the younger one. "On her vomit. She probably wouldn't have felt anything, since she was already passed out. We found bottles of sleeping tablets and gin and wine and brandy and—"

"I'm sorry," cuts in the older policeman, giving the younger one a fierce look.

"That's enough," shouts Joan at the same time, standing up. "Get him out! Get that nasty little scrote out of Dolores's kitchen."

He scarpers into the big room, and the older policeman's face turns very pink.

"I'm awfully sorry," he says again. "He's new. He shouldn't have said that. But it was an accident, like he said." He tucks his hat under his arm. "You should also know that we found something. We think it's intended for you."

He holds out a sheet of crumpled paper to Betty. She looks at his eyes instead.

"What is it?" she says.

"It was in the bedroom. By the desk."

His hand is extended. There is a long pause. Betty fishes for courage and takes the paper from him. The page is thin and has translucent patches, as if water or tears or some other liquid has splashed it. The handwriting is careless, and the angle skewed.

I'm sorry. I'm sorry. I'm sorry. I'm sorry. I'm sorry. I'm sorry.

She looks at it for a long time and hands it back to the policeman.

"I'd better put the potatoes on to boil. Mother'll be home soon."

"Betty, you should keep it," says Joan gently.

"We're out of flour," continues Betty. "She must have gone to buy flour. She'll be hungry if she's walked all the way to Spoole for it."

"If we can do anything to help . . . ," says the policeman.

He sort of bows out of the kitchen. Betty can hear him whispering something in the other room. He sounds cross. It will be all right, though. Mother will come home soon and send them all packing. She will bake bread with the new flour and light the coal fire. They will spear the bread onto pokers and toast it with cinnamon and sugar sprinkled on top.

Someone is shaking Betty's shoulders. She lets her rag doll body flop about and keeps her eyes closed.

"Were you listening?" says Joan, dabbing her eyes with a handkerchief. "Did you hear them?"

Betty opens her eyes and looks at Joan but she can't focus.

"I need toast," she says.

Joan shakes her harder.

"Dolores is dead. Your mother is dead. Didn't you hear them?"

"Toast with cinnamon."

"Betty, don't make this harder for me. I'm upset, too."

She shrugs off Joan and walks to the larder for cinnamon. It is already powdered. Mother isn't patient enough for cinnamon sticks. "Life's too short to grate cinnamon," she always says, even though Betty tries to tell her that cinnamon sticks aren't supposed to be grated.

Betty draws the cinnamon tub to her nose and sniffs. It smells of winter, of the nights that Mother threw back her head and said, "I know, Betty boo boo, we'll have a treat." Betty can't wait for the fire to light, for the cinnamon to melt into the bread. She needs it now. She tips back her head and lets the sweet earthy powder coat her throat. It makes her cough. She can't quite catch her breath. Someone slaps her back.

"Richard, get in here," shouts Joan.

"Life's too short to grate cinnamon," coughs Betty.

Joan hits her back harder. Betty licks the cinnamon from her lips, but her legs stop working and she falls to the kitchen floor. Her chin grazes the oilcloth.

"Richard," shrieks Joan.

Betty lies facedown on the floor that on Tuesday, only Tuesday, she scrubbed until her hands were raw, while Mother lay upstairs in bed breathing.

"Life's too short to grate cinnamon."

Joan cries louder. Someone wearing workman's boots stomps into the kitchen.

"Life's too short to grate cinnamon!"

She can almost laugh about it—how right Mother is. Life is too short for cinnamon grating. Miss Hollinghurst's life was especially short. She must tell Mother that she was right.

Betty wriggles away from Joan's grip and runs into the big room where the two policemen and two ambulancemen are gathered in a circle. A blue light flashes through the nets. In the middle of the big room, drawing the men around it like a Guy Fawkes, is a shape. She looks again. It is Mother's shape. Even through the white sheet, Betty can make out the tilt of Mother's feet and forehead and nose.

"Mother," she calls, lunging forward.

She needs to rip the sheet off Mother's face; Mother hates being too hot and clammy. The younger policeman grabs Betty's waist. He scoops her up and holds her horizontal.

"Mother," she shouts, kicking to get away.

Two ambulancemen carry out the white sheet with Mother still beneath it.

"MOTHER."

The older policeman blocks the door. The ambulancemen are outside now. One of them slams shut the ambulance door. The blue light slides away with Mother.

x

BETTY IS COILED UP on Mother's dimpled armchair beside the globe-shaped drinks cabinet. Someone wraps a shawl around her shoulders.

"It's cold," whispers a man.

"Has he sent you here to hurt me?"

"Betty, you know me."

"Because I won't fight, if he has."

"It's Richard. Joan's husband."

"Oh . . . Yes . . . Don't tell Mr. Paxon where I am."

The yellow streetlamps flicker to life. A phone rings once, twice, then dies. Silence for hours, maybe years.

x

WHEN BETTY LOOKS UP again, it is nighttime. There is a rush of tap water in the kitchen. A glass clanks down on the countertop. Betty uncurls herself and jumps to her feet.

"Mother?"

She rushes into the kitchen. Someone is pouring wine into a glass in the dark.

"Sweetie," says a voice.

The figure has curly hair, and she holds the wineglass near her lips. It must be Mother. Betty is ready to cry out with relief. Then she blinks. Only Joan.

"Did I wake you?" says Joan.

"It's late. You should go home," whispers Betty.

Joan swigs the wine.

"You'll be all right. You have us."

"Go home, Joan."

"Richard's bringing my things here. He thinks I should stay with you for a while."

Her words are slurred, the way Mother's often are. Betty steps forward, and takes the glass from Joan. She pours the wine down the sink and slowly washes the glass. It is as though she isn't in control of her own body; someone else could be acting this out for her.

"You need to go home, Joan."

"What?"

"To Richard."

"It's okay, I'm here."

Joan reaches forward and touches Betty's shoulder awkwardly. Betty pulls back.

"I'd like to be alone."

"I'll sleep here. Dolores would want me to."

"Please."

"I shouldn't leave you," says Joan uncertainly.

"I'd just like to be alone," she repeats.

Joan looks her up and down. Betty looks down at herself, too, and realizes that Joan's big hand-me-down coat is still swamping her. Her feet are bare and streaked with mud. She probably has time to clean herself up before Mother comes home; before the Dansette kicks in and dancers' heels tap on the hall tiles. Maybe Mother will sing along, too.

"I'll come back tomorrow, then," says Joan, gathering up her fur coat. "First thing. Me and Richard. We'll all talk properly then. . . . You look awful. You poor, poor girl."

Betty stands very still and doesn't meet Joan's eye. Joan drags herself out into the hallway. She stops, lets out a single strangled sob, and then she is gone.

In the kitchen, Betty scrubs her hands, pulls off her coat, and washes her legs. Blood has dried on her thighs. There isn't a cloth, so she cups water in her hands and throws it over herself. By the time she is wet all over, the floor is waterlogged, but she still feels dirty. An ache still wraps around her. She changes into a clean skirt, blouse, and knickers from the unpressed laundry pile on the kitchen table, then rolls up her dirty clothes and pushes them to the bottom of the rubbish bin, where Mother won't find them. Mother can never know; what would she think of her, a mother at fifteen?

When she has bolted the front and back doors, Betty stands at the foot of the stairs. The hotel is still. It seems to sleep under a sheet of heavy silence. She steps onto the first stair and changes her mind. She can't go into the bedroom, not until Mother is home and safe. She can't sit in the big room, either, when Mother lay on the floor in there under that white sheet. Instead, Betty walks into the kitchen and picks up the glass that Joan had been rolling against her cheek, the one with a slash of Mother's red lipstick on the rim. She sniffs it. A whiff of Mother's sugary lipstick, that's all she wants, but instead it smells of Mother's breath on her black snowman days.

Betty opens her hand and watches the glass drop onto the floor. She enjoys the smash; it cracks the silence and, for a fraction of a second, the kitchen is full. Then the silence returns, and the hotel is empty again. She drops another glass, then a third, and when there are no more glasses in arm's reach, she lies on the puddled floor and listens to the crunch of the glass shards beneath her.

Cold water fills her ear and an ache sets deep in her eardrum. Something prickles her calves and her back and her ankles. Good. She lets herself sting with pain: she deserves it all.

x

HOURS EBB AWAY. RED morning light creeps through the kitchen nets. Betty doesn't move. She hasn't moved for six hours; she counted them. Mother will be lying on a cold slab of bed in a hospital somewhere. Her giblet is at the bottom of the pond. Then there is Mr. Gallagher and Miss Hollinghurst and Mr. Forbes and Mr. Paxon to think about, and too many other faces to fit inside her head.

She rolls over, and glass pricks her thigh. She has stopped feeling pain. Maybe she bleeds, but it is difficult to tell because she is already damp. She will sit up and check soon. For now, she is too heavy.

Another hour seeps away, or maybe just a fraction, or perhaps a whole day. She doesn't know time or hunger anymore. She is aware that she lies in a fetal shape in a cold puddle. Stupid cow. Don't lie like that; you're not one of those. You had one. You're disgusting. She straightens out, lying in a soldier shape instead. It makes her laugh aloud. A soldier. That's right. You're not a fetus anymore. You're a weak little soldier woman. No wonder he tired of you.

"Mr. Gallagher," she says in a small voice. "Mother. Mr. Gallagher. Mother. Miss Hollinghurst."

She says their names again, again, a thousand times more, to keep them all close.

x

A GIRL'S VOICE FILLS the letter box. So many tongues and throats have caught in that letter box this morning, Betty would like to nail it shut. Some of them postcards or scraps of paper with words of condolence or white flowers. Betty tears off their petals.

"It's me," calls Mary shrilly.

Betty covers her ears with her palms.

"Don't be like this. Mr. Cripps gave me a day off especially . . . I want to help you."

"Help me? You can't even help yourself."

"Don't say that."

"You should've listened. The Paxons are dangerous."

"Why are you saying this? Are you still jealous?"

"I can't protect everyone."

"Betty!"

"I don't care if you end up dead, too. You probably will, but you should have listened."

She isn't certain whether the words came out, but they must have, for Mary gasps and disappears.

×

HOTEL EDEN HAS BEEN empty of Mother for five whole days. Betty must have stood up and let Joan inside, because she is loitering in the big room, and the windows aren't smashed, and the front door isn't broken. Perhaps she unlocked it in her sleep. A dead plant sits in its pot on the windowsill. Mother put it there.

Betty walks over and rubs a leaf between her fingertips, just as someone taps the window. Why won't they leave her alone with the last of Mother? Even Mother's smell is ghosting off. Betty wants it back.

×

JOAN AND RICHARD HAVE been and gone. Mr. and Mrs. Eden live in the hotel now. Mother's perfume smell is replaced with Mrs. Eden's lavender drawer liners. There is no bumble of guests, just visitors sweeping in and out by day. At night, the only sounds come from room six, where Mr. and Mrs. Eden sleep.

When they are shut up in bed, Betty walks around the hotel with Mother's glass bottle of liquid amber. The bottle label says Chanel No.5. She sprays every chair and every mat and every fork in the dining room drawer to make sure that Mrs. Eden's lavender goes away, that Mother is still in charge.

The liquid amber has almost run out when Mrs. Eden tiptoes downstairs wearing her hair rollers. Betty carries on spraying the forks and teaspoons and doesn't look up.

"Betty, stop it. Stop that now! Tancred, come quickly," Mrs. Eden shouts up the stairs.

Betty smiles at her and sprays another teaspoon.

"Tancred," Mrs. Eden calls again as Betty turns the perfume bottle on herself and douses her hair with Mother, eyeballing Mrs. Eden as she does.

Mr. Eden still doesn't come. Then the bottle is empty, and Betty realizes that she is still staring at Mrs. Eden.

These last few days, it has taken a long time to focus on people. Sometimes she can't tell whether they are themselves or not because they morph into Mother or Mr. Gallagher. Just yesterday, Mrs. Eden turned into a bit of giblet, making Betty scream. Even when the faces look like themselves, Betty finds herself staring. Mother never stared. Mother was perfect.

The following night, when Mr. and Mrs. Eden are snoring, Betty looks inside every bedroom (except theirs) and under every bed and opens every closet in case Mr. Paxon has stowed himself there, ready to silence her. She creeps downstairs and checks again that the doors are all bolted.

She is about to turn in when the Dansette winks at her from the sideboard. She winks back. She switches it on and it bleats out the tune that she and Mother danced to, only it sounds bleaker today.

Betty raises her arms. She juts out her left hip, then her right hip. She jiggles her shoulders and rolls her head until her eyes blur and her face sweats. The song ends with a start, and Betty flops onto the floor, exhausted. Someone coughs. Mr. Eden stands in the doorway, his arms folded across his brown dressing gown. Mrs. Eden is next to him wearing peach silk and penciled eyebrows lowered in a frown.

"Have a little sleep, Betty," says Mr. Eden.

x

ANOTHER NIGHT AND ANOTHER red morning pass. People still trickle in and out of the hotel, but they are quieter than usual. Mrs. Eden's nasal voice grates above them all. That woman talks through her nose, never mind looking down it. That's what Mother said once.

"You're right, Mother."

Betty switches on the Dansette for Mother. She drops the needle onto the record. It crackles, and the same "Tutti Frutti" song plays again and again. She pirouettes and dances and weeps. The Dansette weeps, too.

"A wop bop a loo a lop bam boo," she sings, so loudly her throat might have ripped in two.

She picks up the needle and plays the song for the ninety-second time.

x

THE DANSETTE WON'T WORK. Mrs. Eden said it died of exhaustion. Betty could die of exhaustion, too. She hasn't eaten since that cucumber sandwich days ago. She nibbles a hard pear and some broken crackers that she finds in the larder. They are difficult to swallow. Her throat is too dry.

She crawls back to the Dansette, but it is still dead, so she makes her way upstairs and trails her hand over Mother's makeup bottles and furs. Mrs. Eden had said that they'd have to be packed away after the funeral.

"Not if you're packed away first," Betty had replied, but Mrs. Eden had pretended not to hear. Betty had laughed. She threw back her head and cackled because Mrs. Eden was wrong: Betty would never let Mother be packed away.

×

THE DAY OF THE funeral arrives, and Hotel Eden is a kaleidoscope of black. Mr. Eden's tie is ink black and Mrs. Eden wears a dull charcoal hat with net covering her face. It is the sort of net that Mr. Forbes once used to bundle up his chickens.

"What'll happen to his chickens when he's in court?" Betty asks Mrs. Eden.

"Pardon?"

"To Mr. Forbes's chickens?"

Mrs. Eden shifts uncomfortably from foot to foot.

"I don't know, Betty. But his trial is over; you know that."

"Because he's innocent."

"Come on, the cars will be here soon."

"He's innocent. He didn't do it. Mother loved him."

"That girl's talking nonsense again," whispers Mrs. Eden to Mr. Eden. "I think she needs a doctor."

"I can hear you. And I don't need a doctor, I just need Mr. Gallagher."

She shouldn't have said that, and she is relieved when they ignore her. She will keep her promise and never tell a soul. He will be back for her soon, and for Mr. Forbes.

Mr. Eden arranges an armful of lilies on the back seat of his motorcar.

"You can put them by the headstone when we get there," he says, and climbs into the driver's seat.

Betty watches the row of cars waiting to follow the hearse. Or the grand car, as Mr. Eden calls it. Betty is pleased that Mother gets a grand car and lots of eyes on her. She'll like that.

×

THE GRASS IS WET around the grave pit. A big brown box is lowered into the earth. Gallagher still isn't in the crowd; she checked. He will come, though.

A man wearing a white robe says a prayer. Mrs. Eden cries. Mother hates Mrs. Eden. She will hate Mrs. Eden crying, too. "I've no time for that green-eyed woman," that's what Mother says, even though Mrs. Eden has brown eyes. Mother's eyes are a beautiful ice blue.

Betty wanders off to find the nearest tree; it is an oak. She presses her head against its trunk and lets it take some of her weight. The heaviness has returned but she has hardly eaten, so shouldn't she be losing heaviness? Maybe she should have a nap on this branch. Would this be a good place to sleep, Mother? She tries to hoist herself up, but her arms are weak as butter. Mr. Eden appears then. He smiles gently.

"Time to go home," he says.

"Where's home?"

Mr. Eden rubs his chin. Gray stubble pricks through the pores.

"You need to shave," she says, to be helpful.

"Hotel Eden," he says. "It'll always be your home."

"Thank you."

Because that's what you're supposed to say to people who are trying to be kind—and he sounds kind, but she doesn't really feel thankful. She feels nothing apart from heaviness.

"You're looking more like yourself today, Betty."

"Am I? Who did I look like yesterday?"

She wishes she hadn't said that because he is going to reply that she looked like Mother yesterday. She braces herself.

"Don't be cheeky. We were very worried about you."

"Were you?"

She leans against the tree trunk again. She isn't sure how much longer her legs can support her body; it seems to be made of steel. Steel, and they live in St. Steele. It makes her laugh. Mr. Eden doesn't laugh. He looks at her strangely, as if she has turned into a cat.

"What happens when you put steel in fire?"

"We'll get through this."

"Would I melt? Melting would be a painful way to die."

He is too busy steering her to the car to answer. His warm hand rests on the cold small of her back as they weave through the parked cars, the gravel crunching under their feet. It is the same way Gallagher steered her through that fishing village. She catches a noseful of Gallagher's smell, too. She turns and plants her lips on his lips. They land half on them, half on his sandpapery chin. He jumps back. Her lips burn, but not in a good way.

"What are you doing? You mustn't do things like that," says Mr. Eden, in a voice that sounds angry and sad at the same time. It is the wrong voice. Where is Gallagher? Betty starts crying.

Mr. Eden looks at her in a confused way. He glances back over his shoulder, as though considering whether to escape, but instead he stops beside his car and opens the door for her. Betty lies across the back seat. Even lying down, she is heavy.

"Wouldn't it be wonderful to be made of air?"

Mr. Eden gets into the driver's seat and taps his finger on the steering wheel, the way Gallagher did when they stopped for the cows.

"Moo," sighs Betty sadly.

That's what she did to get rid of the cows. She had energy inside her then. Mr. Eden taps his finger faster. He only stops when Mrs. Eden puffs over to them, dabbing her eyes with a handkerchief and saying something about the wind making her tear ducts leak.

Mr. Eden drives back to Hotel Eden. No one speaks.

x

THE WHOLE OF ST. Steele crams into the hotel for the funeral reception. Betty's dress is too tight and the fabric is scratchy. She crawls upstairs on her hands and knees and pulls on her nightdress instead. She considers lying down but she can't: Mother lay on that bed last. Her silhouette is probably still printed on the sheet.

Betty slopes back downstairs and finds herself by the front door as more visitors pour inside. Some of them look at her with soft eyes, but no one speaks to her. Mrs. Eden has probably told lies about her to scare them, just as she did about Mother. Some years ago, she had overheard Mrs. Eden saying that Mother was a dangerous man-eater. When Betty argued that Mother was absolutely not a cannibal, Mrs. Eden had turned very pink and shooed her out of the big room. Betty hadn't told Mother; upset Mother made her upset, too.

She watches the mill of bodies. She thinks that she sees Mary among them, so she wriggles through the crowd and hides herself in the kitchen. It is safest there, with the back door as an escape route and the utensil drawer full of weapons. Agatha Christie would love that utensil drawer; she could kill someone in sixteen different ways using Mother's rolling pin alone. Betty counts the ways.

Some of the visitors squeeze into the kitchen, too, so Betty settles herself in the larder. She sits on the floor, hugging her knees to her chest and tracing her finger in a pool of spilled brown sugar. She draws out Mother's name and Gallagher's name and the giblet baby's shape. Then she closes her eyes and counts the days since Mother went off. There are twelve of them at least. Yes, time has skidded on, the kitchen floor has dried, someone has even swept up the broken glass, but Mother is still gone. Betty hugs her knees tighter, and that moment the larder door swings open.

"What are you doing in here?" says Mrs. Eden. "Come into the big room. And put on some clothes for goodness' sake, or you'll catch a death."

"Let her be," says Mr. Eden in a hushed voice, appearing behind her.

"It'd be nice if you served the teas," continues Mrs. Eden.

Betty doesn't answer.

"Don't be rude," snaps Mrs. Eden.

"Where's my letter?"

"What letter?"

"The sorry letter from Mother."

"I don't know anything about a letter."

"Do the policemen have it? I want my sorry letter."

"Shush, Betty."

"Ease off her, love," whispers Mr. Eden.

"Don't indulge her."

"But the poor girl's in shock."

"It's her mother's funeral, and it's a daughter's duty to serve the guests."

A daughter's duty? Betty struggles to her feet. She walks into the big room and makes for the table in the corner where the tea set is laid out. She stands behind the table, and when people ask, she pours tea into their cups without looking at them. When they don't ask, she still pours it. The saucers fill with tea, too, and so does the dish of wafers. The tablecloth and the cuff of her nightdress drink up the tea, too. Mr. Eden takes the teapot from Betty and guides her back upstairs.

"What you need is a good night's sleep," he says.

"What about a daughter's duty?"

He watches her sadly as though he is about to cry, as though this is his mother's funeral. He pulls back the bed covers for her. She looks hard, but Mother's shape isn't there. Mrs. Eden has probably ironed it away.

"I haven't had a funeral for my giblet," she sighs.

He lingers in the bedroom doorway still watching her. It is the way she supposes a father might watch his child, but she has never had a father, so it is difficult to tell. He comes back in and tucks a loose bedsheet under the mattress, making her warm finally.

Mother used to warm her, too: in the thick of winter, she would tuck the blankets tight around Betty and position the hot water jar at the foot of the bed, all the while singing the words "Betty boo boo" and blowing her warm wine breath over Betty's face. It was comforting, apart from the time Mother forgot to cork up the hot water jar. Boiling water sloshed out and scalded Betty's feet. Her feet blistered and she had to hobble around Hotel Eden for a fortnight after that—she couldn't even manage the walk to school—but none of that mattered because at least Mother had tried.

"You can stay here for as long as you like. This is your home," says Mr. Eden.

She thanks him.

"Nonsense, don't thank me, Betty boo."

She winces. Don't call me that, she wants to say. It is the name Mother gave her; it is disloyal to Mother to let anyone else use it. It is also all she has left of Mother, now that her smell and her shape have dissolved, but Mr. Eden is trying to be kind, so she says nothing.

Mr. Eden closes the door. The bedroom is dim. Long shadows stretch across the walls. Mother's smell returns faintly, but only her wine breath and not her perfume. Betty sits bolt upright.

"Mother?"

There is no answer. Mother must be here, invisible and listening to her.

"You didn't need to say sorry," she whispers.

Maybe Mother is an angel now; angels know everything. Betty can't stay in here. She closes the bedroom door firmly behind her and is about to cross the landing when her eyes fall on Gallagher's old bedroom. She touches his door handle. It is cold. It hits her: what if he never comes back?

No, he must. He will. They are sweethearts. It is his duty.

She remembers her own duty and tiptoes back downstairs. She catches sight of her wild hair and crumpled nightdress in the hall mirror, but there isn't time to tidy herself up or she will miss her duty, so she heads straight for the big room. She pauses at the door, gathering the strength to push through the crowd to the tea table. Mrs. Eden is laughing with the greengrocer's wife. Joan is giggling and wagging her finger at Richard. Betty is furious. She wants to scream at them all to scrub the smiles from their faces because Mother has gone. But then she spots him.

He is standing alone, framed by Mrs. Eden's head and the fishmonger's shoulder. His mouth is moving in slow careful circles, but when she strains to hear his voice above the others, it sounds like long underwater burps, the way she supposes the devil himself must speak. His slitty eyes have long bags beneath them, and he has sprouted even more gray hairs since she saw him last. He turns and meets her eye.

"Him," she finds herself bellowing.

She points at Mr. Paxon. Everyone falls silent and looks at her.

"It was him," she shouts. "He killed them all."

She waits for someone to grab him by the throat, but they are staring at her instead: they are staring at her as if she has blue scaly skin, or as if she has morphed into Mother, or as if she herself is the killer, while Mr. Paxon stands there calmly, slurping his tea.

18

"You must leave," says John Gallagher again.

Mary listens to the nurse's shrinking footsteps. The room becomes unbearably hot. It stifles her. Heat seems to radiate from the walls and permeate the carpet. She presses her forehead to the window and lets the cold soak into her skull and through to her brain. She wills it to run down her whole body and freeze every nerve because she hasn't a clue what to do or say next.

I've come about Nigel Forbes and what we did all those years ago. That's what she should say. Do you think about it often—do you regret it?

"Would you like a cup of tea?" she says instead, turning away from the window. "Or a newspaper? I could fetch one."

She hopes he will agree to the newspaper, it will give her time to gather herself, but he just looks quizzically at her. His right eyebrow lifts. She remembers that eyebrow, the funny wormy one with a life of its own that leapt up and down and crawled over his face like a cater-pillar while the other stayed still. But she shouldn't think of him with such familiarity.

"I'll just dry those," she says, nodding at the pair of damp glasses that the nurse left behind.

She walks around the bed toward them.

"You're not here to dry cups or buy newspapers," says John suddenly, as though he has only just registered what she said. He pauses to choose his final word with care. "Mary."

She blushes.

"You don't need to call me that."

"That's who you are now, isn't it?"

It doesn't sound accusatory or probing or even like a question, just a hard bald fact.

"Come and sit here," he continues softly.

She doesn't want to sit; it is difficult enough to stand still. She has to concentrate very hard because if her legs had their way, she would be bouncing and fizzing and leaping around the room. She pushes the tea towel inside the second glass and twists it.

"Sit down," he says again. "Let's talk properly."

She ignores him and pushes on. Then both glasses are dry, and there is nothing to busy her hands with, so she folds the tea towel once, twice, a third time. She glances at the winged armchair that he wanted her to sit on and wonders whether his wife sits on it often, whether he has a wife at all.

She had asked Holly to look up his name on her computer once, before she had found out about his dementia from that newspaper letters page, but Holly had forgotten and she hadn't asked again in case Jerry found out. She sighs and perches on the edge of the armchair.

"There," says John with a small sigh, as though it were he who had sat down.

"I came here about—" she begins. "You might remember that years ago I . . ."

"Tell me something about your life," he says gently.

"I'm sorry?"

"About your life now."

Her hands tremble. She really could be fifteen again, for was that not what he asked her on the seafront at St. Ives all those years ago? The day slides back to her with surprising clarity, or a version of it that has prettied itself with time. Everything is sharply pixelated: the sea is a bright turquoise, the seagull's feathers are flecked white and gray, and he looks down the lens of her camera with the same hypnotic expression that he wears now.

"I'd like to know a little about your family, your work, what interests you."

"I'm married," she finds herself saying. "My husband, Jerry, works in advertising; he'll be retiring soon. I've a daughter, Cath. She lives around the corner with my son-in-law and granddaughter, Holly. She's going to university in September. She wants to be a historian; she'd be good at it, too."

He smiles at that.

"An academic," he says.

"She's very bright but not at all precocious," says Mary, faster. "She even won a competition for her essay on Etruscan art, of all things. And only seventeen. You'd like her, I think. And you'd like Jerry. He's . . . he's Jerry."

She stops. She has betrayed herself. How would she know who or what a stranger would like? She knows him nowhere but in her head. She has never known him.

"I'm not here about me," she says briskly.

"You're right, this isn't about pleasantries. But I'm interested. Are you well? And in good health?"

She stops, stunned. She could just say it: I have breast cancer. She has an unnerving urge to tell him and then lean on him, this old and withered almost-stranger.

"I'm fine," she says instead, in a clipped way. "As I said, I'm not here to talk about me. I'm here because—"

"I've thought a lot about you over the years," he cuts in.

"I'm here about Nigel Forbes."

There, his name sits between them in the room. It leaves no space for her to think about what he has just said. *I've thought a lot about you.*

"He was interviewed in one of the newspapers a couple of days ago," she continues. "You might have seen it—it's all over the other papers now."

John's expression doesn't change, as though the words *newspaper* and *Nigel Forbes* mean nothing to him. He looks so calm, she is stabbed with envy.

"He wants to clear his name," she says a little harder.

Gallagher does a long blink as if rebooting his brain, and his eyes fix on something over her shoulder. She glances back, but there is only the half-open door and a white wall.

"You do remember it all?" she says.

"Of course," he says in the gruff voice that he used on the nurse. He blinks again and shakes his head slightly. "I'm sorry, I find myself doing that. It's being shut up here."

She looks hard at him. They are so close, she could brush against his wrist if she dared. She doesn't; she doesn't want to, either. Instead, she is pricked with new anger.

"I never forgot him . . . ," she trails off.

He still doesn't reply. *You have blood on your hands, too,* she wants to remind him.

"I'd been so convinced that I did the right thing, but now I don't know. I wanted to hear what you thought . . . That's all. That's why I'm here."

His eyes glaze over. She wonders whether he is having a funny turn, but he nods slowly.

"You did receive the letter I sent you all those years ago?" she presses. "Where I suggested we go to the police?"

He doesn't respond. Don't you feel any guilt? She thinks it, but finds herself saying it aloud, too.

"I do, on occasion," says Gallagher slowly.

"On occasion?" she says in a high-pitched voice that sounds nothing like her own.

"But you're not here about Forbes, not really. You want to know why I left you."

"How can you just lie there like that?" she bursts out. "How did you let yourself off the hook? He was locked up for twenty years, and neither of us helped him. I tried to at the time, just after he was convicted, but—that's not the point. I should have done more. You should have done something, too."

"It's in the past now," he whispers, as though it is difficult to even speak. "There are so many more important things I'd like to ask you about yourself, but, now you're here, it's taking me some time to put my thoughts in order. If you'd just give me a minute to—"

"In the past? You think it's in the past for him, too?"

"You don't want to dredge it up. It's for the best."

"The best for who? What about the best for Nigel Forbes?"

Or the best for me? She won't say that, though.

"I saw the article," says Gallagher quietly. "It was a relief—"

"A relief," she cries in that new voice of hers.

"I never forgot him, either, but—" He stops. "Look, it was hard for me, too, but let's not talk about that now."

"Hard? HARD?"

She bites her lip to stop herself, but what she wants to say is: Do you know how hard it is to live with guilt that is so physically heavy, you'd rather a pile of bricks crushing down on you? Do you know how hard it is to raise a child and cling onto a husband in that state, but never risk telling them, in case you're left with no one again? Or how hard it is, that moment you're at a birthday dinner or an anniversary supper, when it strikes you that you don't deserve these little freedoms because you stole them from someone else? So you find yourself lying in a locked toilet stall at a restaurant because the guilt becomes so unbearable, you can't stand upright anymore. And even when you finally convince yourself, once again, that you did the right thing, and saved the right man, it only gets easier because you harden yourself to it—and to everything else—a little bit more each year.

He still looks calm.

"Say something!"

"I'm sorry," he says. "But this isn't about him, even if you think it is. It's about you and me, and I can explain—"

"That's all? You're sorry?" she interrupts before he can say what he means by the rest.

"I'm sorry about your mother's death. I'm sorry you were locked up in that place, Middlebury. You didn't deserve any of that. I felt very strongly for you, Betty. I mean, Mary." He winces. "If you'd just let me find the words—I get so confused by things these days. I—"

"But you're not sorry you left me there? Or that you didn't come back for me, even after I wrote you that letter?"

Gallagher opens his lips. He moves them, as though speaking, but nothing comes out. He shakes his head, frowning.

"I loved you," she cries, her throat hoarse and the words taut. "Maybe I was just one of hundreds of girls you charmed and tricked, but my feelings for you were real, even though I was terribly young. And I lived with the real consequences of what we did. I didn't tell anyone about Paxon, even though I should have, because I really loved you—I wanted to protect you. Maybe that was deluded, but for so many years, I'd have done anything for you . . . I waited for you!" She swallows. "I waited for you for so long, even after I met . . ."

She stops. She won't bring Jerry into this room again. It is a betrayal.

"Betty, I—"

"No, let me finish! I ruined a man's life for you. I waited for you for years. Even when I was married, I was waiting. And I only stopped waiting when that poor, poor man was released from prison, because I knew then it was over. But even then, I believed I'd done right in choosing you, I believed that there was a good, genuine, sad reason you never came back for me. But there wasn't, was there? Did you have no empathy, no sense of proportion at just how huge it all was? Were you so self-obsessed that you didn't feel a shred of pity or guilt or remorse?"

She stops. She runs very cold.

"Wait," she says. "You said Middlebury. How did you know I was sent there?"

"I didn't."

"You did. You said it, a moment ago."

"You just told me."

"No, I didn't mention it once. I never say that word."

He breathes out slowly and turns his head away from her for the first time since she arrived.

"You knew I was locked up in that place and you still did nothing?"

He doesn't answer. She looks away, too, and stares out the window as she tries to piece it together. A chain of seagulls flies past and, below, a red postman's van threads along an empty road. A car alarm pierces the morning. It screeches on and on.

"Yes," he says eventually, barely audible. "I knew you were there. I honestly believed it would be a fresh start for you."

"A fresh start? You thought that place was a fresh start?" she cries. "I had your child. On a train. It was dead, I had a miscarriage—" She squeezes closed her eyes as she says it. "I was a child myself and I went through that on my own. When I tried to tell the doctors, they told me I was delusional. Delusional! Of course they did, the whole story was so disgustingly unbelievable, I actually started wondering whether they were right and if it was all just in my head—you and me, Paxon, poor Forbes, the baby or whatever it was. But you knew it was true and you knew I was there, and still you did nothing at all to help me."

She stops. She is panting. He doesn't look at her.

"Yes," he says quietly.

"Is that all? Can't you even manage a sentence?"

He sighs.

"Yes, I knew it all. They sent my father your files—I told him. I knew everything."

Mary flops into the armchair. She is tired, too tired to stand. *If only he knew I was here, he would come for me.* That thought had kept her upright through those years at Middlebury. She had even thought about writing to him again for help. She had planned to slot the letter into a bottle and send it out to sea because they wouldn't let her post anything unless it was vetted first. If she wrote his newspaper office address inside the bottle, too, it would be forwarded on and reach him eventually. He would rescue her.

She had put it off, though; she kept putting it off because what if she had sent it and he hadn't come for her a second time?

"The truth is," she says quietly, "you're a coward."

The word hangs in the air. The letters thicken and expand and grow between them. He nods.

"Yes," he says, still without meeting her eye. "I left you because I was a coward."

X

SHE SHOULD FEEL LIGHTER, but she doesn't. Isn't an explanation all she has ever wanted from him? She is gathering the energy to pull herself to her feet and leave when the light changes. A cloud shifts, or the earth moves, and a plank of sunlight slices the room in half. It hits the wall on the far side and fractures, creeping up the wallpaper at a peculiar angle. Everything else in the room looks strangely angular, too: the sharp oblong of the headboard, the rectangular wheelie tray, the cubed bedside cupboards, the blunt creases on his sheets. She stares and stares, until the room becomes a series of angular lines and planes and it hits her.

"Wait. You couldn't have been a coward if you did that war reporting job," she says. "You hated the thought of war."

He scans the ceiling and interlaces his long bony fingers.

"And how could you have known I'd been taken to Middlebury unless someone told you?" She swallows a little gasp. "You must have gone back to St. Steele after they'd locked me up. That's how you knew that my mother had died and where I was. That's how you got them to send my medical records, isn't it?"

His jaw tightens and he stutters over his words. "I—I didn't . . . I was a coward. Leave it, now."

He rolls onto his side, so she can't see his face, just the narrow rhombus of his back. His shoulders shake through the blankets.

"You should leave," he mutters. "Go home to your family."

"Leave?"

John reaches up an arm. She thinks he is about to touch her, and she freezes, every muscle tenses, but he stretches beyond her and pulls a long red cord that hangs from the ceiling.

"What are you doing? Why did you do that?"

His lips open, his fists ball up, and his head shakes from side to side as though his two inward selves are wrestling.

"But you came back to St. Steele for me after I'd gone?"

"An article," he manages. "I just went back to write another article."

"You didn't. You'd already left your job."

"He's free. It's over. Go home now."

"But why did you leave me there? What did I do wrong?" She sounds like a child, but she doesn't care anymore. "You said you'd explain."

The nurse's footsteps are back; they turn up the next set of stairs. Mary crouches so she is level with him, so she can feel his warm, stale breath on her cheek and see the film of age cover his eyes. He opens his lips and mouths something. He tries again, but then the door opens. Mary doesn't move.

"How are we doing, Mr. Gallagher?" says the nurse brightly. Mary watches him, but his eyes are locked away from her.

"I just want to know why," she murmurs.

"Mr. Gallagher needs some rest," says the nurse.

"She was just a silly naive schoolgirl, wasn't she?" she continues, not caring what the nurse thinks of her anymore.

"Perhaps it's best you wait outside. Mr. Gallagher's getting distressed," says the nurse.

"And he was just a selfish man who should have known better. It meant nothing to him, did it? He had hundreds of girls like her, didn't he? I know I'm right . . . I need to know."

"It's best you leave," says the nurse sternly, just as another nurse and a doctor hurry in.

"Just tell me!"

A blue skirt and a pair of stocking-covered legs squeeze between her and the bed so she can't see him at all anymore. She cranes around for a glimpse of his face, but they crowd him. Their voices tangle up.

"Say it, just so it's final. I meant nothing to you, didn't I?"

Someone is clamping her shoulders and helping her to her feet. They steer her out of the room and down the stairs.

X

AN HOUR PASSES, AND John slips in and out of consciousness. When he wakes next, he is locked to the bed with a needle threaded into his arm, connected to lots of clear tubes. A different nurse is hovering in the doorway. He doesn't look at her. Thursday, he recalls. Simon is in Geneva.

"Are you awake?" says the nurse in a hushed voice.

Toes still flex. Knuckles still bend.

"You're a popular man today," she continues. "You've another visitor. Can I send him in?"

Another visitor? He frowns. He hasn't received a visitor today.

"I'm not expecting anyone. Simon's in Geneva."

That moment, it floods back and he is overwhelmed with nausea; she really was here. His Betty. He had wanted to tell her. The explanation was on his tongue. The words were lined up. Then the fog came.

"Yes, Simon is in Geneva," confirms the nurse. "But this gentleman was very insistent."

"What's his name?"

"He wouldn't give it," she says just as the door pushes open.

A tall figure with coils of sandy-gray hair strides in before the nurse can stop him. In his left fist is a golf-ball-shaped key ring sprayed gold. His other hand is hidden inside the pocket of his blazer. His frown is thick and low, his eyes are bright blue, almost turquoise, and his jaw is clenched so tightly that two knobs of bone stick out.

"So you're John," he says as though he has just tasted something bitter.

19

Betty charges at Mr. Paxon headfirst. Mrs. Eden tries to catch her wrist, but Betty is too quick. She is just about to reach him, and thwack him over the head with her fist because she hasn't a harder weapon, when someone pulls her backward. She lunges away from them and raises her fist again, ready to crash it down on his head. It collides with something. There are gasps and tuts, and she realizes that she hit Mr. Eden instead.

"Him," she shrieks, finding her voice. "Someone get him!"

Still no one moves. Mr. Eden catches her arm and pulls her out of the big room, while she tries to struggle away. Joan follows them into the hall and closes the door.

"It was him. He was with Miss Hollinghurst. You have to get him."

"What's she talking about?" says Joan.

"Let's all calm down," says Mr. Eden.

"Fetch Inspector Napier!"

The big room door swings open again, and Mrs. Eden appears.

"The girl's mad," she hisses. "Do something with her, Tancred." Then turning to him, him, very him through the open doorway, Mrs. Eden says: "I'm so sorry about this, Mr. Paxon. She's been acting strangely since her mother passed away: harming herself and screaming and behaving quite like an animal. Do you know that she kissed Tancred at the funeral, actually kissed him? Now accusing you of goodness knows what. I really am sorry."

"No harm done," says Mr. Paxon in a quiet voice, still looking into his teacup.

"But it was him," cries Betty from the hallway.

Mrs. Eden tuts loudly. Joan lowers her eyes.

"Just look at him," yells Betty. "He even looks guilty. Why won't anyone believe me?"

"I am sorry. Now, can I top up anyone's tea?" soothes Mrs. Eden. She turns to Mr. Eden and hisses under her breath, "For Pete's sake, Tancred, be a man for once and sort this out. She can't stay here. Not after this."

The door to the big room is wrenched shut, and Betty can't see Mr. Paxon anymore. Mr. Eden lets go of her, and Joan rubs her temples.

"Your mother died in her sleep. It was an accident," pleads Mr. Eden.

"I don't mean Mother; I mean Miss Hollinghurst. He killed all the girls. Someone needs to tell the judge and stop Mr. Forbes's trial."

"Stop this," snaps Mr. Eden. It is the first time she has seen him angry. "Go and lie down, Betty."

"I'm telling the truth. I would have told you sooner but—I can't tell you everything or someone else will be hurt—I have to protect him—But it's true that Mr. Forbes didn't hurt anyone and that it was Mr. Paxon all along—Get him before he hurts someone else!"

"If you don't calm down, she'll call the doctor," says Mr. Eden sharply. "You won't want that and I certainly don't, either, so let's stay calm."

"Please!"

"There's nothing to worry about anymore," tries Joan. "Mr. Forbes was found guilty and he's being sentenced this week."

"Guilty? But you're not listening. It wasn't Mr. Forbes; it was Mr. Paxon."

The door to the big room opens again, and Mrs. Eden elbows her way back into the hall.

"I've heard enough of this," she seethes. "It's enough to raise the dead."

"Evelyn," warns Mr. Eden.

Mrs. Eden blushes momentarily, then her face hardens again.

"No, Tancred, you've indulged her for too long. She'll behave herself until this day is over, then she's not welcome here. We've done all we can."

"Come on, let's get you upstairs," says Joan, taking Betty's other arm.

"I'm not going up," screams Betty. "It's too dangerous."

"That's enough," snaps Joan.

"If I do, he'll kill you all."

"We need a doctor," says Mrs. Eden. "She's hysterical."

"It was him. Mr. Gallagher knows."

"What Mr. Gallagher?" says Joan.

"Let me take her," interrupts Mr. Eden softly.

Joan helps him usher her upstairs to one of the spare bedrooms. Betty stops struggling and lets it all settle in her mind. It hadn't occurred to her that they wouldn't believe her. A hundred questions, perhaps, but never disbelief.

Joan makes up the bed with fresh sheets while Mr. Eden mans the door. Betty holds her head in her hands and drags herself around the room in circles, piecing together what to do. She could tell them where to find Mr. Gallagher; he would explain it to them better than her, but her head is cluttered and she mustn't risk breaking her promise. Hang, hang, hang, says the voice. If she loses him, too, she will have no one.

"There'll be more," she whimpers, "if no one stops him."

She says it over and over, but Joan and Mr. Eden stop answering.

"I saw him with Miss Hollinghurst. They were kissing, and then he killed her."

"Hush now," says Joan, but she looks at Mr. Eden with wide eyes.

Downstairs, a door bangs open. It sounds as though lots of people are leaving the hotel at once.

"I really saw him," she says, turning to Mr. Eden. "He was near the pond. He was kissing her, and it was definitely him. It was even his hat. He'll get away if we don't stop him."

She crouches and cradles her knees. Her teeth chatter; she is freezing again. There is a knock at the bedroom door. Betty screams. Joan wraps a stiff arm around her.

"It's me," snaps Mrs. Eden through the closed door.

Betty stops screaming, but Joan doesn't stop hugging. Mr. Eden steps out onto the landing. Betty strains to listen.

"Everything revolves around that little madam, I suppose," Mrs. Eden is saying to him. "Just like her mother."

"For pity's sake, Evelyn. Dolores has only just died," says Mr. Eden. "And don't we all know it?"

She says something in a quieter voice that Betty can't make out, then she clicks away. Mr. Eden comes back into the room with a cup in his hand.

"Has Mr. Paxon gone?" says Betty.

"You have to stop this," he says.

"I'm not lying. I know he did it. Ask me anything. I'll tell you; I'll explain as much as I can. But I just don't want Mr. Gallagher harmed. Promise me Mr. Gallagher won't be locked up. He doesn't deserve to hang; not when all he did was love me and do as I asked. It was my fault, you see. He—"

"Hush now, we'll talk about it tomorrow," says Mr. Eden.

His voice is so soothing, she wonders for a moment whether Mrs. Eden is right. Maybe she is just hysterical. What if she didn't see them at all? It could have been any man wearing that sort of hat.

"Here, drink this," he says, handing her a cup of something cloudy. She realizes that she is thirsty and gulps it fast. Only when she has finished does she register that it tasted chalky and unfamiliar.

"What was it?"

"It'll do you some good," says Mr. Eden.

"He didn't pour it, did he?"

"Just something to calm your nerves."

She jumps to her feet and spits onto the carpet to clear the dregs from her mouth.

"You're all in on it," she screams. "You're all his accomplices."

"Stop this," cries Joan.

"It's poison. You're trying to kill me next."

She tries to lunge at the door, but Mr. Eden blocks it. Joan stands in front of the window with her arms folded across her chest. The bedroom goes gray. Everything spins. Betty flops onto the bed. The last thing she hears before she slides unconscious is Joan.

"I can't take her on, Tanc. Dolores was a friend, but this is something else. I'm sorry. I just can't."

X

THE BEDROOM IS EMPTY when she wakes. The curtains are drawn, and the light that seeps through them is hard and yellow. She pats her arms to be certain that no one has killed her, that she really is alive, and she steps out of bed, avoiding the creaky floorboard.

The hotel is silent. She creeps out onto the landing. The bedroom doors are all shut and she isn't certain what to do next. Maybe she should escape, but where? Who would help her? Doesn't she need to make sure first that they all believe Mr. Paxon really is the murderer? What if someone else is killed by him? Perhaps they already have been.

They could be in the big room, a domino run of dead bodies, all spotted with blood. It would be her fault. But she hears a clatter in the kitchen, so someone must be alive.

Betty tiptoes onto the top stair and pauses to listen. As she waits, she catches sight of the mirror on the wall, cocked at an angle. She looks into the glass and sees Mother. Mother!

Mother looks exactly as she does on one of her black snowman days, only her hair is longer and browner. The sacks under her eyes are purple, and her whole frame quivers. Betty bites her lip. Black Snowman Mother bites her lip, too, and Betty sees that it isn't Mother at all.

That second, the front door crashes open. Betty grabs the mirror from the hook and holds it in front of her as a shield. Downstairs Mrs. Eden charges into the hall with a younger man wearing a white uniform. Betty doesn't recognize him.

"Tancred," calls Mrs. Eden.

Mr. Eden steps out of the big room.

"Shh, she's still asleep upstairs," he whispers.

Betty watches them from the top stair. They stand in a triangle in the hall. None of them seems to know what to say next.

"This is Julian; he's a guard there," says Mrs. Eden eventually.

Mr. Eden shakes his head. "I thought we were going to talk about this, Evelyn."

"We can't manage her. We've three hotels to run and a new manager to recruit."

"But we were going to discuss it, not just pack her off."

"We've done our bit. She's not family, and this isn't a stable home for a girl in her condition. Even Julian agrees."

Mrs. Eden nods at the white-uniformed man. He nods back. Betty forces herself not to cry. He lied. He said this was her home, and now he is sending her away. She is about to remind him of that, but the front door opens again and a fourth person appears. Betty's eyes are too blurry to make out who it is.

"Is she here?" says the figure.

"Not now," says Mr. Eden.

"My father's in pieces because of her."

He has George's whinnying voice. She looks again. He has George's stance, too.

"Get him out of here," she shrieks from the top of the stairs.

They all look up at her, stunned.

"Stay away from me," she shouts at him.

She raises the mirror above her head.

"Be careful, Betty. Don't fall," calls Mr. Eden.

"I told you," says Mrs. Eden. "She's unstable."

"Get him away from me. Lock the door."

George steps forward.

"Mr. Eden, please," wails Betty. "Don't let him near me. His father's sent him after me."

"Do you know what you've done, you mad bitch?" cries George, his face taut with anger. She has never seen his face like that before. "My father's all over the place. You can't shout lies like that. They ruin people."

"Wait outside," says Mr. Eden.

"Get him away," screams Betty, the mirror still raised.

"If this is some twisted way of getting your own back because Mary and I are happy," continues George.

"You, get out," barks Mr. Eden at George.

"You'll apologize to him for your vicious lies," says George. "You'll do it in front of the whole village. God help you if you don't."

Wind blows open the front door, and Betty sees that a small crowd has gathered in the street. She can't make them out because Mr. Eden steps forward and positions himself on the bottom stair.

"Come on now, Betty boo," he soothes.

"Stop calling me that."

"Put that mirror back on the wall, and let's sort this out."

"Only if he leaves."

Mr. Eden glares at George. He backs out of the hall, but he waits on the doorstep, still looking furious.

"There's a nice lady nurse in a car outside," Mr. Eden is saying. "She's going to look after you. And so will this nice man, Julian."

The guard scowls. He doesn't look nice.

"After a few days, you'll feel right as a kite again, and then we can work something out," continues Mr. Eden.

"Tancred, don't make promises you can't keep."

"Why won't anyone believe me?" sobs Betty, clutching the mirror to her chest. "I'm telling the truth. Mr. Paxon killed Miss Hollinghurst. He probably killed all of them."

"Make her shut up," shouts George from the doorstep.

Mr. Eden looks at Mrs. Eden. Betty sobs harder. A string of saliva yoyos from her bottom lip.

"I had a long talk with Inspector Napier last night," Mr. Eden calls up the stairs, looking Betty in the eye. "I want you to know that I listened to everything you said."

"So you believe me?"

"Betty, Inspector Napier confirmed that Mr. Forbes's fingerprints are on the knives. They're his knives from his shop, and one of them was certainly used to kill Maureen, just like the judge said. He probably killed the others, too. Do you understand?"

"But it was Mr. Paxon. I saw him myself."

"No, Betty, it was Mr. Forbes. There's not a shred of proof that Mr. Paxon would want to harm anyone. He's a good man with a good life, whereas Mr. Forbes is very troubled. He and Maureen had a love affair, and it's quite possible that he was infatuated with the other girls, too, God bless their souls."

"What about the nights they died? Where was Mr. Paxon? That'll be the proof."

"Betty, he was with Inspector Napier himself when Maureen was killed. Do you see that it's simply not possible? Now the best thing for us to do is—"

"Maybe the inspector's in on it, too. He and Mr. Paxon are good friends, aren't they? Or what if Mr. Paxon threatened him?"

"That's enough, Betty."

"I saw him by the pond with Miss Hollinghurst. It's in the pond, too."

"What is?"

"The giblet. I had a baby, and it's in the pond. I can tell you everything, if you like. As long as you promise that Mr. Gallagher won't get into trouble."

"Who's Mr. Gallagher? What are you talking about? Come on, now. Put down the mirror and come downstairs."

"But I saw Mr. Paxon in the clearing with Miss Hollinghurst."

"As clearly as you see me now?" says Mr. Eden with a sigh.

"Not exactly." She pauses. "But it was his hat. It was him. I even went to London to put it right."

"She's talking us in circles," says Mrs. Eden.

"Maybe she's upset about him and that Mary girl he mentioned," says the guard, Julian, nodding at George, and everyone looks surprised to hear him speak.

Mrs. Eden gives a dismissive wave of her head.

"Sir, you believe me, don't you?" sobs Betty to Mr. Eden, swallowing a thick glob of phlegm and staring straight at him, ignoring the others. "I don't lie. Not when it's important like this."

"I don't think you're lying, but maybe you're a little bit confused after the shock of your mother passing away."

Mother! The mirror slips from her grasp. Mr. Eden jumps back as it falls to the bottom of the stairs and smashes into lots of tiny mirrors.

"Do something! She attacked you, Tancred," shrieks Mrs. Eden.

Mr. Eden looks between her and the small crowd outside. Betty wavers on the top stair. I didn't mean to, she wants to say, but everything is moving too quickly. Her toes curl over the edge of the step. Maybe she could jump down and swoop out the door, up into the sky, and all the way to the clearing again. If Gallagher isn't there, she could fly back to London or across the channel to his father's house in France. He will make everything slot back into place. She raises her arms and is about to dive.

"No," shouts Mr. Eden.

He rushes up the staircase, the guard just behind him. He clamps her waist, and the guard holds her legs, his fingers gouging into her. She is still sobbing.

"Paxon's dangerous. Stop him," cries Betty.

"Sedate her," calls Mrs. Eden.

"It's best we get her on the road," says the guard. "It's a long drive."

They haul her outside to a long black car; there is something familiar about it. A lady dressed as a nurse sits on the back seat. When she sees them, she slides across to make room for Betty. She doesn't smile.

"The car," cries Betty. "It was Mr. Paxon's car! I was leaving the pictures and it slowed down—it was coming from Spoole the same night the girl, Elsa, was killed there. It was big and black and wide. Surely that proves it."

The guard pushes Betty toward the open car door. She cranes her head to check that Mr. Eden heard her, but she spots Mr. Paxon in the crowd, his face gray and bloodless and staring straight at her. She propels herself toward him, but the guard has her tight.

"You," she shrieks. "Admit it! ADMIT IT."

She spits at him but misses. It hits the pavement, and Mr. Paxon doesn't move. He hovers in the air, his feet not quite touching the ground. She blinks and he disappears, or perhaps he was never there at all. Betty wipes spit from her mouth.

"She's feral," calls a voice she doesn't recognize.

Everyone in the crowd grows fangs. The gutter runs with blood. Betty weeps blood, too, but when she rubs it away and looks at her hands, the liquid is clear.

"There," she shouts, pointing.

She can see him properly now. He stands at the back of the crowd, half-hidden by his fedora. It is the same fedora he wore the afternoon he killed Miss Hollinghurst. He must be wearing it to taunt her. She makes one last weak lunge, but the guard still grips onto her arms. He drags her to the car, pushes down her head, and forces her onto the back seat.

The nurse examines her fingernails and says nothing. She has a single long eyebrow that cuts across her face, and she smells of talcum powder. The guard slams the car door. Mrs. Eden eyeballs her through the window and threads her arm through the crook of Mr. Eden's elbow. He shrugs her away and looks at Betty.

"Find Mr. Gallagher," shouts Betty through the glass. "He'll explain. It's all true."

The guard revs the engine.

"You'll help, won't you? You'll find him," she continues.

Mr. Eden looks at her with a sad expression. She reads his reply from his lips.

"I'm sorry Betty boo. It's for the best."

"Don't call me that," she shrieks.

Mr. Eden turns away and strides back into the hotel with his head hung.

"Don't call me that," she screams again. "No one must ever call me that. Only Mother. I'll never answer to it again."

Her long howl rips through the air as the car threads along Newl Grove. Minutes later, St. Steele is a smudge out of the back window.

x

THEY ARRIVE FORTY MINUTES later. The building is red bricked with castle turrets and a fence of barbed wire wrapped around it like arms. The black sign outside has faded. Once, the words read: Middlebury Pauper Lunatic Asylum.

20

Fifty years later

Engines snarl, tracks hiss, and the belly of the train slants sideways, slicing off the sky and drawing the fields closer through the windows. Mary holds on to the plastic tabletop to steady herself. Someone in the next row is munching cheese puffs. They smell rancid. She tries to block out the stench; to keep her balance; and to fill the blank page on the table in front of her with words, then sentences, then a whole letter, but the chewing gets louder.

The train lurches and her sickness rises. Mary pulls herself to her feet, gathers her bag and coat, and struggles along the aisle, slamming into chair ends and people's shoulders until she reaches the toilet. There is no handle, and it takes her a minute to spot the flashing button that opens the sliding door. It smells of chemicals and urine inside, no better than the cheese, but at least she is alone.

She navigates the door shut and locked, turns down the toilet seat with a square of toilet paper, and unfolds the letter again. She takes a deep breath before she continues writing; so far she has only managed three words.

Dear Mr. Forbes

Deciding to write to him had been easy; there had been a succession of much harder decisions before that. First, leaving behind John Gallagher and choosing where to go next. Her feet had dragged her back to the station. She was surprised that the wrens still whistled and the sun still shivered, for it must have been midday, then she had checked her watch and it was still before ten. Funny, she had thought, how so much can shift in such a thin wafer of time.

The train was already at the platform, and she had slipped on, just as the doors shut behind her. The next twenty-six minutes she had spent deciding what to do when she reached Clapham Junction Station. Her clothes were still stiff with shower gel, and she smelled vaguely mousy, so really she ought to have returned home, but how could she slot back in there when everything was still so incomplete?

When she arrived at Clapham Junction, she had checked the board: the train home to Richmond would leave in two minutes or the train to Reading in eight. Another swift connection from there would deliver her to St. Erth by teatime, a short taxi ride from St. Steele. The possibility had made her shiver, though she hadn't a clue how it would help if she went there.

The loudspeaker had bleated, and the announcer had shouted the final call for her Richmond train. She had lingered on the spot long after the ding of the closing doors, then dashed to the ticket machine, bought a single to St. Erth instead, and barreled up the steps just in time to make it. Her lungs had heaved and her hands shook, but she felt more awake than she had in months.

As the train slid away, she had forced herself not to pick through her morning or to think about John Gallagher at all. She had rooted around in her handbag for a mint and unearthed the newspaper that, days before, she had rolled up and hidden there to avoid looking at Nigel Forbes's eyes or face or words. She still hadn't read the interview properly, and she was about to unroll it when it hit her: she should write to

Nigel Forbes directly. She could explain everything and offer to help clear his name. He must still have a lawyer who would know how to go about it.

She had pulled out the blank, slightly creased sheet of paper that she carried in her diary for emergencies, and begun writing, but the words had clogged up after the first three.

Now, in the darkness of the toilet cubicle, her words unspool themselves. *You might remember that I was one of your neighbors in St. Steele,* she begins. *I lived at Hotel Eden with my late mother, Dolores Broadbent.* She stops. It sounds formal and vague, but she only has one piece of paper, and crossings-out would look worse.

For many years I followed what happened to you with . . . With what? Disgust? Concern? Guilty fascination? She leaves a gap, she can find a fitting phrase later. . . . *and like many others I was convinced of your innocence, not only because I knew you a little, but also because I believed I had seen the real killer.* It sounds so blunt that she almost wants to laugh. I saw the real killer? It's something a teenage character in an adventure novel might write. She recognizes that phrase from somewhere else, only she can't remember where.

> *Shortly before she was killed, I saw Patricia Hollinghurst in the*
> *woods with a man. I have always believed that man was our*
> *neighbor George Paxon. I'm sure you remember him—he owned*
> *the biscuit factory and I read that he died around the time of your*
> *trial. I believe he was having an affair with Miss Hollinghurst,*
> *which soured and led him to kill her, and, for some reason, the*
> *other girls before her.*

Yes, she has definitely felt the rhythm of these lines before. In fact, she is certain that she has written them, too. Her throat seals over as she remembers that this is just as she described it all to Gallagher in the letter she wrote to him all those years ago. It had been clinical and factual then, too. She swallows with difficulty and plows on.

I do understand how incredibly strange this will sound to you, but every word is true. I never believed you'd be found guilty and, as soon as I found out you were, I told everyone what I saw and about George Paxon, but no one believed me. It was an incredibly difficult period, as my mother had recently passed away and there were certain people who believed that I was—

She stops. She can't write *mad* or *unstable*, or he might think she still is. *Unwell*, she finishes.

I was taken to hospital and when I was finally let out, I wasn't sure what I believed anymore. For three years, I told doctors and nurses and even other patients over and over that you were innocent and what I had seen, but they all told me I was deluded. It took me a long time to start trusting my memories again, and, at that point, I should have tried again to tell the police; I planned to, but backed out at the last minute. This sounds so weak in retrospect but, in all honesty, I had just given birth to my daughter, Cath, and I was terrified of them locking me back up.

I want you to know how deeply sorry I am. If I can provide a statement or help clear your name in some other way, please contact me or advise your lawyer to do so. I will do anything I can to help you.

I would also like to properly explain why I didn't tell anyone straightaway when I first saw George Paxon with Miss Hollinghurst. The reason was—

She stops. Nothing sounds sufficient. *I have breast cancer*, she writes instead on a new line.

I don't write that for sympathy. I just want you to know that whoever is up there is punishing me, finally. I deserve this.

It was easier than she expected, though she feels no better. She sets down her pen and picks up her bag. Her hands shaking, she pulls out the newspaper and carefully unrolls it, smoothing it on her lap. She should read it all, but his bruised eyes glare at her from the front page, and her stomach lurches.

She hides him away again and smacks the button to open the toilet door. It slides open too slowly, and she dives out into the train corridor. A young boy, no taller than her waist, looks quizzically at her. He steps into the toilet, and she is left alone in the space between the train carriages, unsure where to sit or how to finish the letter or how to muster the strength to read Mr. Forbes's interview in the newspaper.

"Always line your stomach before you attempt anything important."

Jerry's words pop into her mind. He said that to Cath before her school exams, before her driving test, even before she gave birth to Holly. Mary smiles sadly and wishes for the first time that he were here with her. Jerry would know what to do; he always knows. Yes, she wishes he were here desperately, but she switches off her phone before she can do anything about it because if she rang him this minute, everything would pour out. The words would gush until every scrap of her story was laid before Jerry: kind, loving Jerry. He would see who she really is. She would disgust him.

Mary finds herself in the buffet carriage. The sandwiches all contain mayonnaise, so she orders a hamburger, Jerry's favorite, and is handed a warm, damp bun with a flaccid round of pale meat lopping out. By the time she has finished eating, the sickness is quenched and she is ready to read it.

She skims the front-page article, still standing at the buffet counter and avoiding Forbes's mug-shot eyes, but she can't find any words from his own lips, so she opens the newspaper and leafs through, blotting the pages with greasy finger marks.

The first Cornish Cleaver spread is devoted to the history of the unsolved murders. The only comments are from people she doesn't recognize, who call themselves psychotherapists and criminologists and other long titles that were once all bundled into one. A crackly voice announces that the next stop is St. Erth, so she flips through the pages quickly until she finds the interview.

It spans four pages. There is only one new photograph of Forbes, a flat silhouette, but his face is blanketed with such a heavy shadow that she can't even see the contours of his features. She can tell that he is elderly, though, by the hunch of his shoulders. There is a second photograph, too; it is yellowed and fuzzy, but it is definitely him at roughly twenty-five years old. He stands outside his butcher's shop, scowling and wearing a blood-soaked apron and holding a shoulder of cow. She scans the words until she finds the first line that is wrapped with quotation marks. She reads it and almost drops the newspaper. Stunned, she reads it again, then again, and a third time because she never imagined that he would say that.

The conductor is announcing the next stop again and the train brakes are squealing. Mary skims through every quotation, ignoring the journalist's paragraphs of stuffing, as she tries to digest it all. Then she is off the train, her handbag bundled under one arm, the newspaper tucked under the other, not quite registering the hordes and not shielding herself from the rain. She replays the words over and over.

"From today I'm not battling to clear my name anymore," says Forbes. "I wish I could have proved to the world, and in particular to Maureen Cardy's family, that I was innocent but I'm

not angry or bitter the way I used to be. I'm just a tired old
man with little time ahead of me and, what time I do have left,
I want to enjoy with my family in peace."

It takes Mary a long time to leave St. Erth Station. She is still standing on the puddled platform long after the train has rolled on. The rain
has stopped, the other passengers have dispersed, and the lone taxi driver
at the far side of the car park has given up flashing his lights at her.

She shakes dry the newspaper and looks at it again. The words are
the same ones, still stuck down fast. How could she not have read it and
learned all of this when she first saw the headline at Star Newsagents?
How can he sound so forgiving and at ease? She rereads the final paragraphs to be sure that it is not her conscience tricking itself:

> "I've never spoken publicly about this before and I only did
> today for my family," says Forbes. "I wanted my version of
> events to be published so that if, after I've died, they ever find
> out who I used to be, they'll be able to read this story in my own
> words and know that I didn't lay a finger on Maureen Cardy
> or any one of those girls. Whoever killed them was wicked and
> deserved the severest of punishments, but that man wasn't me.
> Sadly he walked free.
>
> "I also want my family to know that, though these years
> have been unbearable at times and though I've often thought
> of taking my own life, I didn't because of them." He added:
> "They might know nothing about my past, but they were my
> salvation."
>
> *Payment for this interview has been donated to the PAI
> Foundation, a charity that supports people affected by impris-
> onment.

The taxi man is still waiting. Mary moves toward him on autopilot. She doesn't register that she is speaking or that the engine is starting or that they are speeding through the country lanes, past a strip of ocean, a herd of cows, over a hill and into St. Steele.

Her pleasantries feel scripted. She doles out the correct change, but she doesn't remember counting it. Then she is walking along a street littered with fudge wrappers and seagull mess and cold, damp vacationers who are scuttling back to their holiday homes as the clouds thicken and blacken. She passes a souvenir shop, the window filled with paper windmills and candy-striped buckets and spades, but she doesn't recognize any of it, not even the sign at the start of the cobbles that reads, Newl Grove.

She only jolts out of her trance when a small girl wearing a bulging nappy and a sandy vest slips on a cobble and howls. Blood pours from her left knee. A mother and father crouch around her, dabbing the knee with a tissue and plugging a green jelly sweet in her mouth. The cobbles are spotted red. Mary stares. The parents see her staring and frown in unison. They pick up the child and walk on, though she still cries. Mary looks at the blood on the cobblestones and at the now-shuttered bucket and spade shop. She presses her nose to the cool glass until it fogs over with her breath. Mother would hate all of those garish colors, that's all she can think. Mother.

She threads her way deeper into Newl Grove, though it doesn't look like Newl Grove anymore. It is narrower; the houses are tinier. She slows as she catches up with the family who are laughing now and hoisting the girl with the cut knee onto her father's shoulders. Mary looks at the houses, so as not to stare, and on a blue front door she sees the number 22. She stops. Hotel Eden was number twenty-two.

She doesn't recognize the building, and it takes her a minute to click that the hotel has been severed into two houses. The house to the right says "22B" above a tarnished brass doorknocker, but the one to the left has a wide blue door with a wooden sign hanging above it; it is the same shape as Hotel Eden's front door. Bumblebee Cottage, reads the sign. There is a tiny painting of a bee next to it. A tinny wind chime jangles somewhere within, and Mary is pimpled with goose bumps.

The curtains are creased and drawn, so she pushes a hand through the letter box and finds herself looking at someone else's carpet, the color of marmalade. She jumps back, ashamed, and hurries along the street, not planning where she is going. Someone is calling her name, but she ignores it; her imagination is playing with her again.

Minutes later, she finds herself sitting on the grass, a pond in front of her, her back pressed against a willow tree. She tries to block out the abandoned excavators and the carcass of a half-built holiday complex that she can just make out through the trees. She tries harder to picture it all as it once was, but it has shrunk and withered, even the pond.

When she clenches her jaw and dares to imagine a fifteen-year-old girl and a man lying here, the image in her mind looks exposed and grubby. Cheap, somehow. She tries to picture the girl tossing a paper bag into the water and she tries to imagine the contents of that paper bag, but it is too difficult to grasp onto, though not in a remorseful way. It is simply disconnected from her own life, as though she is visualizing someone else's history.

She realizes with surprise that the hard ball isn't sitting in her stomach anymore. No one is crushing down on her shoulders, either, and his voice isn't whispering into her ear; it hasn't been for some time. Since the taxi ride perhaps, or since she stood on that puddled station car park and read his words.

She feels inside her handbag for the newspaper that will surely jolt her back to remorse and secret longing—the new normality that is her life now—but it isn't there. Nor is her letter to Forbes. Maybe she left them in the taxi or dropped them in a puddle. Oddly, it doesn't matter anymore.

She is glad to be pressed up against the willow trunk with her bottom on the firm earth, for suddenly she is rootless. So rootless, she has a strange urge to grasp fistfuls of grass, just to keep herself earthed.

Seconds pass. There is a crunch and a pant. Someone is calling a name. It is her name, she realizes. She is Mary Sugden now. The light has almost faded, but she squints and sees him between the arched branches of two trees, striding toward her. She takes him in: the wide kind pools of his blue eyes, his curls of hair, all tangled and tawny and flecked silver, the familiar creases on his face that she could trace with her eyes closed. He is wearing his boyish blue blazer and a sheepish half grin that makes her grin, too. She wants to kiss him. Has she ever wanted to do that so urgently before? He is clutching a bunch of keys and the gold golf-ball key ring that Holly bought him. It jingles louder as he walks closer, closer. She is incredibly light, almost weightless. She jumps to her feet to greet him, a smile eating up her face.

"I've found you," says Jerry with such relief that she clasps his hand.

It is cold and papery. He looks surprised, but pleased, too. She never holds his hand; she hardly touches him at all.

"Thank you," she blurts out.

His eyes are baffled, but his lips are still curved in that thin, pleased smile of his. She clutches his hand tighter. She should explain where she has been and ask how he found her, but her eyes are prickling in an unfamiliar way. Her cheeks twitch. Jerry's face blurs out of focus. Then she cries; she really cries.

21

"George Paxon," he calls again. "Come out here and face me."

John Gallagher steams along the corridor, squinting through the windows. The offices are all dark but for the last one with a dim yellow light inside. A figure is moving around a desk. He is stooped over. His body shudders as he half carries, half drags a bulky object to the center of the room. Gallagher takes a sharp breath inward and flings open the door.

Paxon is on his feet holding a black chair with metal legs. His face is white, and he is slighter than Gallagher remembers. His hair has thinned and grayed, his flannel suit hangs off him, and his brown tie is loose around his neck. It takes him a few seconds to register Gallagher.

"What are you doing? This is private property," he tries to shout, but his voice is raspy.

"What have you done to her?" growls Gallagher.

"Done to who?"

Gallagher's eyes edge around the room, but there is no sign of Betty.

"What are you talking about?" cries Paxon, pushing the chair between them. "And what do you think you're doing in my factory without my permission, today of all days?"

"Where's Betty?"

"You're that reporter, aren't you?"

"I asked you where she is."

"Is this how you bully stories out of people?"

Gallagher stops. "What do you mean, today of all days?"

"Just leave."

Gallagher kicks the chair out of the way and lunges.

"You'll tell me where she is, or I'll snap your neck right now." He grasps Paxon's collar. His neck is surprisingly skeletal. "Murderer!"

"You've got it all wrong," splutters Paxon between coughs.

"Where're Betty and her mother?"

Paxon strains for breath.

"Answer me," he booms, but his grip slackens slightly.

"Dead," croaks Paxon. "Dolores choked."

Gallagher swells with rage. He squeezes Paxon's neck again; so hard, he can feel the bones against his fingers.

"You killed her."

"Me? It wasn't me. It was an accident," squeaks Paxon, his face purple.

"And Betty?"

"She's gone."

"Gone where?"

"Hospital."

"If you laid a finger—"

"A lunatic hospital. She was mad, shouting nonsense. She needed help."

Stunned, Gallagher lets go and Paxon flops into a heap on the concrete. He lets the words settle: she needed help.

"I didn't hurt anyone, I swear," says Paxon.

He smells of liquor, and the whites of his eyes are watery and drooping, like soft wet strawberries. Gallagher glares at him.

"You're going to come clean."

"It wasn't me; I swear on my son's life," cries Paxon, trying to pull himself to his feet. He collapses but tries again. "Please, just let me show you. I can prove it."

He reaches for the desk drawer, but Gallagher swats away his hand. He doesn't fight back.

"You must think I'm a fool," says Gallagher, opening the drawer himself. "What's in here? Another knife? A pistol?"

He looks inside, but there is only a pile of blank papers, a mound of rubber bands, and a packet of new envelopes. A handwritten letter sits on top of them.

"That top letter," says Paxon in a tiny voice, his eyes closed and his head tipped up to the ceiling as though he is silently praying.

Gallagher keeps his hand on Paxon's wrist for a minute longer, then pulls out the letter. The envelope is smudged with greasy finger marks, and the single sheet of paper inside is folded into a tiny square. It says: I'm sorry. I'm sorry. I'm sorry.

I'm sorry. I'm sorry. I'm sorry.

Slowly, nervously, almost not wanting to know what it says, he unfolds the next section.

I'm sorry but all I did was love you.

"What is this?" says Gallagher.

"She was probably drunk," replies Paxon.

Halfway down the page is a letter of sorts, scribbled on a slant. The writing is tangled and smudged.

My darling George, I don't understand why you reacted like that. It
was an act of love to pave the way for us. You'll see that one day.

"I don't understand," says Gallagher, looking up. "What's this supposed to be?"

Paxon trembles and drums his forehead with his knuckles, while
Gallagher reads on.

Don't you know how cruel it was to make me watch you with
them? It never ended—you sat in the same church pew as them, you
laughed outside the factory with them, you even flirted with them
in the shops when I was yards away from you. I'll tell you how cruel
it was, George. It was so cruel that I cut a line across my back with
the same knife I used. I did it to distract myself from the pain you
caused me, but I couldn't because yours was a hundred times worse.

It has taken some time but I forgive you now. Of course I know
that girls like those can be charming and wily, and that's your
weakness as a man. I've faith in you, though, the way Isaac had
faith in God. That's why I did it for you (for us), and now there's
nothing to prevent the four of us living happily together.

I have a little farm in mind in Bodmin. We need never speak
to, or even look at, any other human in the world again. We are
all we need. Once we're settled there, you'll see how selfless those
sacrifices were. Say the word, my darling, and we'll go.

D

Gallagher looks down. Paxon is in a heap on the concrete. He holds
a clump of his own gray hair in his right hand. Blood trickles down his
scalp, running to his ear and smearing his cheek.

"It's the memorial today," he snivels. "All of them mourning those poor girls—and her. Mourning her at the same time as them . . . after what she did. That twisted, vile, disgusting woman. Not even a woman, a she-devil."

"Dolores wrote that? Dolores Broadbent?"

Paxon nods slowly.

"She . . . Her?"

Paxon lowers his eyes, still nodding.

"You're lying," says Gallagher, but he looks again at the handwriting. He recognizes it from the supper menus at Hotel Eden.

"Leave me alone now."

"I'm not going anywhere until you tell me the full story. And where Betty is."

Paxon hugs his knees to his chest with his bony arms. His teeth chatter, and his forehead drops to his knees. More blood trickles out.

"It's called Middlebury. Just go."

"What's called Middlebury? I want answers."

"I loved her so, so much," he chokes.

"Who? Dolores?" says Gallagher, aghast.

"No, my Patty. Patricia Hollinghurst . . . I was going to leave my wife, my son, my factory, everything to be with her. And now she's gone."

Gallagher crouches. He speaks softly, the way he does when he must extract information from the newly bereaved for articles; he feels nothing for them either.

"I need to know everything, George. Now look at me."

He waits.

"Look at me," says Gallagher, firmer. Paxon obeys.

"Start from the beginning and tell me exactly what happened."

Paxon shudders.

"We got close in the spring, Dolores and I. It only lasted a few weeks. I don't know what came over me. I ended it, but she just . . . she hunted me."

"Hunted? Don't be ridiculous; she's a woman."

"She was ALWAYS there; waiting outside the factory with picnic lunches for us, saving a seat in church for me, even sitting in my car. Christ, I found her in a hedge in my back garden once. I should have been firm from the start, but she's so . . . Oh, my poor Patty."

"Slowly, come on."

"I broke it off with Dolores, but she threatened to tell my wife and son, so I had to . . . how do they put it?"

"Keep her sweet?"

"If you like." But he winces. "Then she got it into her head that the four of us—George and Betty, she and I—would all live together like some big happy bloody family." His head jerks up. "You're not going to write any of this in the paper, are you?"

Gallagher shakes his head, but he frowns, too. "So you led her on?" he says.

"Only because she wasn't right in the head. I didn't want to. I shouldn't have . . ."

Paxon rubs his bleeding scalp. His knuckles redden, and his hair clots in bloody clumps. Gallagher glares at him.

"I thought that if I took her out for little drives and night walks on the beach, that sort of thing, she'd forget her silly fantasies and leave me alone eventually. I hoped that she'd meet someone else," says Paxon. "It was easier to keep her close than have her stalk me. I told Patty about it. My marriage was over anyway. I was training George to take over the factory, and I'd have left my wife enough money to get by. I thought it was the most painless way. I just wanted to be happy with Patty. Is that so wrong?"

He swallows hard and focuses on something in the distance.

Gallagher glances around, but the factory is still empty.

"What?" he says, harder.

"She was by the pond looking for Betty. At least that's what she said."

"Dolores?"

"Yes, and she saw Patty and me together. I loved her so much. So, so bloody much. My wife's a decent woman, but Patty—"

"You loved her so much, you were seeing those other girls, too?"

"But I wasn't."

"It says so in that letter."

"Dolores was a lunatic. I didn't even know the girls she killed, except Maureen. I employed two of their fathers, and another was related to my flour supplier, apparently. I'd seen them, maybe chatted to them, but I didn't even remember their names. No, that was Dolores. She latched onto the idea that I was seeing all of them, and she wouldn't let it go . . . So when she saw me with Patty—"

"Surely you could have stopped her."

"But she appeared from nowhere. She was screaming and Patty was crying and Dolores was grabbing hold of me and trying to kiss me. I told her that I loved Patricia. I had no idea what she'd done to the others at that point."

Gallagher flops onto the floor beside him and sucks in his breath.

"She ran away screaming like a raving banshee when I said that," says Paxon. "Patty was so upset. I wanted to walk her home, but she just kept telling me to leave her there, that she wanted to be alone." He shakes his head. "When I left her, she was upset obviously, but she was alive, I swear. I thought we'd all gone our separate ways, but the next morning . . . They found Patty . . . I knew . . . And I saw Dolores . . . She carried on as though nothing had happened."

"Maybe it wasn't her. Maybe it was a coincidence."

"Because she's a woman?" he snorts. "I asked her outright in the end.

She was so tanked up, she started singing. Singing! Singing that she'd killed them all for me."

"You met her again, even though you knew?" sneers Gallagher.

"Yes. No. Yes . . . It wasn't like that. I told her I'd take her out for a drive, but I drove her to the police station at Spoole and told her that she had to confess. But she said that she'd tell everyone it was me—who would believe it was a woman? She promised that she'd rip apart my family and my business."

Gallagher looks disgusted.

"You were scared of her?"

"You don't understand; she was unhinged," cries Paxon. "I said to her, what about Nigel Forbes—he didn't deserve all of that—but she just laughed like a maniac. Do you know what she said?"

Gallagher runs cold.

"She told me that Nigel fell out of love with her, too. And this is what he got. She said he deserved his comeuppance. Then she said that I loved her really, and that I'd just forgotten it for a little while. She said she forgave me."

Gallagher runs his finger over the sharp corner of the letter. "Does your wife know about any of this?"

Paxon shakes his head.

"Your son?"

"No one."

Gallagher takes a deep breath. He folds up the letter, slots it back inside the envelope, and tucks it in his inside pocket.

"You said Dolores choked?"

"In her sleep. They said it was an accident." Paxon shakes his head. "I don't know what to believe anymore."

"Betty doesn't know about any of this, either?"

"No one does, I told you."

"And this Middlebury place?"

"It's an asylum about thirty miles west of here, halfway to Land's End, a big red building on its own."

Gallagher jumps to his feet and makes for the office door. "I don't know how you live with yourself," he hisses. "Or how you've lived with this for so long."

"What are you going to do?" Paxon calls after him.

"An innocent man is about to be given a life sentence. What do you think I'm going to do?"

He marches out of the office, past the sleeping machinery, and the raging furnace, back to his car. He is unlocking the driver's door when, somewhere within the factory, Paxon lets out a long cry.

Gallagher sits on the front seat and thumps his fist against the steering wheel until it stings, as he turns it all over in his mind. He must take Dolores's letter straight to Napier and make sure that Forbes is released. He could drive to Middlebury afterward. He might be able to force them to discharge Betty into his care. After that, he could take her home to London with him. He could nurse her, bathe her, cradle her to sleep, love her. Yes, he must keep his promise to protect her, whatever the consequences for him.

He opens her letter and reads it again, then her mother's letter. He reads them both a second time, but he still can't start the ignition. Something is stopping him from driving to find Inspector Napier. Suddenly he sees it:

He sees Betty. She is hollow and frail and she is wrapped up in his monogrammed bathrobe in the guest bathroom of his Kensington house. Her hair is wet and freshly washed. She is about to pat it dry, but the robe is too long, the towel is too big, and she trips over them. Her hair still dripping, she gives up, pulls on her old grubby summer dress, and walks downstairs to the dining room for supper with him, but she can't quite reach the carver chair. She tries again to scramble onto the seat, but it is too high, almost cartoonish in its proportions. He offers to lift her, but she refuses and, at that moment, there is a burst of light. Camera bulbs flash and pop in the front garden and an army of photographers and reporters jostle for space at the dining room window.

"Dolores's daughter," shouts one.

"The Cleaver's spawn," yells another.

Reggie stands at the front of the pack, his nose squashed against the glass. His teeth are pointy and saliva drips from his mouth. He slurps it back in, still leering at her.

"Give us a comment," he shouts as Gallagher leaps across the room to draw the curtains. "Just one, Betty love. You're your mother's daughter, aren't you? She'd have loved her picture in the paper."

The doorbell rings and Betty huddles under the giant dining table, her palms pressed over her tiny ears. It rings a second time, but before Gallagher can comfort her or bolt the door, someone boots it down. It rips off its hinges and slams onto the hall tiles, cracking them. The door lies flat like a lowered drawbridge, and a dozen feet trip trap across it. Six policemen appear in the doorway and squeeze into the dining room at once.

Gallagher stands in front of the dining table and widens his arms to keep them at bay but they flatten him, too. They reach under the table and grab Betty. She lets out a knotty scream. Her toothpick arms, all veiny and white, reach out for him. He reaches out for her, but the policemen have her tight. They charge out of the dining room carrying her between them, one limb each.

He is still scraped across the dining room carpet, not quite able to pick himself up, when there is another burst of camera light through the curtains. An engine growls to life and a police siren wails. He hears one last girlish scream, and then she is gone.

Gallagher rubs his bruised fist and stares at the steering wheel. "They must never know," he mutters to himself. "She must never know."

He has ripped up her life once; he must never let that happen again. Maybe Middlebury will be a new beginning for her. When she is free again, she can start afresh. He could persuade Father to intervene and ensure that they release her soon, and he could send a little money for when she is out; she need never know it came from him.

A hazy photograph of Forbes the butcher creeps into his mind. Wasn't he widowed? He was an army private, Gallagher recalls, but he pushes away the thought. He can't think of Forbes now; his loyalty must be with Betty. He owes her. He loves her. And for that, she must never know the truth about her mother.

Gallagher jumps out of his car and hurries back into the factory, a letter in each hand.

"Paxon," he calls. "Paxon! I've decided what we'll do."

The only sound, as he paces back toward the office, is the crackle of the furnace. Through the frosted window he sees the black silhouette of Paxon. His chin rests on his chest and his toes are pointed like a ballet dancer's. His body rocks slightly, and he is suspended high above his desk. He could be flying were it not for the brown silk tie knotted from the rafters and looped around his neck. An upturned chair lies beneath his feet.

Gallagher coughs. He coughs again. He coughs unstoppably until his eyes water and his chest is raw and his lungs are ready to jump out of his throat. When the coughs stop, he is left with a surge of guilty relief. He dries his eyes. He paces around Paxon's office, careful to avoid looking at his dead eyes, as he rifles through the papers on the desk. He searches the drawers next and looks inside the filing cabinet and bin for further traces of Dolores's guilt, but finds nothing. Good. He still clutches the two letters in his sore right fist.

The eyes follow him out of the office. He tiptoes back along the corridor to the factory forecourt and stops in front of the furnace. Slowly, carefully, he opens his fingers and drops the letters into the flames, watching until they shrink to black ash. Calm, so calm, Gallagher walks back to his car.

x

BY THE TIME HE reaches Middlebury, the sun has sunk and risen again and the sky is indigo. The building stands solidly in front of the sea, strangled by ivy and surrounded by barbed wire. He parks under a lone sycamore tree, naked with winter, and retrieves his binoculars from the glove compartment. He waits.

There is little to look at. To the front of the building is a strip of bleached sand and steely sea. Surrounding it from every other angle is dead scrubland, where the yellow grass has parched or diseased. He turns off the engine and is glad of the sea's company; it laps and weeps and keeps the ghost of Forbes at bay for now. He winds down his window so the sea is louder and the smells of salt and earth drift in. An hour passes, and Forbes creeps back to him. He hates his company already.

x

GALLAGHER STILL WAITS. HE waits for two days, drinking his hip flask dry. He thinks that when he sees her, he might run down to the sand and reassure her that she is not alone; he is protecting her. But how could he look at her and not tell her the truth about her mother? He can't risk her finding out; it would crush her. Then Forbes floats back to him.

Forbes is still with him when the sky darkens. Neither of them sleeps. When it is light again, Gallagher raises his binoculars to his eyes and watches as pairs of stick figures trickle out of the building and walk on the sand. There is always a guard in the pair; the guard always wears white. Sometimes the non-guard cries or sits on the sand or paces in fast, tight circles, but the guard always stands still. Betty and her guard still don't come.

On the third day, she appears. He dives out of the car and notches up his binoculars, though he knows her at once by her thick waves of brown hair that brush the small of her back. Her arms aren't bound like the others, but her head is bowed. She wears something blue that he can't quite make out. He is desperate to call her name, but he chews on his tongue instead; he promised himself that he would only check on her from afar.

Betty and her guard slope to the beach. Gallagher drops his binoculars and shields a hand above his eyes, half willing her to turn around; surely she would recognize his car. She doesn't turn, though. Her head lifts when her feet touch the sand, and she doesn't cry or sit or pace. Instead, she glides to the shore and stops so close to it, her feet are probably licked by the cold tongue of ocean.

The guard stretches his arms above his head, and Betty tilts up her face to the sky. Gallagher can't make out her expression, and he wonders for a moment whether she is in pain, but then she wades into the shallows until her ankles are covered, and, her head still facing the sky, she kicks up a great fountain of ocean and shouts.

"I love you, Mother," he hears, or thinks he hears.

Epilogue

Jerry stokes the dustbin fire with a rake and watches as the last of the old bank statements curl up and blacken. The back garden smells of autumn.

Mary had sprinkled a handful of dry leaves onto the bonfire before she left, and stared as the flames crackled and hissed. Neither of them had spoken, but his arm had snaked around her waist, hers around his. Then Cath had tooted the horn; Mary had smacked him on the lips with a kiss and dashed out to Cath's car, shouting that she'd buy him steak for supper.

It was peculiar, getting to know the new Mary. She had just stopped aging one day—that day two years ago. Time had reversed on its heel, and each week, even as he drove her to and from hospital appointments, she became younger, more exuberant, freer somehow. A miracle recovery was what Dr. Sanders had called it after her first round of radiation. An understatement, he had thought at the time.

He smiles at the thought, pokes the bonfire ash, and tosses on a second handful of leaves, then he ambles back into the house for a second lager. The top snaps off, the foam fizzes over, and he is dabbing the froth from his fingers with a tea towel when the doorbell rings. He opens it with a silly grin. Mary must have forgotten her purse; so forgetful these days.

"Oh," he says in spite of himself when he looks out.

"Hello," says the man, a stranger with a grave expression. He sticks out a pudgy hand that Jerry considers, then shakes. "Sorry to drop in unannounced. It's Mr. Sugden?"

"That's right," says Jerry with a nod.

"You must be Mary's husband," continues the man, glancing into the hall and turning over a large padded white envelope in his hand. "Is she home?"

The man's eyes are purpled with tears, and his hair is oily, but his black suit looks expensive.

"No, she's not," says Jerry carefully, looking at the envelope. "Can I help?"

"It'd be easier if I came in," says the man, a nervous edge to his voice.

He turns over the envelope again and traces his finger along the seal. There is no name, not even an address on it. Jerry looks at him for a second longer, then steps back to let him inside.

"What's this about?" he says when the front door is shut and they are standing on either side of the telephone table, a potted orchid between them. "Are you a friend of my wife?"

"No, but I think my father was," says the man. "I've just come from the church. That's why I'm . . ." He gestures to his black tie. "Sorry, I haven't even introduced myself. Simon Gallagher."

Simon sticks out his hand again, and Jerry takes it a second time. Was. Gallagher. He lets a tiny sigh escape. John Gallagher is gone for good, then. And he is instantly guilty at his relief.

"My father left this package with one of his nurses. It's for your wife," says Simon. "I didn't even realize he had visitors apart from me."

"What's inside?" says Jerry, surprised at his own bluntness. He composes himself. "I'm sorry. None of my business. My condolences."

"Thank you. I just wondered . . . do you know whether they were close?"

"I don't think so," says Jerry. "Old acquaintances, that's all."

"Oh," says Simon. A pause. "I haven't looked inside. I didn't even know it was there."

"I'll see she gets it."

Simon looks crestfallen.

"I was rather hoping that I might give it to her myself. I wanted to ask her if he'd said much about me when she visited him." Simon props a palm on the telephone table. "He was a very closed man, my father. Sometimes I think I hardly knew him at all. I just thought that . . . I don't know what I thought."

"She'll be a while, I'm afraid," mutters Jerry. He clears his throat. "She's out shopping with our daughter and . . . Well, she only saw him once at the care home." Then he adds as casually as he can, "Your father didn't talk about her, then?"

"He didn't mention her once," says Simon, as though still surprised. "I thought the nurse must have made a mistake when she gave me the address and this," he adds, raising the envelope. "Dad didn't have many friends, even when he was younger. I was writing his memoirs and—" He stops and shakes his head. "Listen to me going on."

"His memoirs?" blurts out Jerry, horrified. "He's written an auto-biography?"

"Well, I was ghostwriting it, but he changed his mind last minute, so the finished book has a grand old audience of four. Him, me, my secretary, and an editor. But what can you do?"

He spreads his hands and forces a laugh, but it sounds hollow. Jerry smiles placidly. Simon holds out the envelope and he takes it. It is heavy; heavier than he expected. Whatever is inside is hard and blockish and rectangular. Simon still doesn't move.

"Can I get you a drink?" says Jerry as politely as he can. "A beer? Soft drink?"

Simon shakes his head and looks at the door with a sigh. "No, I should get to the wake. I was going to ask if your wife—if Mary— wanted to come. As I say, I didn't know about her until today, otherwise she'd have been invited, too, of course. It's a shame she's not here."

"A shame," agrees Jerry with a nod, opening the front door.

Simon is just reaching the gate when he turns back.

"I almost forgot," he calls. "You don't know anyone with the initials BB? Perhaps another of their old friends?"

Jerry shakes his head tightly. He waits until Simon's silver saloon is a spot at the end of the road before he closes the door, presses his head against it, and lets out a long shaky sigh.

x

JOHN GALLAGHER HADN'T LOOKED at all as Jerry had expected. He had pictured him, as he raced to Eugenie Heights, as a tanned hulk of a man with shining black curls, crystal eyes, and a suave silk suit. Then he saw him.

"So you're John," he had blurted out.

He had wanted to laugh. This was the man who had held his wife captive all these years? This pale worm in an orthopedic bed? He had tried to mask his surprise when John spoke and he recognized his voice from the television. He masked it again when John admitted that he had loved Mary, a schoolgirl then with a different name. It all sounded so seedy.

Jerry had always known that, inwardly, Mary was never fully his; that she was bound by something or someone else, only he hadn't considered that the man would be so old and so unthreatening, or she so young when she knew him. He hadn't wanted to know.

He still didn't want to know anything more than where Mary was—

he needed to find her urgently; he had found out from the doctor's letter about the cancer and that her treatment was to begin the next week—but as he stood over John's bed, he let himself listen to the story about the innocent wife-beating man who was wrongly imprisoned for those famous murders, and the biscuit factory owner who Mary believed was the real killer. There was something improbable yet unsurprising about the story. Everything slotted together; finally he understood why she was as she was.

But when John got to the bit of the story about Mary's mother, about how he covered it up and carried the guilt for Mary to save destroying her life further, and her memories, Jerry had gripped the windowpane and sunk onto the sill. He closed his eyes, too.

When he opened them again, John looked different. He was bigger and more forceful. Jerry's expression must have been transparent because it had made John smile in a slow, strange way. I win. I loved her more than you ever could, said that smile.

Jerry had jumped to his feet and made for the door.

"Send her back to me," John had called after him. "I need to explain it all properly to her."

"Do you really think I'm going to ask her to come back here? She's ill. Seriously ill."

John had winced but hadn't asked more. "Still, it should be her choice," was all he said.

Jerry had glared at him one last time and stormed out. He hated that John was right. But he had intended to tell her. Then he had seen her. His Mary. She had held his hand. She had really cried.

"How did you know I was here?" she had said, tightening her grip on his hand.

"I saw you on the street back there. You walked so fast, I couldn't keep up."

"No, how did you know about St. Steele?"

"John told me," he had said. He paused. "You disappeared and I was looking everywhere for you . . . I found his name and address on that bit of paper in your old diary."

She had turned white, but she still hadn't dropped his hand.

"I always knew you weren't from Reading," he had admitted. "Your accent . . ." She had sucked in her breath. He had opened his lips. "I'd have understood if you'd just told me about your mother dying when you were young and wanting to start fresh with a new name and everything. John said how close you were with her and how hard it hit you."

"John," she remarked, as though trying out the name on her lips for the first time.

"He was an old friend of yours."

"He was an old lover," Mary had corrected him gently.

"An old lover," he had agreed quietly through gritted teeth.

He could have said the rest, but she had cried again. He would tell her later.

"And you can really accept me lying to you all these years?" she said between sobs.

"Oh, Mary."

He had pushed his face into her hair that smelled different; it smelled of coconuts.

"Did he say anything else?" she had asked, her eyes far away.

She was watching a branch moving in the distance. Something was rustling. A magpie had appeared in the clearing. It swooped low, and its wings brushed the pond. The water rippled.

"Just that I might find you here."

"That's all?"

"That's all," said Jerry with a careful nod; he would tell her later. "But you didn't need to run off. Of course you should visit a dying old friend, lover, whoever he was to you. I'd have understood . . . it all."

"I should tell you the whole story."

They had walked for two hours around the clearing, through the woods, along Newl Grove, and down to the shingle. They walked until their feet were soaked, until their shoes were gritty, until the sky was black, and until every noise stopped except the whisper of the waves and the lilt of Mary's silvery voice.

He had let her spill out every scrap about her guilt and about the asylum and the breast cancer, which she truly believed was her punishment, and all the while he pretended he knew none of it. About Nigel Forbes, too, and George Paxon, and John Gallagher, whom she had thought loved her but now realized never cared for her at all.

"I didn't even know him," she finished. "It was all fantasy; I built it up in my head."

Then Jerry opened his lips—it was time to tell her what John had really done for her. But the rain had started again, and she pointed at a sign that said, Rooms available.

"Let's stay the night," she had cried breathlessly.

There was only one room left, a single. They shared the narrow bed and locked together as a whole while they slept and while the owner's Yorkshire terriers scratched at the bedroom door. When they woke, they kissed.

"We'll fight this; I'll come to every hospital appointment with you," he had whispered in her ear before they rose.

They ate their slippery bacon rashers and cold toast and strong tea in silence.

She still didn't speak as he drove her home, but neither did she look out at the streets with a wistful face, as he had expected her to. Instead, she rested her hand on the gear stick, on top of his hand.

"We're going to be okay, aren't we?" she had said, as though she were realizing it herself, rather than asking him.

And all of her stayed in the car with him; all of her was his, finally. He couldn't risk losing her now.

x

JERRY FINISHES HIS LAGER in one and turns over the envelope in his hands. He opens a third bottle and a fourth. He wipes down the countertops, he stokes the bonfire again, and he throws on a branch to resurrect it. Then he sits on the hard splintered bench between the conifer and the pear tree, and, in a single movement, he tears open the padded white envelope. The ripping sound cuts into the peace of the morning. He pauses and looks around before reaching inside to pull out the contents. It is a book. The pages are stiff and the cover is blank but for a row of X marks where he supposes the title should be, and beneath them:

PROOFCOPY

a memoir by John Gallagher

Jerry flips open the first page, then changes his mind and shifts to the back. There is an index. He scrolls down his thumb to *B*, to *E*, to *M*, to *S*, but her name isn't listed. He looks for St. Steele next; for Cornwall; for Cornish Cleaver; for Nigel Forbes, but he finds none of them. He thumbs through the front pages. Two are blank, one has the author's name again and something about copyright laws. There is a fourth introductory page, too, which is blank but for these ten words.

For BB. Some things are too precious to be contained.

Jerry smacks shut the book and jumps to his feet. He grips the cover, raises his right arm, and draws it back. As he slams his arm forward again, releasing his fingers and hurling the book across the garden, he closes his eyes and lets out a bellyful roar; he'll be damned if he lets her go. He can't. Not now that he finally has all of her.

There is a clunk and a hiss, as the flames bolt up out of the dustbin. Jerry opens his eyes and crosses the lawn to the bonfire. The flames are already licking the cover; the pages are wilting and charring nicely.

He doesn't notice the smaller, thinner envelope that fell out from between the pages as the book flew across the garden; he doesn't notice that the envelope has landed on the rock garden; and he doesn't see that it is white and letter-size with three blockish forward-slanting words on the front, written in bright blue ink.

To my Betty.

Acknowledgments

Thank you to Mum, Dad, Amy, Mollie, Nan V., Guppa, Nan P., Grampa, and Andrea for your unstinting belief and encouragement. To my first readers, Eleanor Drew, Paul Sellars, and Hannah Walford. For your part in turning this into a reality, thank you to Fiona Brownlee, Robbie Guillory, Richard Skinner, Karolina Sutton, and everyone at Literature Wales, and Jackie Cantor and the team at Gallery Books. Huge thanks to Norah Perkins, a most wonderful agent, who was the best support imaginable during the bumpy bits—and has made it so fun along the way. Thank you to my friends—especially Kathryn, Kim, Alix, Meabh, Gemma, Sarah R., and Nat—for listening patiently to me witter on about this for years, and for never once saying "Isn't it done yet?" Thank you to Sarah B. for seeing it through the final hurdle and being the most loyal and enthusiastic cheerleader. Thank you to Wills for your support and for reading this in its many drafts. And last but by no means least, thank you to my amazingly talented Faber friends, without whom it wouldn't have been possible to, as we say each session, "keep going."